Deep Within the Morning Glory Blue

By

Selyna Malinky

authorHOUSE™

1663 LIBERTY DRIVE, SUITE 200
BLOOMINGTON, INDIANA 47403
(800) 839-8640
WWW.AUTHORHOUSE.COM

First published by AuthorHouse 04/11/05

ISBN: 1-4208-2526-7 (sc)

Printed in the United States of America
Bloomington, Indiana

This book is printed on acid-free paper.

[1] Reprinted by permission of PFD on behalf of: The Estate of Laurie Lee.(c): as printed in the original volume.

Cover image by Fred Voetsch; www.acclaimimages.com, with the grateful thanks of the author.

CHAPTER ONE

Isobelle could not really say when she first felt that she was being watched. She was in the train taking her towards Moorgate. The day was refreshingly cold, but with the intense sunlight that made her feel particularly warm and drowsy within the seal of the train. There was an unusual quiet within the carriage, with only the occasional lazy flutter of a broadsheet page turning. Although the train swayed purposefully on, it was as if the compartment had slipped into that comfortable realm of half-sleep, half-wake. It was in this languid state, staring out the window with half an eye at the imposing Alexandra Palace, that she became slowly aware that someone's eyes were upon her. She did not wish to look, partly because she was enjoying her current lethargy, but also because she felt sure that she would catch some male commuter examining her intently. Not that she could get upset or annoyed about them looking, for she herself secretly enjoyed people-watching and loved weaving a history around some of the characters who were regular passengers on her route. Keen on the expression of poetry, Isobelle gleaned many of her subjects from observing her fellow passengers.

Poetry, she thought dreamily, was the only way to describe her situation now and what better lines than those of Laurie Lee in April Rise:

If ever I saw blessing in the air

I see it now in this still early day

Where lemon-green the vaporous morning drips

Wet sunlight on the powder of my eye.[1]

The thought of eyes brought her reluctantly back to the present. She still had that sensation of being watched, but strangely enough, she felt that it was neither an insulting nor a demeaning examination. She could not

---

[1] Reprinted by permission of PFD on behalf of: The Estate of Laurie Lee. ©: as printed in the original volume.

explain it to herself, but intuition seemed to be assuring her that all was well and she need not fret. However, now her curiosity was beginning force itself upon her, pulling aside the dreamy mantle that had enveloped her protectively since boarding the train at New Barnet. Slowly Isobelle looked around the assorted commuters, most of whom were wrapped up in their own particular worlds of reading or daydreaming. At first she thought she had spotted the culprit as her eyes met those of a young businessman, but almost instantly she realised that he had looked up from his newspaper to obtain bearings on his surroundings whilst turning the page. His eyes slipped naturally back down to the sports section. Where are you, she silently questioned as her glance extended further down the carriage. No one seemed to be staring pointedly her way, so perhaps they had averted their eyes in anticipation of her sweep. Oh! Well, she sighed to herself, perhaps I have to be a little more devious.

The train was by now pulling into Finsbury Park, a connecting station for overhead and underground trains to various points in London's City and West End. People began to shift, ramming newspapers hurriedly into briefcases, buttoning coats, searching out gloves, eager to be the first off and leading the way to the next mode of transport. Isobelle watched them, suspecting that this was the end of the issue, when all at once she noticed that she was indeed being examined. What threw her momentarily, though, was that this someone was a woman. Rationally, there was no cause to be surprised, for women are often wont to appraise other women. She had often done so herself. She believed that women tended to be a lot more perceptive about each other, a belief that she logged in her mind following a discussion with some male work colleagues who confirmed that they very rarely studied other males for fear of accusations or violence.

This woman, standing near the doors appraising her, surprised her more so in that she was rather stunning and certainly stood out from the other occupants of the carriage. She was stunning not just because she was attractive in appearance, but also in her dress and the manner in which she held herself. She shouted elegance, so much so, that Isobelle thought that she could have been plain and still turned heads as she passed. Her clothes had the look of quality and expense, although there was nothing showy about them. She wore a long black woollen coat with a wide collar over the shoulders, unbuttoned at the front to show a red tailored business suit, a plain round-necked dress of calf length with a long jacket. A simple pearl beaded necklace set this off.

Impressed with her style so far, Isobelle began to take in the features of the woman herself. She was of tall stature, which was enhanced by the long coat she wore. But the role of the coat had another purpose, as it was the ideal colour to compliment her natural blonde hair and fresh cream complexion. Her hair was set in a French bun, not often seen in this day and age, but Isobelle thought that it certainly did not look out of keeping on her. She had high cheekbones on a classically beautiful face and her lips were a red that cleverly matched her suit. This inspection of the woman seemed to have taken ages, but Isobelle knew that in reality only seconds had elapsed. It was at this moment that Isobelle realised that the woman was fully aware that she had been considering her, for those red lips had broken into a beautiful wry smile. And, although Isobelle could not see them clearly, she was sure that the woman's eyes were sparkling mischievously behind the lenses of dainty, but fashionable, rectangular glasses. Isobelle turned down her eyes, feeling the rapid heat of a fierce blush burning her cheeks.

The train drew haltingly to a stop, with the commuters pouring from its doors in reluctant haste to get to work. Isobelle looked up again, glimpsing the sheen of the woman's blonde hair as the stream carried her off into the vast sea that was London. Isobelle held fixed in her mind the picture of her standing with that teasing smile which seemed so in place with such a glorious morning. But why, she questioned herself with some irritation, had she blushed. After all, it had been the woman initially staring at her that had led to Isobelle's examination in return.

CHAPTER TWO

Isobelle had worked as a Management Accountant in a smallish finance house based in London Bridge for some 5 years and was reasonably content with her lot. Her two immediate work colleagues, Meyra and her line manager, Paul, were decidedly friendly and she had a good relationship with both. Paul was the kind of manager who let Isobelle prove her capabilities without pressuring her and this had benefited them both. The gained confidence in her worth helped produce work, which was well considered by her customers within the business and their praise in turn helped her financially.

She was aware that she was never going to rise to the upper echelons of the firm, but she had a job that she liked, a small flat that was her own and enough money to buy a few luxuries each month. In terms of her future, she assumed that one day she would meet that Prince charming who would sweep her off her feet, but she was not duly concerned that it had not yet happened. She did have male friends, but they were just that, friends. Some indeed were happily married. It was not that she thought of them as sexless beings, merely that she did not have romantic or otherwise inclinations towards them. That said, she liked them as people and sincerely hoped that they felt likewise about her.

It was not to say that she had not had relationships in the past, but they were the relationships of growing up where two people met, enjoyed close time together before moving on, tasting other options before making their commitments. Isobelle had no regrets with her past, even though some of the relationships had been ill matched and stormy, because she knew that she had learnt a lesson from each and that it was not at a time when it could have effected her life significantly. She had allowed two relationships to develop sexually, but had not found either to be erotic or passionate. She did not, however, solely blame her partners for this, but put it down to inarticulate inexperience, especially in her case, which she believed would one day be resolved when she met Mr. Right.

During the course of her day, Isobelle found her mind occasionally distracted by memory of the woman on the train, but she could not fathom why it had effected her so. She was quite grateful when she was roused out of her reverie by a call from her sister, Fiona.

"Hello, Issy. Fancy meeting up after work for a drink? I had to come into London today to meet Piers for lunch. As he is having to work a little later this evening, I had hoped that you could keep me company for a while."

Fiona was her only sister and three years older. They were split by a brother, Gordon, who worked out in the Middle East. The Piers referred to was Fiona's fiancé.

"I would love to, Fi. Where would you like to meet?" Isobelle was not a frequent pub-goer, so her knowledge of potential watering holes was somewhat limited.

"How about I drop by your office around 6 and we can just find somewhere then?" Fiona, throughout their lives together, had always been the more assertive and decisive, a feature she continued in her engagement with Piers to seemingly good effect.

The remainder of the day went quietly for Isobelle whilst she worked with Meyra on a budgeting project. At 6 pm she met a bubbly Fiona in the atrium, who greeted her with her usual hug and kiss to each cheek.

"Brr! You feel cold," Isobelle complained good-humouredly as their cheeks momentarily brushed. "Look, I really don't feel like an alcoholic drink; would you mind if we go to the coffee shop in Hays Galleria?"

In the end they settled for Malibu and cokes in the nearby Halcyon bar, which was fairly quiet considering it was a Thursday night. They managed to find a table near the window overlooking the River Thames, the various coloured lights of Tower Bridge, the HMS Belfast Museum and the City on the opposite bank competing for their attention.

"How are your wedding plans going?" enquired Isobelle. Fiona and Piers were due to be married in June, some three months away.

"Well, I think most of the planning is complete. It is whether it all comes to fruition on the day." She paused, ruminating. "I believe that the only new development since I last saw you is that we have booked Middleton Hall for the reception."

While Fiona continued to relate details of her forthcoming wedding, Isobelle marvelled at how radiant Fiona had become since meeting Piers. They had met about eighteen months ago at a cocktail party thrown by the company for which they both worked, Melhuish & Jamieson, a small UK banking concern. Like Isobelle, Fiona was employed in the accounting side, although as a department head. She had been introduced to Piers, their leading derivatives trader, and from that instant they had been together in every available moment. Isobelle was thrilled for her sister for they had always been close and still continued to be, meeting up like this frequently. What is more, she really liked Piers, a very calm and gentle man despite his profession and a perfect match for Fiona.

In between suitably injected signs of affirmation in her sister's enthusiastic discourse, Isobelle regarded Fiona's features. If it were not for the hair, many people would not necessarily know that they were sisters. The hair and the eyes were the give-away in that both of them had red hair the colour of deep claret and eyes of rain-washed peppermint leaves. Although they had similar hairstyles all through their teens, Fiona had then elected to adopt a shorter, more raggedy elfin-type style, which suited her longer face. Isobelle loved her own hair long, enjoying the sensation of the fine strands cascading over her shoulders and down her back like a rippling satin sheet. Along with the ruby hair they had both inherited the freckles, although Fiona's tended towards the prominent, whereas Isobelle's were like a sprinkling tossed over her small nose. Fiona's face was long and sculptured, with lips that spread beautifully when she smiled. She was a very handsome woman. Isobelle, ironically, had a face that was more fairy-like, with full desirable lips that seem to adorn all French glamour models. One of her previous boyfriends had described her 'as having the near wantonness of Angelina Jolie with the innocent mischief of Imogen Stubbs.' Isobelle had not been quite sure how to react to the remark save to know that she had yet to experience wanton!

Fiona's figure was a tad fuller and more curvaceous that Isobelle's, but Isobelle was well aware that her own trim figure was as a consequence of her love for swimming, a pass-time that she managed twice weekly. Recently when she had persuaded Fiona to join her and they had shared a changing room, she had seen that Fiona's breasts were much larger than

6

her own and that her hips were wider. Although they were about the same height, they both appeared right with their different shapes. Piers was always hugging Fiona and telling her how cuddly she was and Isobelle could understand why he felt that way. On impulse she reached out her hands, covering her sister's, squeezing them tight with affection for her.

"I am more pleased than you can know that everything is falling into place and to see you looking so happy. I can't think of a nicer man than Piers for you, and you know how possessive I am about you," she told Fiona, her voice tripping with emotion.

"Thanks, Issy. When you say it I really know you mean it. Piers is very fond of you, so I hope you will come to us often afterwards. I told him how we had spent so much intense time together when father died and how we had become so close as a consequence, so he knows and is pleased that you are a large part of my life." Last January, their father had been in hospital for two weeks in a coma before he died, during which vigil they talked as never before about everything. At that time an unspoken bond had grown between them which they both strove to maintain and protect. "Incidentally, mother has been asking who you intend to bring as your guest to the wedding. I keep telling her that it is not necessary for you to bring anyone, but then she starts on about how Piers must have some friends that would suit you. I do try and ward her off, but you know what she's like when she has a bee in her bonnet," she added with an understanding grin.

Isobelle smiled imagining just how her mother must have sounded, but confident that Fiona would have shielded her and would never dream of pairing her up with anyone against her will.

"I told her that you are an independent woman and that you might bring a friend of either sex as company and that you would refuse to come if you thought you were being fixed up. I said that I would be devastated if you did not attend for any reason, so I hope that I put her off enough."

"Thanks, Fi. I suppose she is only like it out of concern, but it does tend to grate that she thinks I am incapable of surviving on my own. I have not really considered if I will bring anyone yet, but if I do I will let you know first. I could bring Meyra from work as she has not been to a Christian wedding, but if you don't mind, I will leave it a bit longer."

"Leave it as long as you like, Issy, and bring who you like," Fiona said kindly. "Besides, you could always bring Meyra and tell mother that you no longer like men. That would set the cat among the pigeons for sure!" she continued, chuckling.

CHAPTER THREE

Isobelle did not feel in the mood for anything cooked by the time she arrived home. Piers had met them about 8pm and insisted that she stay with them for another drink. It had been a nice evening, but Isobelle was quietly pleased when he said that they ought to make tracks home. He offered to drive Isobelle home, but it would have been way out of their way, so he kindly dropped her off at Finsbury Park station. While tossing her feta salad and preparing a dressing of mixed pumpkinseed oil, walnut oil, olive oil and squeezed lemon, she replayed the evening's conversation with Fiona. It was difficult knowing whom she would take to the wedding…Meyra had been interested in the arrangements and mentioned that she had yet to go to such an event, but Isobelle knew that if she did go, Meyra would need constant attention as she would know no-one there. Isobelle felt a little selfish, but she just wanted to go alone and spoil her sister on her big day and not have to worry about anyone but her and Piers. With a sigh, she mentally logged the fact that she would need to telephone her mother, but she did not have the resolve to argue tonight.

She decided to slum it, carrying her salad and orange juice into the lounge to eat. Placing the Brandenburg Concertos on the CD for background, she sank onto the settee and began to nibble thoughtfully at her salad. All this ruminating over the day led her mind back to the morning's incident and the woman who had been watching her. She intrigued Isobelle, for she knew she had not seen her before on the train. She would have definitely noticed someone as beautiful and well dressed. But what had the woman seen in her for her to stare so. Perhaps she was reminded of someone, or maybe she had just been daydreaming while locked in on Isobelle's features. Then again, the smile later suggested a playful connivance, which would dispel the daydream theory. She knew that she was not going to solve anything tonight, so finishing off her salad, she decided on a shower and hair-wash.

Showering was always a luxury to which Isobelle looked forward; the near unbearably hot water flooding over her body without break. It was not a sexual feeling, but highly joyful. It literally washed away the ills of the day and she knew she would emerge steaming and happy. This was one reason she hated the idea of roughing it on a holiday and why she did like her swimming. The showers at the Leisure Centre were excellent, making the drudgery of changing after a swim a lot more tolerable. As she was soaping the promise of peaches over herself, she once again found that she was thinking of the woman's smile. What is more, despite the heat of the shower, she noticed that the fine hairs on her arms were upright and that her nipples had hardened. Slightly heady from the stifling temperature, she allowed her fingers to stroke slowly back and forth over their firm contours. Despite not having large breasts, she had large pink nipples and areolas which both jutted out like mounds which she knew were pretty unusual from her observations at school. For a brief moment she imagined the woman's red shiny lips over them, before she suddenly jerked herself out of her reverie, feeling an embarrassed flush balloon over her face. Whatever had possessed her! Acting as though someone might have caught her in this embarrassing performance, she began washing her hair vigorously in an attempt to ignore just what she had felt. Even when she completed her shower, she saw that her hands were trembling, although she could not trust herself to truthfully answer why - guilt or passion? She barely dared shave her pubic hair, something she had always done since her appendix operation as a teenager, but she carefully persevered, putting her whole attention into the task and blanking out all else. Despite this, her hands were still slightly trembling when she emerged from the bathroom, smelling of English roses and bundled in a long, soft bathrobe.

Making herself a cup of rosehip tea, Isobelle began to convince herself that it was nothing to worry about. It had been perhaps too hot in the shower and she had hallucinated. Maybe Fiona's joking implication to her and Meyra in a relationship had mingled into her recollections of the day. Well, no harm done, let it lie, she thought before taking her rosehip and herself to bed for a good read before sleep.

CHAPTER FOUR

Whilst the mind can be tweaked and manipulated during the daylight hours, glossing over truth and confusion with tenuous explanations, the night-time provides for no such tomfoolery. The night, in fact, has no pity, driving roughshod through excuses, poking and prodding relentlessly at fears and passions until the troubled sleeper wakes bathed in sweat and bewildered. Even then, the night works its spell, for in the darkness, doubts become concrete and troubles swell into battalions. Was it dream or reality, or a blend of both which frantic eyes seek in the blue black chasm of a once friendly room?

And so it was for Isobelle as she woke with a start, wrapped in damp sheets with beads of sweat on her forehead. The dream had been in vivid Technicolor, running and re-running a single sensuous scene. The woman had smiled as in the train, before seeming to effortlessly glide over to her. All the other passengers had disappeared and the next thing she knew was the woman kneeling closely facing her; Isobelle had been drawn to the glossy wetness of her slightly open lips. She had seen with clarity the gentle creases etched on those lips and the small golden hairs silhouetted just above them. As she had felt herself tilting in tiny movements towards those heavenly lips, she could even smell her perfume, it's heady aroma teasing Isobelle those few inches before their soft, quivering mouths finally met. And there it cut, only to play again, so real and so tantalising, taunting her so much that before she could even think, her hand moved instinctively to satiate the intense yearning which had arched her body with its fierceness.

Isobelle lay spent on her rumpled, soggy bed staring up at the ceiling but making out nothing as her thoughts rollercoastered through her brain trying to make sense of emotions so alien to her. Never in her life had she experienced such powerful sensations that left her so utterly drained. And never had she had such charged thoughts about another female, not even at boarding school, which was always considered a breeding ground for such liaisons. The amazing thing she was unable to fathom was that this

11

woman had only appeared in her life momentarily and yet had left such a mark on her. She knew nothing about this woman; she did not even know her name. And how could she smell her perfume in the dream when she had not been that close to her in the train? Isobelle was not ashamed or upset in any way about the fact that she had reached an orgasm, for she had not been in a relationship for a while and had happily spent evenings exploring her body. No, she just felt particularly guilty about the subject of her orgasm. It was astounding that she had been so totally overwhelmed by the intensity of the orgasm when she had never thought of another woman as anything more that a friend. Did this make her a lesbian? She certainly did not view herself as one and as she had not actually made love to another woman, she supposed she was not one. With her breathing now regular and her mind beginning to rationalise, she felt it was time to make a move and busy herself. So much for the shower last night; another was definitely in order.

Isobelle had never been much of a jeans or trousers person. She adored being feminine and believed that dresses and skirts suited her best in that pursuit. Dresses were her favourite and her wardrobe held a number of plain, stylish ones for winter, along with some opulent floral ones for summer. Although the sun was bright for the morning, she could see that it was burning off a frost from the grass outside. So today she selected a royal blue dress with matching jacket, pondering on whether the added attention she had applied to herself was because she hoped to see the woman again. But the morning sunlight had also burnt off the night's naked candour and Isobelle lied to herself that she always paid this much heed to her appearance.

Following a more leisurely breakfast of porridge accompanied by rosehip tea, Isobelle browsed through her bookshelf for something to read. She had just read Laurie Lee's 'Selected Poems' and after the beautiful prose therein, dripping from each page like freshly pressed apples, she thought that it might be a hard act to follow. Picking another of her tried-and-trusted favourites, Sharon Olds' 'Sign of Saturn', she gathered up her coat, scarf and gloves, setting off for the station with a spring in her heel. Although she was convinced that the woman had not boarded the train at this station, Isobelle could not help but scan the crowd surreptitiously, focusing in on any blonde hair within the waiting commuters. As expected, there was no sign of her even though she kept watching until the train drew in. Making sure she got on precisely the same carriage, with an excitement that she was attempting to suppress, she found the same seat was once again vacant. Acting nonchalantly, she opening her book of poems and forced herself to read the first line. Only then could she look up and begin her eager sweep of the carriage. So confident was she of seeing the woman again that when she could not she felt her heart miss a beat in disappointment. Perhaps had she got on at a later station, she reasoned, for she had not been aware of her stare until close to Finsbury Park. That was it. Clutching at straws and giving up on clandestine glances, she strained her neck, eagle-eyed at each successive stop to glimpse her. She had not contemplated this journey without seeing the woman and probably even feared the thought last night, but a dread was beginning to build up in her that she would not appear. It was Friday today, so she would have to go the whole weekend before the opportunity would arise again. Inwardly she groaned. She could feel one of those discomforting aches similar to those she felt as a girl when she would wave good-bye to her parents in the Middle East before flying back to boarding school in Wales. It was that ache of wanting someone or something so badly it hurt. And yet, once again she had to remind herself that she did not even know her name, let alone anything else about her. Was this yet another first, a 'love at first-sight' first she asked herself? This growing desire just to see her was certainly potent, stronger than that in any former relationship. With a start, she became conscious that she was even beginning to accept that it was a woman.

Friday's do have a habit of dragging at work as the business wound down almost as quickly as the staff for the weekend break. Fortunately no excessive demands were made on her during the day and she was grateful that she had no meetings scheduled, as she did not trust her powers of concentration at all. Fortunately Fiona rang towards the end of the day to thank her for her support the previous evening, taking Isobelle's mind momentarily away from her longing. She could not believe that it was only last night that she met Fiona; it seemed a lifetime away.

"Are you alright, Issy? You seem even quieter than usual," asked Fiona, her voice reflecting her concern. Instinctively, Isobelle almost told her then, but her head quickly took over from the heart and allowed her a neutral reply.

"I am fine, honest. Just a bit tired, Fi, as I did not sleep so well. I should be fine after some zzzz's tonight."

13

"Well, we will be around this weekend if you feel like popping over at all. Just ring and let us know. You know that you are always welcome."

"I know that," replied Isobelle. She truly did. "Thanks, Fi, you are a gem and an angel and I am so pleased to have a sister like you to look after me."

"The same applies," she said, pausing before cheekily adding, "And anyway, if I did not look after you, who would?"

CHAPTER FIVE

"Goodnight, have a great weekend!" resounded around the office as eager colleagues melted into the evening river of humanity following a pied piper promising fun and recreation. Isobelle felt hollow and sad. She knew she had no right to be, but that ache of something missing was growing while the likelihood of seeing the woman soon was diminishing. The idiotic thing was that even if she had seen the woman again, what would she have said or done. She would have been far too shy to approach her; perhaps she would have tried an encouraging smile or a shy secretive wave. She knew for sure that she would have accompanied any such action with the mother of all blushes. The thing is, she reminded herself, that she may have twisted this wholly out of proportion and that the woman's smile had been that of someone being friendly. I do not care, she told herself, for she knew that now she would happily settle for seeing her again. Friendship would be a welcome gift and anything else would be a fairy-tale treasure. But what did she want, she questioned herself. Where did she wish to go with this? She sighed deeply, so much so that the commuters around her looked up in surprise at her melancholy. She could not think past seeing the woman again and if she ever did, she would let the situation guide her then. Impulse was always available to make fools of us all, she thought. Isobelle took up her book of Sharon Olds poems, but no matter how she tried to concentrate, the words were just blurry black psychiatric shapes on the page.

"What is that you are reading?" asked a dusky voice in front of her.

Isobelle's eyes shot up, blinking rapidly as they tried to focus. She felt her heart begin to race as the vision began to register the image that was before her. It was her woman and she still had that mischievous smile on her glorious lips as if there had been no interlude since their last meeting. Seeing that Isobelle was struggling to answer her, for her vocal chords had failed her in her moment of need, the woman leaned forward and prised the book gently from her rigid fingers.

"Ah! Sharon Olds. I thought I was the only one in England who read her poems, yet here is a fellow admirer. Are you an admirer?" Her voice was quite extraordinary to Isobelle and certainly not as she had imagined, although, to be frank, she had not really determined how it might sound. It was low and huskier than most women's she knew, but that said, it was not in the least masculine. It was very much a feminine voice, but unique. Not the same pitch as the voices of women who have smoked a lot; less raspy, more fluid. Beautiful.

"Yes," croaked Isobelle, trying hard to control her own voice, "I have admired her poems for a long time and often re-read them." Unable to resist, for she had to know, she added, "What is your name?"

"Evelyn. Evelyn Hertford, which is ironic as I now live in the county. And you?"

"Isobelle. I'm Isobelle Swanson," replied Isobelle, overjoyed to know both her name and the fact that she lived in this county. Evelyn Hertford. Even her name was one evoking class and Isobelle was enjoying bouncing it around her mind.

"Mmm! Isobelle. That is a good Celtic name. It fits so perfectly with your hair and eyes. Do you hail from Ireland or Scotland?" she enquired. She was still holding Isobelle's book, idly running her thumb back and forth over its glossy cover.

"My parents hail from the Scottish Borders region. My mother had the red hair and green eyes which she passed on to my sister and I," replied Isobelle. "I cannot begin to guess where you are from," she added, but thinking that it might appear rude, she stammered, "sorry, that sounded terrible, not what I meant to say".

"Absolutely no offence taken, Isobelle. Well, my parents are Irish, but as with many of the Irish gentry, they do not really have a distinct accent," she said with a warm smile. "I hear slight tones of that lovely borders accent in you though."

Isobelle felt her cheeks colour with the joy of what she perceived was a compliment.

"Do you mind my asking what you do?" Evelyn followed. Isobelle took this opportunity to look closely at her eyes, a missing part of her puzzle when conjuring up Evelyn's image the previous night. They were a summer blue - the only colour that Isobelle could match them to was of a tropical sea as it moves from the deeper green to shallow blue hue - it was the blue of that turn. There was a slight depth near the iris, lighter as it moved away. She could almost see the sun-reflected spangles of mirth in their corners.

"Nothing exotic, I'm afraid. I work as a Management Accountant in London Bridge. It is a job that I do reasonably well and it provides me a decent wage for the little luxuries I seek," replied Isobelle, slightly defensively, for she imagined that they were possibly leagues apart in their incomes. "I would hazard a guess that Management Accounting is not your line," she appended.

"Management Accounting is a worthy profession," Evelyn returned, sensing Isobelle's slight discomfort, "but, no. I am an Architect that specialises in water tower and barn conversions. I am intrigued about your luxuries, though. Other than food, what do you spend your money on?"

Isobelle was still reeling over the fascinating nature of Evelyn's work. An Architect that specialises in water tower and barn conversions certainly was not the type of profession that mingled with hers…. those kind of people only ever seem to surface in quality TV documentaries. And here she was asking what she spent her money on.

"Oh! Again, I buy the usual mundane things. I suppose it is the choice of things that makes them different. I like to purchase music, pictures, sculptures, books galore, things for my flat and, of course, clothes and toiletries to keep me feminine and sane," she burst out, wishing instantly that she could delete and rephrase such a silly end of sentence.

Evelyn seemed not to notice. "Well, Isobelle, you have certainly achieved the desired effect with your clothes and toiletries. What statues do you collect?"

Isobelle was cursing herself as she once again felt the heat of embarrassment rise from her chest through to her neck and face. Why am I unable to accept a compliment without turning into a robin each time! Evelyn will think she is dealing with a shy schoolgirl rather than a competent woman. "One day, in a gallery in Mill Hill, I found a small nude called 'Chrissie

Resting' by a sculptor named Tom Greenshields. I was mesmerised by the beauty of the piece and had to buy it. I enjoyed its presence in my flat so much that I later bought another, 'Claire Stretching'. I am very proud of them both, but they were expensive for me, so these two shall have to get on as a pair."

"They sound delightful," Evelyn said, "although I have not heard of Tom Greenshields. I will definitely have to look into his work. Were there male nudes as well?" Once again Isobelle saw that naughty twinkle in her eyes and had to quickly look away to stem any second wave of blushing.

"I believe he has male nudes, but I just found these female figurines so exquisite. I suppose I am more familiar with the female form and could recognise the detail to shape." She realised that she had leaned foreword to whisper these words to Evelyn as they were not the kind of sentiments to share with her fellow travellers. In doing so she was conscious of the mesmerising effect of Evelyn's perfume.

Jerking up, she glanced out of the window. Where was the train? How long did she have with Evelyn before she had to get off? She began to panic as she recognised that they were, in fact, drawing into her station. Her mind was in a tangle trying to think of the best question to ask to ensure that she would see her again, but her emotions had numbed her reason and transformed her back into that bumbling schoolgirl. As the train came to a stop, she hastily gathered up her coat, her mouth finally managing to come unglued enough to ask, "Do you travel into town everyday?"

"No, not often, I'm afraid. Here, this is your book of poems", she answered as her thrust the book into Isobelle's hands. "The poem on page eight is one that needs plenty of attention!"

CHAPTER SIX

Isobelle stood deflated on the platform watching the red warning lights on the back of the train fade into the night. So Evelyn did not travel this line often. How many times was that? Would she see her again, or might she be destined to occasional chance meetings when the fates took pity upon her. Already she could feel that ache of longing begin to squeeze and tug at her insides. She knew that forever and a day she would be angry with herself for not having asked outright where Evelyn lived, but it had just been so difficult to do so on the train. Wait though, start thinking girl, shouted a voice of reason in her brain. You know her name and that she lives in Hertfordshire, so start the detective work. Sometimes she wandered how she had ever got her accountancy CIMA examinations for her common sense dissipated so often into thin air.

With an air of purpose, she gathered herself together and headed off towards home. As she walked, she could feel the corners of her mouth stretching into a smile, like a Cheshire cat so the saying went. After all, she had not expected to see Evelyn at all after the disappointment of the morning trip in, yet she had appeared, provided a name and some details about herself over which Isobelle knew she could now dwell. It was just a shame that she had not kept her eye on the stations so that she could have timed her questions better. But she recalled that it was not a normal conversation, that half the time she was tongue-tied, captured by Evelyn's perfume, or pinned within the tight embrace of her eyes. Still, all was not lost and the weekend, formerly to be dull, now held plenty of promise.

She placed her book of poems on the occasional table while she removed her winter trappings, remembering only then Evelyn's cryptic message as she had hurriedly passed the poems back to her. She had said something about a poem on page eight. Quickly Isobelle snatched up the poems and sank into her settee, a little quiver of excitement running through her. Rustling through the pages with fumbling fingers, she sighed with pleasure, for there, tucked firmly into the back of the page was a business card:-

Evelyn Hertford BA (Hons) BArch (Manchester) RIBA
Conversions: Barns, water towers, etc.
Restoration & Refurbishment

And under that was the greatest prize of all, a telephone number. Checking in the telephone directory, Isobelle saw that it was a Brookmans Park code. Armed with this information she almost felt light-headed. As she began to pull together the ingredients to make herself a vegetable goulash, she knew that Evelyn had put the ball in her court now and that the next contact would be up to her.

Throughout the preparation of her meal she mulled over what she would do next. She assumed that Evelyn saw something in her to be staring at her and then come and sit by her. Moreover, she had given her the business card when she knew that it was most unlikely that Isobelle would be calling on business matters. So, by inference, she must want her to call. As she began to eat, Isobelle deliberated her feelings towards Evelyn. It was a formidable attraction, of that there was no doubt. She could not think of herself as being a lesbian as the whole concept was so remote from her life, but then again, she imagined that not all women were born lesbian and that some must have found out through similar jumbled emotions to those she was experiencing. It was certainly not the stereotype lesbian relationship she had heard about through school, for both Evelyn and herself were very feminine women. She could not envisage a butchy bone between them.

The strange thing was that last week, the idea of wishing to caress another woman's hands, never mind kiss another woman's lips, would have been inconceivable. It was not that she was homophobic, just that she had never considered it. Still, swivelling the argument around, it could be that it was just Evelyn who had seduced her with her smile and presence and that it could equally have been a man another time. There was no saying that just because it was Evelyn, that she had been seeking a woman. No, in her mind it was the person, Evelyn, who attracted her and so she was not going to categorise herself.

Nevertheless, she knew that if she took the relationship any further then it was going to be difficult, but at the moment she could not really think beyond her current happiness. She had berated herself in the train about behaving like a schoolgirl, but inside she actually felt that young craving that comes with a new and promising romance. She felt positive that

Evelyn was facing equivalent sensations towards her, but she also knew that it was possible to mis-read signals in the headiness of romance. They would initially be cautious with one another, both hesitant about making that opening move that could lead to a giddy euphoria or a shame-faced rebuttal.

Isobelle had decided. Tonight she would delight in the moment, savouring each word and action of their meeting, recalling every detail of Evelyn's dress, drinking in every venerated scent from her body. Tonight was for wallowing in that exhilarating wine of a new love; she knew that she was already intoxicated for she could taste the sweet apple of desire on her lips. This was the passage of adoration which painters and poets the world over had tried to capture in the colours and inks of their passing - the flighty gesture of fingers, the twinkle within the eye that saw only love, the bruised strawberry blush on tender cheek. Many had come close, but the sanctity of that moment would only ever reach perfection in the subject. And so it should be. Isobelle tried, taking up pen and paper, but her young and joyous mind lacked the necessary vocabulary:-

Their eyes have locked after so much shy avoidance
And she knows that this moment will be
the most delicious; she hears her heart thump
With the expectation of the kiss.

Her breathing's laboured, husky; her chest is tight
With truly painful yearning of delightful intensity
playing on her tongue, which moistens full lips
in the expectation of the kiss.

And so, through slightly parted lips is born a sigh,
Within which last vestiges of doubt and reason flee.
As determination tilts her forward, to kiss
Her lover and her own sex.

So, Isobelle had decided. Tonight was for her and tomorrow she would make the call. She would invite Evelyn to visit her on Sunday.

CHAPTER SEVEN

Because Isobelle's mind was no longer rebelling against her feelings for Evelyn, the night became her friend, prompting her with notions and situations of kisses and hugs in places she did not recognise. In harmony with her conspiratorial mind, it committed scams and ruses; a gentle draft to mimic the sleep-saturated breath of one beside her; tender fingers of twilight disturbing the drift of her hair. So crystal-clear was the trickery that when she awoke in the morning, she honestly thought the she was embracing Evelyn and not her pillow.

She forced herself to await the more reasonable hours of mid-morning before she allowed herself to take up the business card and, with quivering finger, dial Evelyn's home.

"Hello, Evelyn Hertford here. How may I help you?"

Isobelle relished each and every word, delighting in the warm, yet business-like introduction.

"Hello, it's Isobelle, the other woman in England who admires Sharon Olds poems," she joked spontaneously.

There was a low chuckle on the line. It made Isobelle's toes curl with the pleasure of it. I have made her laugh, she thought with a naive pride.

"Well hello fellow fan. I am glad you called. I am working on some designs here that are a little complicated and you have provided a welcome break," she replied with a soft, but distinct voice.

"Glad to be of service," sympathised Isobelle. "Hopefully I can be of more use to you in your hour of need…I wondered if you would like to come over tomorrow, have lunch with me?"

"That is very kind of you, Isobelle, but I have a bit of a problem." Isobelle's heart sank momentarily. "It is just that the owner of the designs that I am working on is planning to call me tomorrow for an update. Unfortunately

I have to be within proximity of these designs, so I think that I should stay close."

"Not to worry," whispered Isobelle, vainly trying to hide the disappointment oozing out of the three words.

"That is not to say we cannot meet," said Evelyn, throwing a lifeline, "do you have a car?"

Isobelle did not, having never had a real need for one in London.

"It is a bit of a trek here from the station," continued Evelyn, "so what do you say if I come and collect you about 10, we have lunch here, I take my call and then after we go for a walk? The weather has been so nice this week and the forecast is cold but sunny tomorrow. We can wrap up warm."

Isobelle tried to keep the youthful exuberance from her voice as she almost shrieked "Yes, that sounds terrific!" before Evelyn had finished her sentence.

Evelyn chuckled adorably again, picking up on Isobelle's obvious enthusiasm. "In that case, young lady, you had better tell me where you live!"

Following the telephone call Isobelle floated from room to room with an inane smile fixed firmly on her face. Before the call she had experienced that doubt, the inevitable taunting that is part of the package of infatuation; *would she be pleased to hear from me or consider it a bit soon for a friend to call?* The fact that her fears had been unfounded added to the sheer positivistic spirit of the conversation. After she had passed by and switched the CD player on and off a few times, unable to decide which style of music would best suit her mood, she determined that she should do something positive and exercise some of her energy. She busied herself getting together her sports swimsuit, towel and various toiletries that she would require before setting off for her swim. It was a good time to go swimming, she pondered, as most people were shopping on a Saturday morning and the pool was usually fairly empty.

Clearing her mind of everything, Isobelle dived into the invitingly translucent waters of the pool and spent the next 45 minutes scything her way up and down the lengths, pausing only occasionally to change her strokes. By the time she had completed her gruelling work out, she felt exhausted but all the better for it. At least she could think straight.

On her way home, Isobelle stopped off at the supermarket to stock up on a few essentials to keep her going through the coming week. In the main entrance to the store was the flower stand where she bought herself some white Chrysanthemums for the living room. While she was admiring the blooms, an eager-to-please member of staff, comforting in her authoritative uniform approached her.

"Are you looking for flowers with a person in mind, dear?" she enquired with a sweeping gesture of her arm at the selection.

"Yes, er! Yes, for a friend," muttered Isobelle shyly, trying to imagine what the assistant would say if she knew the truth. Her embarrassment worked to her advantage, for her eager helper took it to be a lover for which she was buying.

"Well, dear, roses are for love and purity if you avoid the yellow; daffodils for unrequited love; tulips are a declaration of love; stocks are bonds of affection and carnations, especially red, say that my heart aches for you. Would any of those choices be suitable?" She stood waiting, leaning forward slightly as if helping to prompt Isobelle like one of her curved blooms.

"That is fascinating," admired Isobelle, impressed with her knowledge of their meanings. "Yes, I would definitely like two bunches of the red carnations and two white. What do the white ones represent?"

"They are for innocence and pure love, dear," she announced as she selected the requested bunches.

My heart aches for you and pure love...that will do nicely decided Isobelle.

That afternoon she spent deciding on what to wear the following day. As Evelyn had said, the country was going through a rich spell of sunny days, but there was a price to be paid. Behind glass they beckoned you out to enjoy their warmth, lulling you into slipping on light jumpers, before sending cold tendrils through thin layers to chill the very marrow. No, it had better be garments that were smart yet practical. With the sensual euphonies of an Enigma CD following her throughout the flat, she finally picked her outfit. It would be a pink gingham blouse with khaki canvas jeans, topped off with a thick rose patterned French-collared jersey. Over that she would wear her university duffle coat and on her feet some walking boots. During the course of discarding one top for another, the thought struck her that it would be wise to wear her better lingerie, just in case! To this end she picked a pink flowery bra with a lacy top and matching panties - her lingerie. Now that was a word to savour, lingerie. It sounded so gracefully and exclusively feminine that she could not imagine a better word. Grabbing her notepad, she scribbled down:

> *Here lies the truth, the real apple*
> *Pouting pink to float on "who me" blond.*
> *A take-away dream of silken treasure*
> *Suspended, ripe, with rosy blush,*
> *Slips juicily when unhooked to fall,*
> *Tempting the Eve(lyn) in us before decay.*

A giggling Isobelle was ready. Tomorrow could not come quickly enough, so she spent the early evening preening her body and hair, before curling up in her bed wishing for the mantle of sleep and the arrival of her girlfriend. Girlfriend; she drifted off into slumber with her mouth still forming the word.

CHAPTER EIGHT

Sunday morning found Isobelle up, ready and eagerly awaiting Evelyn's arrival before the clock had struck 9am. Music would have to be her minder over the next hour, for otherwise she was fully aware that she would be struck with apprehension about her choice of clothing and would be frantically dipping into her wardrobe for alternatives. It had to be suitably dreamy and quixotic to match her current mood and, searching through her CDs, only Enya could fit that bill. As she was lured along by soft Celtic harmonies, she deliberated the amazing change to her life over the few days. It was partly the fact that she was finally, in her eyes, experiencing the symptoms of 'falling in love' and that it was happening so quickly, but also the fact that it was obviously with a woman. The latter element she felt that she had dealt with sufficiently for the moment, but the fact that she was falling in love was again a new-ish occurrence. She would not insult the past relationships in her life to say that she had never sensed the gangly awkwardness of meeting someone with whom the chemistry seemed to gel, but it had never been with this intensity before and with someone of whom she knew relatively little. But, she had to admit, now that she had come to terms with herself over the actuality that she was enamoured by another woman, she could not believe how excited the passions made her feel. It was the odd mix of the girlish adolescence and responsible adult tussling with one another for supremacy of her faculties.

Isobelle was looking down from her second floor window when a white Land Cruiser pulled into the curb outside the apartments. While she was weighing up whether this could be her (she had not thought to ask what she may be driving), the driver's door opened and out slid Evelyn. Absence certainly had made the heart grow fonder in this case, Isobelle judged, for Evelyn's radiance was almost enough to make her legs unsteady. Evelyn, meanwhile, had stopped to check a piece of paper she was holding, before moving gracefully towards the entrance way below Isobelle. By the time the shock of the buzzer disturbed the still of the flat, Isobelle had grabbed her coat, the flowers and was out the door.

"Hello, Evelyn!" she greeted with enthusiasm, "I have been so looking forward to today!" Inside she was asking herself why she was so able to sound so juvenile. Evelyn, conversely, appeared to be amused and flattered by her effervescence. To try and make amends, Isobelle coyly offered the carnations, "These are for you. Did you have any trouble finding me?"

"Absolutely no trouble at all and thank-you, you are very sweet. These will look beautiful in my lounge," she replied with that resonance of voice that Isobelle had tried and tried unsuccessfully to mimic in her mind. *If I was not smitten by your looks,* thought Isobelle, *then I am slain by your voice.*

"Did you want to come up for a drink before we go?" asked Isobelle out of politeness.

"That's a kind offer, but if you don't mind it would be better if we got back to my place soon....I would like to make sure I am there for the telephone call."

"No, that's fine with me," declared Isobelle, pleased that they could be on their way to Evelyn's home straight away.

In the Land Cruiser, having marvelled at all the instruments it contained to ensure an effortless drive in paradise, Isobelle teased, "I thought that you would have a sports car of some sort, commensurate with your profession."

"You may tease, young lady, but many of my colleagues do actually have the Porches, Jaguars, and the like, but I have found that many of the jobs with which I get involved are in such inaccessible places that a sports car would be a liability. Whereas this trusty Toyota has taken me to hell and back in perfect comfort without a complaint! Besides which, I am not really a sports car person," she added.

Normally Isobelle would have considered anyone calling her 'young lady', as Evelyn had a couple of times, condescending, but strangely enough she was not at all bothered by it. In a way, it provided her with the excuse to be naughty and impish. While Evelyn had been talking, Isobelle had taken the opportunity to ease round slightly in her seat so that she could surreptitiously study her. She was wearing her hair down today although she had back-combed it on the right side. With the sun enlivening its fine flaxen strands, it was all Isobelle could do to refrain from reaching over and running her fingers through it. She wanted to smell it, for it looked so clean that she knew that it would consist of lemons and citrus. She wanted to taste it, run some bunched strands across her lips and tongue.

"Are you looking for spots on my face, or have I smudged my lipstick," said Evelyn with a wry grin, breaking through Isobelle's reverie.

"I would have trouble finding spots on your face," grinned Isobelle, "it is nigh on perfect. I can't believe that you could ever experience the pimply curses of plain girls such as myself!"

"Ahh! That is where you are wrong," she retorted. "Although I rarely get them on my face, I have been known to get them on my back. That is why low-backed dresses are not for me. And anyhow, who on earth gave you the notion that you were a plain girl? Far from it. I personally think that you are the most attractive girl that I have ever met. Shame about the duffle coat though!" She finished with a laugh that was so infectious that Isobelle almost forgot to blush at her compliment.

"Do you mind my asking how old you are?" Isobelle questioned, using her impishness to the full. "I will set the pace to show good faith - I am 24."

"Mmm! 24 is delicious, so much innocence to corrupt," she returned. "And me, I am 27 going on 28. Probably ancient to your 'spring chick' eyes. But now it is my turn to be cheeky. Let me see.....so, does this ruby-haired, green-eyed maiden have a host of men fawning after her?" Her voice seemed to strain, almost imperceptibly when asking the question, as if dreading the asking but driven to do so. Isobelle knew how Evelyn was agonising, because she too needed to ask the same question, likewise afraid of what the answer might be.

"Well," Isobelle said, after a slight pause to gather her thoughts, "27 going on 28 is just fine....a stabilising influence to a young and potentially wayward girl such as myself. And as for boyfriends, this princess is still under the spell. She's awaiting that kiss that will open her eyes to the one she loves."

Isobelle could almost touch the relief that rushed out of Evelyn. She managed to turn quickly to look into Isobelle's eyes as she answered in little more than a whisper, "I hope that is the fairy-tale where all ends happily ever after."

"And you?" Isobelle had to now ask, "with your drop-dead gorgeous looks and air of unrivalled sophistication, you must have architects designing pleasure palaces all around you?" Her heart began to thump against her breast. *Answer me quickly, my love, before it bursts.*

"What, this Ice Maiden? I have no time for such frivolous past-times when I am striving to be better than the best. I cannot say that I have not had approaches, but my work has soon driven a wedge in between and so far, I have never tried to stop it. So I am the ice maiden to look at but not to touch." As she said that there was a sad edge to her voice, which Isobelle picked up on immediately.

"Does the title trouble you or the fact that you have not met the right person?" Her heart was still reminding her of its concern.

"It is neither of those…it is something else which I'll tell you about later, not now," she replied a little distantly. This did nothing to allay Isobelle's fears and still her heartbeat, but she could tell that this was not the time to force the issue. Evelyn seemed to read her mind as she added, smiling comfortingly, "There is no love in my life at present."

CHAPTER NINE

Evelyn's home left Isobelle open-mouthed with amazement. "What on earth is this?" she asked peering up at the tower before her. It had the appearance of a red brick lighthouse, but was positioned on a hill with forest all around. Evelyn was enjoying her look of bewilderment. She did not have the opportunity to invite many people to her home.

"It was a water tower, built by prisoners of war in 1903. It was used until the early 1990's, but then was abandoned for a few years. My father found out about it and made an offer. It took a while for the paperwork to go through, but eventually he managed to buy it."

"Do your parents still live here?" asked Isobelle, shocked to think that she might have to share Evelyn when she thought that she might have her to herself.

"Good grief, no! We were all too demonstrative a family to live cosily in here together. My father tended to use it when in England on business. I think he probably brought his lady friends here, for mother never visited it. She preferred to remain in Ireland. Father was also an architect and about the time he retired, I was offered my position down here. Probably on orders from mother, I was given the tower being so convenient for my work and no doubt making sure father stayed under her control! Come along, let me show you the interior as I don't often get the chance to show it off."

If Isobelle had been amazed at the outside of the tower, she was absolutely mesmerised by the inside. Each of the floors, although not particularly large, were decorated with an eye to making full use of the space. Much of the wall furniture was purpose-built to accommodate the curves of the tower, which reminded Isobelle of the picture books of her childhood. This was particularly so in the kitchen; she could almost imagine Mrs Tiggy-Winkle cooking in her toadstool house. The bedroom was situated near the top of the tower before it broadened out into where the water tank initially would have been positioned. Isobelle was looking forward to seeing this room as this was where Evelyn's private space was; here the intimate parts of her were folded in draws, tucked under pillows, hung in deep wardrobes. Her eyes swept this restful room of blues with hints of gold, cataloguing various items in her mind - the 'Home and Country' magazines on the bedside table, the 'Blond' by Versace on the dressing table, her gold hairbrush with further strands of gold caught in the bristles. She knew she would revisit it all later as the night beckoned her to contented sleep.

The final room was a lounge. The water tank had long been replaced by a huge space completely surrounded by windows and commanding an absolutely breath-taking view over the neighbouring countryside. There was a narrow veranda outside the window for warmer days, for it was obvious that many of the glass windows were in fact doors, which could slide open on silent runners, bringing the a sense of tree-house openness, and, no doubt, some cooling breeze. Today, however, they were firmly closed, but the warmth of the sun ricocheted off the polished wooden floor to provide the effect of a modern museum. Evelyn stood to one side observing Isobelle's speechlessness with a pleased smile tilting up the corners of her mouth.

"You are one of only a few to see my home," she said, uncharacteristically shy. "I am very possessive about sharing it with others, so only special people get to visit."

"Then I am very fortunate as we have only known each other a short time," replied Isobelle, still drinking up the views over undulating Hertfordshire. "Who else do I share the honour with?" As soon as she had said it, she regretted it, as she was sure it was hinting the pang of jealousy she felt.

"Well, lets see," she taunted, pretending to be deep in thought. "There was the local rugby team, all the handsome colleagues at my office, several dozen passing coach-loads, oh! And of course the amateur dramatic society. Now was that all or have I missed the Australian netball team?" She must have caught Isobelle's flustered look which she failed to hide in time and so relented. "In truth, I managed to persuade my mother to visit, a favourite aunt who has since died, my lady mentor at work who holed up with me one weekend on a conversion project, and finally, a policeman."

"A policeman?" questioned Isobelle. That was about the last visitor she would have imagined.

"Yes. Look let's have some lunch and I will tell you about it. It is an unfortunate part of the package that comes with me, so if you are to be my friend, then I should let you know what you are letting yourself in for."

It certainly reeked of mystery, but Isobelle followed Evelyn down towards the kitchen in the knowledge that she would know soon enough.

"I have put together a selection of cheeses with French bread and hummus. Is that alright with you? Do you like cheese as I can always make a salad if not?"

"Cheese is fine. I am vegetarian, but fortunately most cheeses no longer use animal rennet in them. Certainly makes my life easier."

"How long have you been a vegetarian?" asked Evelyn as she placed the paraphernalia of the meal in a modern dumb-waiter, which was whisked up to the lounge above. She selected a wine with a raised eyebrow at Isobelle. "Glasses in the cabinet behind you."

"About six years," replied Isobelle, following Evelyn's breathtaking figure up the stairs.

They seated themselves facing one another at a round ash dining table, making small talk which they both were aware was the hors d'ouvre to the explanation that Evelyn had promised.

"Now the reason for the policeman's visit," announced Evelyn. She paused for a minute to seek the best starting point to her narrative. "Back when I was at university in Manchester, there was a man on my course named Richard Bleach. He was what many women might consider good-looking and he certainly knew it. However, it was me he set his sights on, which was unfortunate as I was not attracted to him and considered him very rude and arrogant." She took a sip of wine and Isobelle found that she could not take her eyes off the dusky red of the wine against Evelyn's lively red mouth. The tip of her tongue quickly licked the taste of pinot from her bottom lip before continuing.

"Like many arrogant people, he could not accept rejection. He saw it as a challenge and bombarded me day and night with visits, invitations and weird gifts. I kept refusing the invitations and returning the gifts. I hoped that he would eventually tire of his efforts and give up, but he did not, he just got nastier. If I were at a party where he also happened to be invited, he would purposely fondle his girlfriend while looking directly at me as if to say, this could be you. I gave up going to parties after that. Then there were the messages left on the university notice board which could not be proven to be him....you know, special massage with my room number provided and similar sexual innuendoes. Then there were the rumours he carefully passed around. About my father and his mistresses, which was true. About my being kicked out of a private school for drugs, which was untrue, and so on." She halted at this point and dabbed at her eyes with a tissue. She kept her head hung, staring vacantly down at the remains of her barely eaten meal. Isobelle hardly dared move for fear that the spell would be broken, but she longed to put her arm around Evelyn. She suspected that this was a purging act, that the story had not been told often and Evelyn needed to finish it. She was being gracious enough to tell Isobelle the worst and then let her go if she was afraid of the blacker elements of the friendship; an out-clause before any further intimacy made it impossible.

Evelyn continued, conjuring a darker and rapidly uncontrolled image of Richard Bleach. Of following her through inky cloisters in darkened winter evenings, of ceaseless pebbles rattling her study window as she laboured frightened, through her course work. Then came the telephone calls where no one would speak, knocks on the door which yielded no one and type written notes of pornographic flavour. Evelyn had wilted under the pressure, "My work was suffering and so was I," she moaned, as if experiencing its hurtful heaviness yet again. "I had complained to the university authorities, but although sympathetic, they could do nothing unless he was caught in the act, so to speak."

It was fortunate for her that just such an event took place, for as he slipped one of his spiteful notes under her door one night, her floor neighbour spotted him as she returned from a party and duly reported the incident. Quietly and quickly, he had been advised to leave the university and never return unless he wished charges pressed. That respite to her daily fears meant that at long last she could concentrate on her course, which was later reflected in her final examination results and subsequent offer of a very prestigious position at her current firm.

"For a time everything seemed to be on track again, although I admit that I never felt entirely at ease. I imagined that I spotted him in all kinds of places, sending me into uncontrollable shakes. However, for about a year all was well and I was getting to a stage where he was no longer appearing in my nightmares. I was regaining confidence in myself again." She stopped, taking another hasty sip of her wine, as if steeling herself for the continuation of this painful extraction.

"I was in Central London where I had just finished a meeting with a client outside of the Swiss Centre, when I glanced up and spotted him. Of course he tried to hide himself in the crowd, but I knew it was him." Feeling faint with nausea, she had made her way home using as tortuous a route as possible. She had never seen him around her home to her knowledge, so she prayed that he had only found her through the company and that her tower was still her sanctuary. Scared and nervous, she had been unable to sleep that night, regularly peeking through her windows to make sure that he was not outside, waiting. The following day she had intimated to her secretary and colleagues that a dreaded old boyfriend was trying to make contact and that on no account was anyone to give out her address. It was company policy not to do so and she was sure that many of them did not know her address in any case, but it paid to be safe.

"I had suffered in silence at university for a long time before I had said anything," she continued, "and it did me no good at all. This time I decided to act straight away, so pretending that I had a client appointment I went instead to Scotland Yard and asked at reception if they had a department that dealt with stalking cases. The Receptionist advised that I go to my local police station, but must have taken pity when she perceived my obvious distress and managed to find someone to speak to me." Evelyn had been disappointed at first that it was a man that came to listen to her, for she guessed that a woman might be more sympathetic and understanding of the horror of the situation. But her mild prejudice was swept aside when the policeman had informed her that he had dealt with stalking cases for 6 years and sincerely hoped that he could help her.

"Of course, knowing Bleach's name helped, for he advised me to go to a solicitor and take out a court order preventing him from coming near my company or myself. He was an enormous help and comfort, giving me his card and mobile number so that I could reach him instantly if ever I saw him again. He assured me that he would try and locate his whereabouts and have a quiet word of warning to him. Well that was all some years ago and I am relieved to say that I have not seen him since. However, I have had phone calls at work from telephone boxes where no-one would speak and there have been occasional nasty letters to the office, but over time I have learnt to handle and ignore these. It is the overwhelming fear of him turning up here that stokes my nightmares even after all this time." At last she looked up at Isobelle, her eyes smudged with the tears that had escaped her best efforts to withhold them.

"The policeman came to my house to advise me of safety precautions and to collect a couple of the letters for evidence. Even now that caring policeman will occasionally call me to check that I am well, so I will not stand to hear anyone say a bad word against our police force," she stated while mustering a strained grin. "So, I have laid my soul bare of my troubles on your gracious shoulders. Will you run away from your new friend, Isobelle?" Her eyes bore into Isobelle's, imploring her; *do not be frightened by this, say you will stay.*

Isobelle felt absolutely drained by this sad tale that had so hurt the woman she wanted. How anyone could ever wish to terrify such a lovely creature was totally beyond her.

"Oh! Evelyn," she said, her mouth dry with the wine and the torment of the story. "How could you possibly believe that I would run away from you. Besides, I seem to recall that you promised to corrupt my innocence and I am holding you to that promise!" With that, Evelyn reached over and squeezed Isobelle's hand, running her draughtswomen's long fingers along Isobelle's equally lengthy keyboard-friendly ones as she slowly retracted it back to her lap.

"It is a beautiful day, Evelyn. Let's go for that walk," ventured Isobelle, her fingers on fire.

CHAPTER TEN

They walked across a gently sloping field towards a nearby wood, their breath forming vapours in the crisp afternoon air. As they had left the tower, Isobelle had linked arms with Evelyn, pulling her close so that the heat from their bodies gave succour to one another.

"I wish that I had been your friend then," declared Isobelle, her mind cast back to Evelyn's cruel days at university. "I don't suppose I could have helped much, but I would have been a good friend to lean on. Did it help to tell me about it?"

"Yes, it did help. I wish I had known you before too. I think you would have been an excellent antidote to the pain I experienced" she replied forlornly, griping Isobelle's arm tighter as if to accentuate that belief. It was odd how things turned out, thought Isobelle, for she had from the beginning regarded Evelyn as so self assured and confident, herself being the gangly, uncertain one of the two. Yet, here Evelyn was, wearing her apprehension like a shy new girl on the first day of school. In an outlandish sort of way it gave Isobelle heart, for now she knew that she could give something positive to their friendship. She had been worried that she might be out of Evelyn's league, but she could see that her strength and her support would be as valuable to Evelyn as the tower, the Land Cruiser and any other financial trappings in which she had wrapped herself.

They walked for the most part in a comfortable silence, enjoying each other's proximity as well as the absolute sanctity of the occasion. Spring was dancing her way through the countryside, tossing coloured mantles here and there, gold, russets, lemons, and a myriad of shades of green, to drape the prudish trees from their winter bareness. Splashes of yellows and purples as late daffodils jostled with hyacinths for the passer's attention. If I could bottle these hours, they would have to be called 'Pure Unadulterated Happiness', reflected Isobelle.

The crisp country air had woven its magic, for by the time they returned to the tower, they were rosy cheeked and both in good spirits.

"I want to prepare a meal for you now. You must be hungry," declared Evelyn. "Do you like pasta with a mushroom sauce?"

Isobelle said yes, after which she was urged to explore the tower if she so wished. In the sumptuous bathroom of pink tiles and huge fluffy towels, she examined the appurtenances that were Evelyn; her deodorants, perfumes, tweezers and toothbrush. She pressed the flannel to her face, closing her eyes and absorbing the soapy scents, imaging its feathery passage over Evelyn's body. Places she longed to visit. She uncapped jars and unscrewed bottles, smelling each fragrance, anointing her arms with a trail of essences committed to memory. She gently kissed the needles of the toothbrush while dreamily gazing at the shower and bath, satisfied that both could hold two people comfortably if the situation demanded it.

She felt herself redden at the brazenness of her contemplation. Next she made for the bookshelves; bathrooms, bedrooms and bookshelves, the 'b's in our being, the bits and bobs of our characters and make-up, the bytes in our complex software. Isobelle rang her curious fingers over spines of eye-catching colour, classics, mysteries and adventures, romances, art and painting and naturally the tomes on architecture's great. Her finger tips soaked up the titles, noting how in so many cases their tastes did coincide; Thomas Hardy, the Brontes, Emily Dickinson, Elizabeth Browning, Patricia Cornwell, le Carre, Vermeer, Van Eyck, Fragonard and Ingres - names that were mirrored on her shelves at home. It comforted her to know that they enjoyed so much in literary common.

She did not visit the bedroom, much as she wanted to. That was a place she needed to be invited into, a room to be shared. Instead she made her way to the kitchen to share the news of their interests in books and to see if she could be of help. She found a very composed Evelyn, a woman well in control of her kitchen and aromas which reminded her noisily that she had built up an appetite.

"Could you just reach some glasses down? I have just finished a most interesting book called 'A Village Affair' by Joanna Trollope. Have you read it?" Isobelle confessed not, the only Trollope she knew being Anthony Trollope.

"Well, you must take it with you. If our tastes are that close, then you are bound to like it. Let's eat!"

Again they ascended to the living room where Evelyn controlled the lights to provide the atmosphere of a candle lit supper. It had the desired effect, although Isobelle was convinced that she would have felt romantic in blazing neon.

"So, what did you find of interest in your travels around my home?" She grinned, perceptively, as if she had insight into Isobelle's reverence of her possessions.

"Ah! I was introducing myself to your home. I started with your bathroom and then extended the courtesy to your bookshelf," She was pleased that the dimmed light hid her latest flush; the guilty schoolgirl caught kind of flush. "Do you have a busy week next week?" she hastily continued, deflecting further prodding on her bathroom venture.

"Mmm! I do. I have to travel up to Derby tomorrow as I have to spend a few days checking out the progress of a conversion. I probably will not be back until late Thursday evening."

This news was like a thunderbolt striking Isobelle's heart, for she had not even considered anything but that Evelyn would be nearby. Alas, now she was going to be miles away until Thursday. She tried to keep the fretfulness out of her voice.

"I'm sorry, I did not realise. If you have got to pack you can drop me at the station after supper."

"Don't be silly, Isobelle. I have already packed and I will not be heading off until mid morning tomorrow, so there is nothing for me to do except enjoy the evening with you. I am quite happy to drive you safely home later. No need to fret."

But I do fret, her mind cried out. *I will not hear from you for nearly a week!* She managed instead a weak smile and muttered some words of thanks.

"Why so disconsolate?" Evelyn queried. "Would you like another glass of wine?"

"Nothing…well, I suppose I am saddened that you are off as soon as I have met you. It would have been nice to have seen you again this week." She nodded at the proffered bottle of wine.

"That is so sweet!" Evelyn exclaimed. "But if it is any consolation I too am upset that I have to disappear so soon after our getting together. I was hoping that you would give me your telephone number and post code so that I can contact you while I am up there."

Isobelle's heart skipped and gambolled once again. She would miss Evelyn for sure, but at least Evelyn had also reflected on their parting and had expressed her wish to keep in touch. Evelyn, as if to reinforce her desire to remain in touch, found a notepad and pen." Do not think you can leave the premises until you have listed your particulars," she joked, her hand affectionately squeezing Isobelle's shoulder.

Taking the empty plates she threw a "Hope you like oranges", before gliding out of the room. While Evelyn was out of the room, Isobelle jotted down her full address and number, adding a flourished kiss underneath. Then, listening to the kitchen-borne sounds of Evelyn opening fridge and cupboard, she reached over for Evelyn's wineglass. She gazed at the raspberry red of Evelyn's lip prints, smudged slightly on the rim of the glass. *Where her lips were planted, there lay mine.* Isobelle, eyes closed and overcome with the occasion, placed her lips over the exact spot, lipstick to lipstick, and drank of Evelyn's glass and wine. So absorbed was she that she failed to notice that the kitchen was quiet and that Evelyn's soft footsteps were tracing their way toward her. Gracious Evelyn, for she must have noticed, said nothing but a tender, "Caramelised Oranges. I made them for us last night, so I do hope you still have room." She placed two crystal dessert bowls on the table, before reaching for her wineglass, which Isobelle had hastily and surreptitiously tried to return to its former place.

Watching Isobelle's eyes closely, she too sipped from the spot still warm from Isobelle's mouth. Isobelle could only press her legs firmly together in a vain attempt to stem the twinges of excitement cascading through her most intimate parts.

She took the spoon up with a hand that was not hers…not hers in that it failed to respond to the shaky mixed messages that her brain was attempting to relay. It shook and trembled, far too distracted to help her taste the caramelised oranges.

"Here," hummed Evelyn's voice, "let me help you." And spooning an orange from her own dish, she offered it slowly, hesitantly to Isobelle. Isobelle fed and returned the favour by nourishing Evelyn, each giggling shyly at first, but then sensuously biting, delighting in those segments that were thick with sugar and seduction.

CHAPTER ELEVEN

Later they adjourned to the sofa, where they sank down comfortably at either end, legs curled up, still eyeing each other fondly. The chiaroscuro of the room was charged, pulsing with a longing from each of them that was almost tangible. And yet neither dared to move, fearful that their advance might upset the balance and send their yearnings into that domain of aches, tears and denial. They each craved to speak, but what words would match this silence and which one could trust their voice not to let them down. Isobelle knew she would burst, her heart would go spiralling away if she did not take the impetus of her appetite and turn it into words.

"On the train," she whispered, hesitantly, but loud enough to carry in the stillness, "why were you staring at me as you did? I felt it, but it did not trouble me."

Evelyn held back a moment, the confession teetering on the end of her tongue in a day of divulgence.

"I do not visit my office much during the average week," she began, "but last week I needed to do some research in our library. The first day was on Monday. I do not usually try to drive into work, but take the train and it was there that I first saw you get on at your station." Again Evelyn paused, her morning glory blue eyes fixed on Isobelle's. Taking a perceptively deep breath, she carried on. "I could not take my eyes off you. At first I was captivated by your hair, how naturally, gloriously red and so obviously natural. And how long and fine it was. It rippled when you moved, it seemed to send rays of sun bouncing off it to almost blind me."

Isobelle was in heaven. Her delicate ears burned with the fiery messages they were receiving. She barely dared breath.

"Then I saw your face….." Here again she stopped, but slipping gracefully off the sofa, she opened a desk drawer a produced a small boxed collection of books. She returned to the sofa.

"When I saw your face, I knew that I had seen it before and had adored it then….Have you ever read Cicely Mary Barker's Flower Fairies?"

"Yes," Isobelle replied, "my mother bought me a treasury when I was about ten. I read it time and time again."

"Well, I have to say that these are my pleasure," she said, her face holding the bliss so reminiscent of someone able to divulge their hobby to an interested listener. "Whenever I am down, they comfort me. Each season has their own fairies and each their own verse. I know so many of them, which is why when I saw your face I knew that you were the Black Bryony Fairy, one of Autumn's." As Evelyn said this she had located the page and passed one of the thin books across to her. Isobelle looked at the little figure dressed in orange and black and was surprised to notice that the face did indeed bear resemblance. The fairy needed longer hair, a greener shade of eye and a smattering of freckles over her tiny nose and she would be her. Isobelle noted with irony that Black Bryony used to be considered a cure for freckles.

"I just could not stop looking at you. My stomach went into knots that were quite painful, but it could not deter me from soaking up every detail I could about you. I found it difficult to get off the train at Finsbury Park, especially when I saw that you were continuing on to Moorgate."

She described the restlessness during her day, how she had returned over and over to the image of Isobelle and how she knew that she would have to see her again. Isobelle could hardly believe that Evelyn had been going through all the same tangled emotions that she had, the worries and questions on their attraction and their gender, the distress at the thought of no possible further sightings, the uneasy, sweaty nights - all of it a few days before Isobelle.

"I could not wait to take the train each day in the hope of even the slightest glimpse of you. I did not see you on Tuesday or Wednesday and I agonised that perhaps you had been on a one-off trip into London on the Monday. I could not understand what was happening at first; if you had been a male I would have believed I was falling in love. But with you I just did not know. I have never fallen in love with a woman and I was in total confusion as to what I was experiencing. All the symptoms were those of falling in love, the pangs of wanting to see you, the lack of appetite….I had even decided that if I did not see you on the Thursday, then I would take Friday off and wander around New Barnet in the hope of spotting you."

"But then you saw me again on Thursday," added Isobelle; she felt amazing light-headed. "I sensed someone watching me, but it was not until just before Finsbury Park that I noticed that it was you."

"Yes. I was so pleased to see you again that I had my eyes fixed on you the whole time. I wanted so much to try and begin a conversation with you, but I was too cowardly. I cursed myself later as I was concerned that I might lose you again. However, at least I had established that you travelled into town more regularly than a one-off."

"But I did not see you on Friday morning," blurted out Isobelle.

Evelyn broke into a smile at this point. "Were you looking for me then?"

"Yes, Evelyn. I had just spent a night going through exactly what you had earlier in the week. I was praying that I would see you again. That was probably why I came across as so eager in the evening when we met. I kept thinking about your parting smile on Thursday. There is a quote by Arrigo Boito; *When I saw you I fell in love. And you smiled because you knew.*"

Evelyn sighed. "That is so apt. On Friday morning I could not find my car keys…I'm usually so careful, but my mind has been in turmoil. Anyhow, I ended up missing the train and feeling so disconsolate. I had mustered all my courage and determined that I would approach you this time; I could not bear the weekend without an opportunity to talk to you. I could tell that you were younger than I, so I did not want to push myself on you. I, of all people, am conscious of how horrid it is to have unwanted attention directed your way. I decided to provide you with my business card and let you call me if you so desired. I was terrified that you would not call, but I sensed in our meeting on Friday evening that you did like me. You were so shy and youthful that I just wanted to take you in my arms and hug you!"

"I imagined that I must have appeared a bumbling idiot to you," grinned Isobelle. "Most of the time my mouth was too dry to speak. Incidentally, were you not expecting a call from a client today? Have they rung?"

Evelyn suddenly looked a bit sheepish. "I am sorry to have to say this, but I told a white lie. There was no client going to call. No, I have not really entertained anyone here for so long and I suppose I knew I would be more confident on home turf, especially since I had made up my mind to tell you about Richard Bleach from the start, particularly if we became friends. I deliberated that if you came to me, then it would require more effort on your part and that you would only accept if you really wanted to come. Does that make sense…do you forgive me my little lie?"

"My goodness! You said you would corrupt this innocent youth and you certainly wasted no time!" replied Isobelle in mock amazement. Then, "Actually I am glad you told a white lie. I have been so happy with you today. I had hoped that you would feel about me as I do you, but I didn't dare believe it would turn out like this. How have you coped with the fact that I am a woman?"

"This is all new territory for me…..there was confusion, perhaps even a little disgust at myself; self denial I suppose. But as the week went on I began to accept it. Why shouldn't I fall for you? It still seems strange, which is why I wanted to meet you this weekend. I knew that I had to go Derby for most of this coming week and I thought that if we were able to get to know each other, I could have that time to ensure that this was no short-term crush, but instead something deeper. Of course I did not know of your anguish, but I was conscious of it not being fair to try and seduce you if you did not have the level of feelings about me. I just do not know what I would have done if that had been the case."

Isobelle pondered a minute before responding. "As for me, well I know for sure that I do not dislike men and conversely, I have never particularly fancied a woman. I do not really consider myself a lesbian, as I do not want any other woman now. We do not appear to fit the stereo-type as you and I are both feminine, so I just look on it that I have met someone with whom I think I am falling in love and that she happens to be a beautiful woman. I have not dwelt upon the repercussions, but I really do not want to. How often do I fall in love? I very much want to enjoy it. I will long for you while you are away though. Will you promise to keep in touch?"

With her alluringly husky voice, Evelyn promised. "I shall take your flowers with me for my hotel room to remind me of today."

One of the remarkable mysteries of this highly charged evening was the way in which they had both begun their flirting at either end of the large sofa, but at this particular point had managed to find themselves still facing one another, but within easy reach of one another. Neither had done so intentionally, but it had happened. The re-adjustment of a wayward blouse, leaning forward for a glass on the coffee table, switching a leg - they all had their desired effect. So when Isobelle elected to grasp this moment, she found herself ideally positioned.

"Take the flowers to remind you of today," she whispered thickly, "but take this to remind you of me." And so, keeping her hungry green eyes open, she tilted towards Evelyn, lips slightly parted, knowing that whatever happened in the rest of her life, this instant would be a celluloid memory in her mind forever. Isobelle's warm fingers met Evelyn's cheek first and without any pressure of movement, drew her face towards that of Isobelle. This was the moment when they knew that their lives would change, that they would be a part of one another and responsible for each other. This was a moment of sheer, luxurious bliss. As their lips met, sticking together in their dry anticipation, a quiet moan escaped from Evelyn, a moan of rapture that Isobelle drew in and swallowed. Slowly they kissed, sensitively and lingeringly, the upper lip, the up-turned corners; licking with quick and smooth flicks of their tongues, the earthiness of the wine mingling with the sweetness of oranges. As they explored more, they wanted more and as the sought more, they grew more frenzied. Now their lips opened in abandon, their mouths accepting each other's darting tongue, their fingers in each other's hair, Isobelle pulling Evelyn's lips harder against hers and Evelyn biting little nips at Isobelle's. They twisted and turned their heads for better angles, trying to mould their lips and mouths into one, to become each other; eyelashes brushing cheeks, hair teasing eyes, noses brushing against one another. They tasted one another's saliva, their tongues secking more until that point when they had to slow to breathe. That was the witching moment when sweltering green eyes met scorching blue, when in close embrace they could see beyond the physical, the unspoken but communicated words which assured them. Do not hurry this, for there will be time a-plenty.

While they read the messages of their eyes, they replied through kisses, small staccato ones of avowal and longer legato ones of commitment. It felt as if a night-time had passed when Isobelle spoke again. "You had best take me home, or I won't be accountable for my actions!"

CHAPTER TWELVE

The headlights pierced through the pitch-black shroud of darkness, following the country road as it twisted through an almost ethereal world of looming hedges, gnarled tree trunks and tortured claw-like branches. Inside the Land Cruiser, Isobelle almost purred with happiness though, her arm on the back of Evelyn's seat, fingers tracing through the strands of her hair. Her whole being was in heaven, her lips bruised with the confirmation; a harpsichord filling the vehicle with reedy treble and sonorous base dancing along with her perceptible delight.

"What is this enchanting music, Evelyn?"

"It's the Italian baroque composer, Domenico Scarlatti. It is so wonderfully uplifting that I often play it in the car."

Isobelle picked up the CD box and examined the title by the cheery coloured lights on the dashboard of the Land Cruiser.

"If you like it, then I shall go out and buy this in my lunch-hour tomorrow. It will make me feel closer to you. I shall listen to it and relive every sacred second of today."

Evelyn removed a hand from the wheel and gave Isobelle's leg a tender stroke in response. Isobelle caught the smooth hand in hers, interlocking her slightly shorter fingers between Evelyn's long slender ones and then bringing it up to her lips. She ran one of the perfectly manicured nails along her lips, the lacquered surface even and cool. She opened her mouth and let the finger slip in, running her inquisitive tongue along its length, following the whorled pattern of the skin.

"That is so sexy, but if you keep it up, I'm sure we will both end up crashed in a ditch!" laughed Evelyn.

"In that case, I would have to administer first aid to you. Let me see, first I would have to loosen your clothing and check there were no constrictions...."

I think that could be difficult, keeping my mind on the job! Mmm! Then there would be no other course of action but a protracted kiss-of-life from which I would not stop until I felt your heart beating frantically in your breast. Finally, I would have to wrap myself around you to keep you warm - to avoid shock, of course." Isobelle giggled with the thrill of it.

"That sounds delicious," tittered Evelyn, "but I am not altogether sure I want to go through the accident to receive this life-saving treatment…can't we just have a practice run sometime?"

"Of course. Every responsible adult should update their first aid skills. I shall make it my duty to update yours!" Isobelle's grin was large and lecherous. "Tell me, what do you do when you go on these trips? I hope it is not some other young lover that you are corrupting!"

"No, I think that I could only manage one corruption at a time! This is a barn conversion just outside Derby for a middle-aged couple. As I cannot be up there all the time, I go occasionally for an intense period, covering expectations and any problems with the site manager and owners. I expect that I will spend most of my days on site. In the evening, I usually go to bed fairly early as I am usually bushed, but on this particular trip I have this special client that I must ring every night to whisper sweet nothings to. She has made me promise, the punishment for failure too lurid to detail!"

Isobelle playfully slapped Evelyn's arm. "She must be so absolutely stunning to hold you to such a promise. Although I will be madly jealous, a promise is a promise. Perhaps on your return you will have to outline exactly what it is about this damsel that attracts you so!"

"That could take a long time in the telling, "smirked Evelyn, "but I am game. Anyhow, you will have your hands full looking through the flower fairy books for your lover's likeness. I am only seeking solace in another out of despair!"

Isobelle had begged Evelyn to lend her the flower fairy books to see if she could find one that encapsulated Evelyn. Not only would she enjoy locating this fairy, but she would delight in handling the books because they were Evelyn's.

"This is a lovely car, so comfortable. You are very lucky, although I do feel guilty that you have had to drive me home and then back to your place. Will you be okay? Do you think you'll stop for coffee?"

"It is a pleasure…I will go straight back if you don't mind, because I know if you lure me up into your flat I shall be regaled with all sorts of temptations which I would not be able to resist and then I would never get home. I shall have my thoughts of you to occupy me on my return journey."

"And so I should think so!" said Isobelle with a feigned severity. "Do not think, madam, that I will be swathing my being every night with considerations of you, be bleeding out every wanton ache for you, unless I know that you are experiencing the like. You will miss me or be damned!"

"Talking of which," countered Evelyn, "don't you find it remarkable that we have undergone such similar emotions in much the same way? After all, neither of us has ever had a relationship with another woman, but both of us were struck almost identically. I admit that I probably brought on your interest when you discovered me staring, but there was still something that captured you, that lightening strike that took you beyond the idea of just friendship. I know that people are always falling in love, but I would have thought rarely almost spontaneously together like this."

Isobelle's heart sang the most energetic of heart songs. She is falling in love with me. Although it would appear obvious to a Shakespearean Chorus, standing silent in the wings, to each of them it was a revelation, despite the passion of their kiss.

"The last few days have been incredible to me," agreed Isobelle, "but even though some of it has hurt me inside, I would not change it for anything. I am so, so glad that you smiled your seductive smile and blissfully happy that we met. I never want to lose anything of those days, whatever may happen in my life. But I do know one thing and that is that I am exultant when I am with you."

"Do you think you will say anything to your family?" queried Evelyn, her hand resting easily on Isobelle's leg again. "You mentioned that you were close to your sister, Fiona."

"To be honest, I am not sure. My mother may take it hard…..she's always trying to be a matchmaker for me with sons of friends, but I do hope that Fiona will support me. She and I are so close that I sure she is more interested in my happiness than other people's impressions. However, I think I will play it by ear. It is a big step after all. What about you?"

"With my parents living in Ireland, I do not tend to see them that much, so for the time being I will keep it between us. Perhaps later when I next decide to visit home, I will ask if I can bring a friend. I think my father would accept us, not exactly being in a position himself to hand out the moral standards, but my mother would probably be like yours. Still, together we shall face them and not divided fall!"

"That's my girl!" agreed Isobelle, noticing with a sinking feeling that they had just entered her road. With that wrenching feeling that is evoked with imminent farewells, Isobelle grabbed at Evelyn's hand and clasped it tight to her chest, only releasing it reluctantly when it was evident that Evelyn needed it to change down on the gears. She scanned every contour of Evelyn's face in the muted light of the Land Cruiser, determined that she should not forget a single stray hair, the up-turned corner of a dear mouth, the fluttering blink of fair eyelashes, the slender sweep of alabaster neck……four days without being able to cast her eyes over this adorable creature. Why had fate not introduced them after Evelyn had been to Derby? She determined to stay upbeat while Evelyn was still with her - eke out every precious minute.

As lovers' minds flit and dart, so did Isobelle's, coming up with a worrying thought. "Do you mind if I kiss you before you go - I couldn't bear our not doing so? If you turned off the engine, the car would be very dark and I'm positive we would not be seen."

"I am prepared to take the risk if you are, "grinned Evelyn switching off the car. Being in a cul-de-sac, there was no traffic to fill the Land Cruiser with unwanted light. The windows of the overlooking apartments were either dark with emptiness, or close-curtained against the drawing cold of the Spring night.

"Can I ask a favour of you?" questioned Evelyn. "I know it sounds peculiar, but do you have a handkerchief on you?"

"Yes. I put a clean one in my pocket this morning. Why do you ask?"

"I was hoping that I could have it as a keepsake," she replied, suddenly sounding coquettish. "I have one of mine for you with my favourite perfume on." She fished a small broderie anglaise handkerchief from her bag and handed it shyly to Isobelle.

"What a brilliant idea!" exclaimed Isobelle, "you are so thoughtful!" Taking Evelyn's delicate handkerchief, she located hers from the pocket of her jeans…not the best, a small white one with tiny embroidered pansy in the corner. "Wait, I have an atomiser in my bag." Fortunately, having sorted her bag out the evening before, the perfume was easy to locate. "There!" she added, spraying a modest amount over her square. "I hope you like it."

"I absolutely love it," said Evelyn inhaling the scent before placing it reverently in her purse.

They regarded each other's silhouettes in silence, prolonging that inevitable parting. Isobelle raised her hand, and traced her fingers over the cool skin of Evelyn's face, following the path of her high cheekbones to slide down her svelte nose to those ready lips. Polarity did the rest, its field pulling them together in a slow, memorable kiss, a kiss where Isobelle rejoiced in the tiny sigh which once again escaped Evelyn.

"Will you ring me when you arrive back home? I just want to know you got back safely," whispered Isobelle into her ear.

"There's no need, my sweet, I have driven at night so many times. I rather enjoy the quiet of the road."

"Yes, but you did not have someone who cares passionately about you before. Ring me and send me a kiss goodnight."

CHAPTER THIRTEEN

The initial daylight hours of their parting were not too unbearable for Isobelle as she had an agenda, tasks that she wanted to carry out in protraction of her developing love for Evelyn. Work was a necessary deviation from her dwelling on the miles between them, but a hindrance from the tasks she felt merited her immediate attention. The lunch hour could not arrive fast enough. Grabbing her handbag she all but ran over Southwark Bridge, totally ignoring the panoramic views up and down the river which the cameras were encapsulating for the early season visitors. Isobelle's first mission was the music shop where she made straight for the Scarletti, selecting a CD on harpsichord pieces. As she waited in the queue, she could imagine its melodic notes soothing her this coming evening as they had the last in Evelyn's Land Cruiser.

Next stop was the bookshop, where she found a book on the Flower Fairies. Although Evelyn had lent her copy, Isobelle still wished a copy of her own, so that when she returned Evelyn's, she knew she would retain that common bond with her. Rationally, it sounded silly, she knew, but to her it was perfectly understandable. Such ministrations were the life-blood of any lovers, that insatiable edacity for anything, be it inanimate or a chance to evoke the senses and bring your beloved that much closer. That desideration to almost have them a part of your very being.

It was while at the bookshop that Isobelle had quite a shock, but an uncannily welcome one. As she was ascending the stairs from the basement floor, she became aware of posters on the walls advertising forthcoming novels and biographies. Her eyes casually swept from one to another as she climbed the stairs, half taking in the titles and faces portrayed, that is, until they alighted on one. It was a black and white photograph of a stunning woman, the delivery very much of the 1950's - what was totally arresting about it was that the pose was so familiar in many of the positions she had seen Evelyn adopt. The resemblance was so similar that it momentarily took the wind from her sails. Who was this woman? Being black and white, she could not guess the colour of the hair or eyes for sure, but the shape of the face, the lips, eyebrows, jaw-line were all Evelyn. The hair on the photograph was luscious, dropping onto her shoulders in large curls, whereas Evelyn's was fine….it was one of those instances where, under infinite examination there were many disparities, but the semblance of the whole was quite alarming.

"Who is the photograph of, that one over the landing there, please?" she asked of the assistant as she proffered her book for purchase.

"Oh! That one….that is Veronica Lake, the actress. There is a book out on her life. She is very attractive, don't you think?"

"Indeed she is. She looks so amazingly like one of my friends that I would love to get such a poster. Do you have a spare one of those I could possibly buy?"

"That's actually a promotional one. Let me see if we have a spare in the stock room…I don't think you need buy it though," she offered, helpfully.

To Isobelle's delight there was a spare, which the assistant rolled up for her. She thanked her profusely, setting off back to work with a sure spring in her heels.

It is often said that close friends and colleagues can detect the change in demeanour, that increased sense of life with the utter dichotomy of listless distraction, the colour in the cheeks against the loss of appetite. These were indeed noticed by Meyra and Paul, but it was fair to say that only Meyra recognised it for what it was. Isobelle knew she was behaving differently despite her efforts not to, but the fact was that she was different to that girl of last week. It forced her to recognise that hers was an unusual situation and that it was not going to be greeted by all with the same veracity as news of a boyfriend would. At this particular time she did not really care, but she was wise enough to know that it would be prudent to hold her tongue until the her future with Evelyn had developed. However, anyone who has been in love also knows that a great part of the joy of such an event is imparting it with others and wallowing in the pleasure that they express on your good fortune. This she definitely felt was not something she was ready to deal with for the time being.

After work, she made a detour to the West End to visit a poster shop where she found a tasteful frame large enough to house the poster of Veronica

Lake, for she was impatient to hang it in her bedroom. Only it was not Veronica Lake, but Evelyn Hertford that would regard her with that over-the-shoulder look of innocence which appealed for an affectionate embrace. Isobelle just knew that she would spend ages studying the poster and wishing she could supply that hug. Her mood continued to be buoyant as she walked from the station to her home. It was a favourite time of the year, for the streets were liberally dotted with trees of both cherry and apple blossom, the cherry vibrant and contrasting to the subtler pinky-white of the apple. As the wind rustled the rosettes, petals spiralled down like a soft snow. Nature's bid to propagate quickly was a shame in the case of the blossoms, as they flourished in the very month that England usually encountered its worst in winds and rain, leaving the trees in their glory for such a brief period. This year was an exception. The weather had been predominantly sunny, even warm during the day, although the chill wore on rapidly during the evening. This might effect the less hardy plants, but not the blossoms which proudly displayed their frocks with shameless abandon.

After eating, Isobelle poured herself a glass of wine and placed her new CD in the player before sinking into the cushions on her sofa. Closing her eyes, she allowed the music and the memories wash over her, massaging her mind and body with a relaxation that transported her to a tranquil plane between wakefulness and sleep. It was from this languorous state that the telephone ring jerked her, dragging her sleepy eyed into reality once again. This could be Evelyn, compose yourself she advised, taking a couple of deep breaths to calm herself before lifting the receiver.

"Hello, darling, I am missing you," came that voice that involuntarily made Isobelle's toes curl with absolute bliss

"Hello, Evelyn, I was just imagining us in your car last night....I bought a Scarletti CD. And, you will never guess what I also found today in a bookshop?"

"Well, I would have to guess a book, but on what I give up!"

"You are partly right, I did buy a book, but it is not that I am referring to...no, it is a poster of you, or rather your likeness."

"Ahh! Let me guess....was it Morticia, or perhaps Boudicea? Go on, give me a clue!"

"Alright Evelyn, a few clues as I'm sure you will not guess. She is an American actress from Baltimore, slightly schizophrenic in her teens, starred with Alan Ladd and died of hepatitis after a series of B rate films at the age of 54. Certainly she does not sound like you...well apart from the schizophrenia, but her features are so alike yours. Can you guess?" asked Isobelle.

"Mmm! I would guess Alan Ladd was in the 1940's. Let me try Googie Withers. Am I close?"

"Not even close, sweetie. Googie was English. No, try Veronica Lake."

"Veronica Lake? I do not think that I have come across her. Is she as pretty as me?" Isobelle heard the mirth in her voice.

"I was wondering when you would ask that. Yes, she is stunning. It was because I cannot have her that I want you - did you not realise?" Isobelle teased.

"It is a good job you cannot see me now...I am pouting and my eyes have gone as green as yours! Miss Lake had better watch out on my return!"

"On a serious note, how was your day? Could it have been as productive as mine?"

She heard Evelyn chuckle. "Actually, for once all is going to plan. I always dread delays as it often means that I have to extend my stays. I especially did not want that this time as I want to be with you over the weekend. Still I feel very weary, so I am going to run a bath and then go to bed clutching your handkerchief. What about you, darling?"

"Me, I'm going to put this likeness of you in a frame in my bedroom, and then I am going to follow your lead. I am also going to have to consider what term of endearment to call you, since I see that you have already laid claim to darling!"

Evelyn chuckled as she always chuckled, deep and beautifully. "I am sorry, I did not mean to monopolise it. Let's see, there is sweetheart, honey, dear, dear-heart, love, lover, poppet, treasure.......I have run out."

"Of that selection, I think I like love and poppet best. Perhaps in time I will discover one so embarrassing that you will flush as much as I seem to when I am in your presence. I wish you were with me now. I really want to kiss you and hold you." Isobelle closed her eyes all the more not to be distracted from Evelyn's voice.

"And I long to hold you, darling. We will soon and we have our keepsakes to remember each other by…when we meet later this week we will enjoy each other all the more. I am going to kiss you goodnight down the telephone now, so be ready to catch it.

Isobelle was and did.

CHAPTER FOURTEEN

Justification is the way we live and Isobelle knew that she would have to justify her actions over the coming weeks, but exactly when she would be held to account was the rub. To a certain extent she did have an element of time, for their relationship would be seen by most as that of two good friends. However, she was of a tactile nature and so the thought of guarding against glances that relayed massages of their love and desisting on affectionate touches was not thinkable. Her symptoms and behaviour left her in no doubt that she had fallen in love with a woman and that she should accept it and the consequences as should her family, friends and acquaintances. Obviously it would not be easy for there were undoubtedly elements of homophobia in society, but she knew that fortunately society was learning to be a lot more tolerant.

Her only big concern was the acceptance of her family, particularly Fiona, so she would have to handle that revelation with kid gloves. The very idea of Fiona being upset or disgusted by her affair was frightening, so much so that she tried hard not to dwell on that scenario too much. If it happened, then there would be little she could do but rue the loss of Fiona's close sisterliness. But that would have to be the consequence as she was not prepared to lose a love as tangibly intense and real as this in order to protect other's conceptions on what moral values she should possess. Knowing Fiona as she did though, she could not foresee a rejection of any kind. If anything, she would possibly try and discourage her with the impediments likely to arise as a consequence of such a pairing. Nevertheless, the prospect of telling her was still intimidating. The appropriate time to tell Fiona would be dependent upon the commitment that she and Evelyn were to show one another. Neither of them had encountered such an affinity so that the experiences would be fumblingly new and the reactions probably more diverse and varied than a conventional relationship. Isobelle was unequivocal in the depth of her fervour for Evelyn and she was fairly convinced that this passion was reciprocal. However, they had yet to undergo any potential hostility or rejection, catalysts that might shake and worry at the very essence of their new love. Although unimaginable, it might well lead on to doubts and second thoughts.

In a situation in which she might already have divulged their love for one another to her family, she could hypothesise the 'I told you so' smugness that would accompany the words of commiseration - Such a relationship was bound not to last....It must have just been a phase that she was going through, and other similar platitudes. A sad, uncomfortable parting with the 'Let's be adult, remain as friends', followed by matchmaking suppers with eligible young men unknowingly paraded with the express idea of placing her firmly back on the straight and narrow. Such a future would be unbearable and she resolved to ensure that she did all she could to retain Evelyn's love.

Her mother would no doubt use the question of children as a potential obstacle; after all, how can two women produce children and what of the mothering instincts? To a certain degree, Fiona had helped her famously, for once married, the pressure would rest firmly on hers and Piers' shoulders to produce a grandchild. At present Isobelle had no inclination to children, although she had no dislike of them. She assumed her hormones were just not responsive yet. And, if the occasion should arise, she was sure that there were ways and means for lesbians to have children through insemination or adoption. As long as the relationship was stable and loving, she could see no reason for objections to be raised. It was something to discuss with Evelyn in the future.

Mulling over the word 'lesbian' directed her to consider what she actually did want from their future together. Without a shadow of doubt, she wanted Evelyn. She adored her potency and seeming aloofness, which so rapidly could change to shyness and humility. She loved the way she knew in her bones that they would live well together, sensitive to each other's strengths and weaknesses, but neither assuming authority. Evelyn had a calm about her, a tranquillity that was reflected in her poise. *I am so fortunate to have met her* thought Isobelle - *I am so sure that I will benefit my life from just being with her*. What is more, Isobelle knew that she had plenty to give in return. Being hardly conversant with the world of lesbianism, she assumed that there would be clubs, bars and meeting places specifically for them. Perhaps also advice on the Internet. However, she reasoned that at the moment she did not want to frequent these venues, but would rather try and maintain a certain level of normality. Whatever she felt about the justice of it, woman to woman relationships which strayed beyond the fenced off areas of friendship were not the expected norm although society was moving towards greater tolerance. Even she had her perimeters, as she admitted to feeling herself quite threatened and apprehensive of the femme/butch relationships. Evelyn was every bit a beautiful woman and it seemed so natural that she be attracted to beauty. So, what she felt more comfortable with was not heralding her lesbianism by mixing exclusively with lesbian groups, but admitting it and hoping that their lives could go on as they had been. She just did not want them to be indexed as different, but just be accepted for what they were, namely two women with a lot to offer. She suspected that her outlook was probably considered naive and, no doubt, one that numerous lesbians of longer standing had once striven for, but this was to be her path now and she felt confident that she and Evelyn could deal with it. That was not to say that she did not respect the tribulations which the early lesbians had battled through to make society more accepting, the Stonewalls of the world; but, Isobelle argued, that was partly why she wanted to treat their relationship as naturally as possible. It was because that is what those lesbians had struggled for, the right to determine their choice of partner and not be excluded by society as being unconventional.

And so the week wore on and with it the weather grew greyer and colder, scattering Isobelle's certainties as the blustering winds and heavy, impulsive thunderstorms scattered the filigree blossoms into untidy piles in the gutters. The often quoted *'Absence makes the heart grow stronger'* was more often said by those not actually exposed to the absence. Most lovers know otherwise, that any absence when building on a relationship is in fact extremely wrenching. Emotions are playing ping pong; these are the days in which so much is uncovered about one another before the criterion of the relationship are forged, before the love is sealed and acknowledged by others. Any break in this process only lends the mind to idle speculation, the niggling question of 'What if?', the reproach of favourable attributes not mentioned and the infernal fear of a changed mind or regret.

Isobelle found herself living for the steady rock of confirmation in Evelyn's telephone call each evening, after which she would torture herself with misguided interpretations of words said and nuances in tone. And who was to say that Evelyn might not be approached by someone more beautiful, more worldly then her? What then? As if to torment herself further, she would listen to ballads of bleeding hearts and desperate angst; evenings huddled in a chair, sharing the tears that Connie Francis lamented in 'Who's Sorry Now' or 'Carolina Moon'. All the while her stomach gyrated and spiralled, perturbed by her anguish and sending her time and time again running to the bathroom.

On the Wednesday morning she had received a pale mauve envelope containing the message:

"I think we dream so we don't have to be apart so long. If we're in each others dreams, we can be together all the time."

> See you soon, my darling,

> Love Evelyn.
> xxx

This mauve envelope was now almost bent beyond recognition as the letter was slipped in and out to be read, re-read and read yet again. It had been clutched tightly and wetted with salty tears, but each reading served to strengthen the ache under her ribs. It was like a narcotic though, for she could not avoid looking at the words at least once an hour, as if in the period between reads the words might curl and change to voice the unfounded concerns pricking at her conscience. She was well aware that the rationale for these worries was spurious and that in the scheme of things Evelyn's absence was fleeting, but the heady mixture of love, longing, missing, and ennui had no place for reason and good sense. No, it knocked chairs over, it spilt a cup of coffee, it caused the light bulb to go. It gnawed and worried at her, turning four days into a twisted eternity.

CHAPTER FIFTEEN

Wednesday evening's call from Evelyn did little to help her disposition and she sincerely hoped that the anguish in her voice was hidden from Evelyn.

"I am truly, truly sorry, my darling, but I am not going to be able to return until Friday. I did try to clear everything up by today so that I could drive back tomorrow, but a problem with some roof joists has caused a delay. It should be cleared up tomorrow and I will rush back on Friday. Are you cross with me?"

"Oh! Evelyn, how could I ever be cross at you….it is the fates I am cross with. I do so long to see you and hold you again. And you must not rush back too quickly; be careful driving as I want every luscious part of you back in one piece!"

"You are working Friday, are you not?" asked Evelyn.

"Unfortunately, yes."

"Well, I have to drive back into town to the office on Friday, so what say you pop round after work? I can show you my office and then we can go for a bite to eat before driving home. Tell you what, bring your night things and stay over so that you need not rush home. How does that sound?"

Isobelle's heart was lifted once again. She felt the makings of a smile erupt through her body, before settling contentedly on her full lips. "Evelyn, my love, that will be heavenly!"

What a difference an hour, a piece of news, some hope makes; driven out was the turbulence that turned common sense opaque, to be replaced with an unbridled happiness and a need to prepare herself. To elevate her further out of the trough and up the peak, there arrived another of the pale mauve envelopes on the Thursday morning. This time she carefully opened the letter, fingers fluttering over the folded sheet, to recite:-

'Give me a kiss, and to that kiss a score; Then to that twenty, add a hundred more: A thousand to that hundred: so kiss on, To make that thousand up a million. Treble that million, and when that is done, Let's kiss afresh, as when we first begun.'

We have a lot to catch up on,

Your love,
Evelyn.
xxx

Thursday evening could not come quickly enough. For once, domestic chores were not deemed as chores, as Isobelle sailed around the flat dusting and tidying, loading the washing machine and arranging the ironing. Appropriately, Patsy Cline's 'Crazy' accompanied her as she selected her clothes carefully, with both the bitter weather and impressing Evelyn in mind. Friday would see her in a tailored trouser suit in a muted gold for work, but she would pack warm fitted trousers and soft brushed cotton blouses for casual. Wisps of lilac and chantilly lace found their place in her bag along with comfortable socks, thick cardigans and low-heeled shoes. Toiletries and make-up were ready for popping in last thing the following morning. The night attire was a bit of a problem, as she generally slept with nothing on to restrict her, but she did own a pair of pyjamas patterned with blue forget-me-nots. They would have to suffice. Her eyes dwelt on the pyjamas as she considered what Evelyn was likely to wear in bed. Living alone, she doubted on any slinky translucent nightie, but she could imagine her in a long satin number - with her lovely blond hair and elegant figure floating in muted lighting, she would surely look like a Christmas card angel. The image was enough to make Isobelle hug herself with the anticipation. Her Christmas card angel…her guardian angel, her angel.

What would it be like to spend a night with her in the tower? Would she be expected to sleep on a sofa in the lounge, or would Evelyn take her to her own bed. And what then? Isobelle had no hesitation in knowing that she wanted Evelyn as she had no other, that she pined for her and that the thought of touching and caressing her nakedness was so electrifying she felt positively faint. She called to mind her fantasies in the shower after she had first seen Evelyn and the impact that brief encounter had afforded her. It had been all she could do not to drop to her knees, her legs had been shaking so much. Of course, if Evelyn did invite her to bed, would she know what to do? She assumed that she would do the things that she found excited her and hoped that they effected Evelyn in the same way. Still, she thought, we are both experimenting in this, so we will have to help each other. After all, the trepidation would be no different to that of any couple making love for the first time.

Friday was a busy day at work for which she was grateful as she was buzzing inside like a light bulb. She knew that she was glowing and, from the looks she received from her colleagues, she was also aware that they perceived a dramatic change in her. Fortunately they were all too polite to enquire why. The one thing she had decided for certain was that if the weekend went well, then she would tell Fiona about herself and Evelyn. Guilty that she had not spoken to Fiona all week, she gave her a quick call.

"Hello, Fi, how are you doing? Sorry I did not get to see you last weekend, but I ended up visiting a friend's house and did not get back until late."

"No problem, Issy. It was nothing firm anyhow. You know that you only need call and you will always be welcome around at our house. I hate to think of you alone all the time, but if you were with someone, that was all well and good." Isobelle could hear the unspoken question in her voice.

"Yes, Fi, I know what you are thinking!" laughed Isobelle, "and you are partly right. I have met someone special to me and I am going to this friend's house again this weekend. I was hoping that we could meet up for lunch next week and then I will tell you all, but I need a promise from you first."

"Now this sounds exquisitely interesting," purred Fiona. "What promise must I commit to?"

"Just that you won't say anything until after we meet, particularly to mum. You know she will be on my case if there is the hint of romance in the air."

"And is there?" she questioned cheekily.

"Wait until next week. How would Monday lunch suit you? We can go to the Thai restaurant just down the road from here."

"Let's see…..Monday's fine. And fear not, Issy, my lips will be firmly sealed from everyone until then, although I will be bursting to know the full details!"

"Fi, you are a gem. How are your plans going? Have you sorted out your honeymoon yet?"

"So far everything is going swimmingly. Piers said that he has booked somewhere hot and luxurious with beaches and beauty, so that takes care of all my needs! I know what to pack for, but outside of that it is a surprise."

"Knowing how sensitive Piers is, I'm sure it will be somewhere divine."

Isobelle was somewhat relieved that she had made the commitment to tell Fiona, otherwise there would be too many opportunities to keep putting it off. And she really did want to share this news with Fiona. She was certain that Fiona would be genuinely happy for her now, especially as Fiona herself was so exultant - she would dearly want Isobelle to share in that blissful state. Isobelle only hoped that she would continue to feel the same way after Monday.

CHAPTER SIXTEEN

That evening she unusually left the office by 5pm, in itself raising a few eyebrows and whispers from her more discerning colleagues. Since it was not a particularly pleasant day and also because she was lugging around an overnight bag, she allowed herself the extravagance of a taxi.

"Portland Place," she requested, before relaxing back into the seat with an excited shiver of anticipation. Seeing Evelyn again just could not come soon enough, although now that the time was almost upon her, she was enjoying the build up of exhilaration. Isobelle directed the taxi to a recently sandblasted building of pomp and grandeur, decorated in columns and stone carvings so popular in Queen Victoria's day. Although Isobelle's favourite period was Regency, she could see that this imposing building was a noble forefront for an eminent architectural design company. However, on walking through the doors, she was awed to find herself transported into a lobby of Art Deco, with large clean sweeping lines of stone and shiny metal, of triangular clocks and a sweeping staircase guarded at the base by two black marble panthers. She was bewitched by it, more so since it was unexpected, but she could not help at the same time feeling excessively sorry for the poor cleaners having to perpetually retain a gleam on the acres of metal. She walked self-consciously across a swathe of marble in a Middle Eastern geometrical design to the reception, where four receptionists were fairly dwarfed by the proportions of a long, slender wood and chrome desk.

"Hello," she announced, "I'm here to see Evelyn Hertford, if you please."

"Ah! Yes," said the receptionist, a very efficient, middle-aged lady dressed in the style of the lobby. She noticed that the others were likewise garbed; obviously a uniform. "You must be Miss Swanson," she continued with a friendly smile, "Miss Hertford asked us to look out for you. If you would care to take a seat I will let her know you have arrived." She gestured to some curved easy chairs, each so long they had to have been purpose-built. "Can I fetch you a drink at all while you wait?"

Much as Isobelle would have enjoyed a coffee, she realised that Evelyn had paid her a kind of compliment in inviting her to this office and Isobelle was eager to make her proud of her trust. The very last thing she wanted to do was risk spilling coffee over herself, thus creating embarrassment all round. She always remembered the time some taxation inspectors had visited their office, and how, after a visit to the toilet, one of them had unknowingly traipsed around the building trailing some toilet paper caught in his trousers. Everyone had virtually wet themselves with stifled laughter, her included, but at the same time she felt ashamed that her amusement was at his expense, especially over something that could so easily happen to anyone and which could leave such an everlasting impression.

She was so absorbed in her reverie that she did not notice the receptionist return, starting as she coughed discreetly.

"Oh! Sorry, I was miles away," she apologised with a grin.

"That's quite alright," the lady replied. "Miss Hertford asked if you would mind going up and meeting her. If you take one of the lifts directly over there to the Fourth Floor, she will be waiting for you. Now if you do not fancy carting your bag up there, I can look after it for you in reception."

"That's very kind of you, but to be honest, I'm not altogether sure how long we will be. Besides it is not too heavy, so I will hang on to it, if you don't mind."

"I understand, by all means." She offered Isobelle a laminated pass and a clipboard. "For security, I'm afraid. Would you mind signing in for me?"

Soon Isobelle was ascending in the heavily mirrored lift, hardly conscious of the upward movement. Before she knew it the doors were sliding back to present a large foyer of chrome and ultramarine. Corridors led off on each side and standing, absolutely radiant by the one on the right was Evelyn. Isobelle's heart almost stopped, for Evelyn just looked so stunning that she surpassed the visions that Isobelle had held in her mind.

"Isobelle," Evelyn greeted, striding quickly over to meet her. She held Isobelle's shoulders and kissed her on each cheek, whispering, "Quickly, come to the office. I so want to kiss you, you raven-haired beauty!"

Smelling her perfume mingling with the hibiscus scent of her hair was a heady concoction for Isobelle and she had to be guided, almost trance-like to Evelyn's office. As soon as Evelyn had closed the door, she cupped Isobelle's face in her cool hands, pulling her face close to her own. At first Isobelle thought that Evelyn was going to at last kiss her and closed her eyes in readiness. However, after a few seconds she opened them to find Evelyn's eyes roaming over every feature of her face, her thumbs tenderly massaging Isobelle's cheeks as she did so.

"Oh! Isobelle," she breathed, "how I have missed this face, these eyes, this beautiful hair and your wonderful soft lips." As she said this she raised a hand and her fingers traced each in turn, finally gliding over her mouth, the manicured nail sending currents through her sensitive flesh. Isobelle darted out her tongue and ran it over Evelyn's finger, the whole time staring deep into her blue eyes. Eyes that were glazed, eyes that spoke of her desire for Isobelle. *How silly I was that I should have ever felt so worried when she was away in Derby,* thought Isobelle. *While these eyes convey her love so clearly, I shall doubt no more.* With a surge of tenderness for her, Isobelle leaned forward and let her lips graze against Evelyn's, nuzzling delicately at her bottom lip before kissing her brassily, her tongue tracing Evelyn's lips and ever seeking out her own moist tongue. She tasted Evelyn and kept wanting more; Isobelle could feel her own fuller lips pulsing. The skin on her face seemed to tingle, a delectation that coursed down the back of her neck and along her spine. It felt effervescent. The blood in her head pounded to the point that she almost felt dizzy.

"Evelyn," she managed to groan, "you just do not know what you are doing to me inside." Evelyn managed a lazy smile, her forehead against Isobelle's, noses almost touching.

"I think I do, darling, because a similar thing is happening in me."

"I am so pleased you are back. My whole being was screaming out to see you again. Do you have much to do here?"

Their eyes were still inches from each other's, and Isobelle drank in Evelyn's warm breath as she replied. "No, darling, I am almost done. I just have to take some papers to my boss and give a quick update on my week and that will be it. Would you like a drink while you wait?"

Isobelle smiled inwardly at the thoughts she had had earlier on spilling coffee and being embarrassed. Now she felt on top of the world, confident. "Yes, poppet, I would love one. Do you have anything cold?"

Evelyn pointed to some cabinets. "If you look in that cupboard there is a mini bar. Please help yourself to anything. I shall be as quick as I can and then the weekend is ours." She smiled so tantalisingly as she parted from Isobelle that she almost pulled her back again. It was only the knowledge that to delay would mean less time together at the tower, a far safer venue for privacy than this office. She poured herself a fresh orange that was refreshingly cold, running the glass over her fevered brow. Meanwhile, Evelyn had managed to pick up a file and walk to the door without taking her eyes off Isobelle. Hesitating, she moved towards Isobelle and carefully took the glass from her hand. While still watching her, she tipped the glass, the orange bold against her red lips, the lipstick leaving its mark on the rim. "Make yourself at home," she grinned, "I will be back soon."

Taking her glass to Evelyn's executive chair, Isobelle settled and swivelled to take in the room. As of yet, she had not really noticed very much, her attention until now being much more pleasurably occupied. The layout of the office, in terms of fixed fittings, encapsulated the style of the rest of the building in its dynamic industriousness. However, Isobelle could see that Evelyn had been able to indulge in her own touches, such as in a couple of well-framed Vermeer prints and some easy chairs which looked far too comfortable to be Art Deco. She guessed that Evelyn did not spend a great deal of time in this office, for she had noticed a mahogany architect's pedestal desk at the tower and assumed that she did much of her design work at home. Behind her, there were large windows affording a panoramic view over London, making it look a lot more inviting than on the ground level due to the larger sweep of the sky. Swinging back to Evelyn's desk, Isobelle perused all the bits and pieces that covered it; she noticed that there were no photographs, but she was unsure just how close she was with her parents. While pondering this, she suddenly noticed that there was doodling on a telephone note pad…with a thrill she noticed that the centre of the doodle spelt her name and she could make out little hearts radiating out from it. This very palpable display of a private moment gave her a flood of affection for Evelyn. It made her feel secure and safe in their love, knowing for sure that their parting had not lessened Evelyn's regard for her. She smiled to herself and hugged herself with joy, a shiver of beatitude coiling through her body.

Before she knew it, Evelyn breezed back through the door, dropping a large file on her desk. She came round behind the chair in which Isobelle was sitting and began to play with her hair, letting her fingers slip through its fine red strands. She bent her head down and pecked a kiss on Isobelle's ear.

"Are you ready to go, young lady?" she uttered in a low voice. "Because I want to take you home."

Being driven home in the comfort of a Land Cruiser as opposed to the train was a luxury in itself, but seated beside someone as beautiful as Evelyn made it bliss. At first, shy with each other once again, they talked about their work and the week that had just passed. Weather even featured in their conversation before Isobelle asked, "Would you mind if I put on some music?"

"By all means. I think we're both like those clockwork toys that have been wound up, waiting to be released. Perhaps music will calm us. Is there something you like?"

Isobelle looked through the collection and exclaimed in surprise at how many were ones that she had herself. "We're peas in a pod," she grinned. Selecting a CD collection of Celtic bands, she sank back in her seat, idly watching Evelyn in concentration as she manoeuvred through the north London traffic. She was so graceful, this blond angel beside her. Sometimes she felt that she wanted her so much that she wanted to become her, absorb her thoughts. But then she would not have the absolute pleasure of being able to kiss such a heavenly body. Instinctively, she reached over and rested her hand on Evelyn's leg, the material of her dress cool under her palm. Evelyn turned towards her and gave one of the smiles that turned her from a woman to a worshipping schoolgirl inside. As a song came up that she particularly liked, Isobelle could not help herself from singing. After only a few seconds, Evelyn joined in with her and before long they were in full vocal flow as they began to pick up speed on the road out of town.

As the countryside unfurled around them, they fell into a respectful quiet, drinking in nature's spring attire in the daylight of the lengthening days.

So often winter in England can seem exhausting; going to and from work in perpetual dark wearied the soul, so that any bright days brought the populous scurrying about like lizards to lap up the rays and revitalise.

"I adore being in your presence, poppet, even when we do not speak. I feel so comfortable and, strangely enough, protected. Did you have much time to think about us and your future with me while you were in Derby?" Isobelle felt tentative asking, there was always the fear of the unexpected answer.

"It was harder thinking of the barn conversion," laughed Evelyn. "Seriously though, I did spend most of my evenings considering our future. I know we shall find the going rather difficult at times and certainly with you and your family being so close it would be disastrous if they were to make you a pariah. But my heart and my head are unanimous in wanting to build a life with you. I have never, ever experienced the intensity of emotion that I have for you and frankly I do not want to lose you. I know that together we can overcome most adversities if we stick by one another. What do you think, darling?"

Isobelle exhaled noisily having held her breath in expectancy, spluttering "I think that speaks volumes! I was so worried that you might re-consider. I am anxious about my family too, but I am a big girl now and have to think about my own future. I know that they will be concerned for me, but I am positive that they will accept us once they realise that we are serious about one another. If not, then it will be unfortunate, but it is your love that feeds me now."

Evelyn took her own hand from the wheel and laid it over Isobelle's, squeezing it being the only response required. After a while, Isobelle asked, "Evelyn, what of your family, will you tell them?"

Evelyn appeared not to have heard at first. Just when Isobelle was about to let it go, she replied. "I believe that I will in time. Maybe sometime we can go over to Ireland together, but not just yet. My parents and I have never been that close - the irony is that my line manager at work, Irene Jessup, has been more of a parent than they have ever been. When I was going through all the problems at Manchester, I needed to confide in them, but because they were so involved in my father's philandering, they never had the time for me. The last time I visited home was about two months ago and the reception I received was more akin to that of a guest than a daughter. They come from a generation and breeding that made no show of outward affection and tried to sweep weaknesses and scandals under the carpet rather than confront them. In a way I feel extremely let down by them. If I told them about us, they would just pretend that they had not heard. They would ask me about the men I had met, whether you had a boyfriend, that kind of thing."

"Well, don't worry about that, my love," comforted Isobelle patting her leg. "Let's not think of anything that detracts from this weekend."

"Sounds good to me," Evelyn said with a brave smile.

CHAPTER SEVENTEEN

In Elizabethan plays the Fates play their role, often mischievously, directing the hero and heroine into awkward situations or sending out misplaced messages to confuse or beguile. But they are usually not malicious; there is a method in their deceptions and in the conclusion, all is made right. The lovers are brought together and the curtain closes on their sealed kiss. The Elizabeths on the throne have changed in that time, but have the Fates, for off-stage they have been awaiting their cue and now they decide it is the hour to make their entrance?

The weekend changed as soon as Isobelle and Evelyn turned into the drive. Clearly visible was the damage to the tower, for several of the huge lounge windows were smashed, the large glass fragments scattered around the base. Isobelle glanced at Evelyn and saw that she had paled visibly.

"Oh! No," she groaned, "don't say that he has started again!"

"What…do you think it is that Richard guy again? Would he do this?"

"I grew to believe he would do anything," she said bitterly. "Let's go in and then I will have to call the police."

They ascended through each room cautiously, Isobelle leading the way, her hand gripped in Evelyn's. Neither thought that anyone would still be here, especially since the door had been firmly locked, but their fear was such that neither was prepared to be foolhardy.

"So far, nothing appears to be disturbed," said Evelyn. Isobelle noticed that Evelyn's self-assuredness had slipped away, leaving a frightened girl in her place. She gripped her hand tighter to let her know she was not facing this alone any more.

"Come on, sweet pea," she coaxed, "only the lounge to go. Let's get the worst over with."

One of the incredible mysteries of glass is the way in which, when smashed, its volume increases significantly. Evelyn's lounge literally looked as if the proverbial bull had thundered through this china shop, for there were shards of glass everywhere. Admittedly the windows had been huge in the room and two of them had been smashed, but the sheer amount of pieces over the room belied their size and number. It was all over the sofas, the furniture and on the floor.

"How do you think it was done?" Evelyn asked quietly, a trance-like expression on her face.

"I would think that was part of the reason," replied Isobelle, pointing at a huge rock near the dining table. "It looks as if it has got something wrapped round it. Shall I go and take a look."

"No, I must ring the police. I have Detective Keenan's card in my purse… I must ring him." She seemed all at sixes and sevens with the possible intrusion into her life by this Bleach maniac, so Isobelle decided that she must show her strength and help Evelyn now when she required it. She led her down to the kitchen and got her to find Detective Keenan's card. Then she gave his mobile a call, praying that he was not on holiday or too busy to answer. Fortunately he answered the phone quickly, his calm, authoritative voice comforting under the circumstances.

"Hello, my name is Isobelle Swanson and I am a very close friend of Evelyn Hertford," she declared.

"Yes, I know Evelyn. Is she alright?" There was genuine concern in his voice.

"Well, when we arrived back at the tower this afternoon, we found that two of the large windows had been smashed. It looks as though it has been done on purpose and we think that there is a message on one of the rocks. We have not touched a thing though, so unless you want me to go and check, I am not sure what it says."

"No, leave it just as it is. I am about an hour away, but I will ring the local police and meet them across there. How is Evelyn taking it?"

Isobelle looked over at Evelyn who was sitting at the kitchen table, still pale, staring at the table surface. "Not very well, I suspect. I think this nightmare was something that she thought had largely gone away. I will get her some sweet tea and care for her."

"Right, that sounds like a good idea. I'll see you both in an hour or so, although the locals may be there sooner."

As soon as Isobelle had put down the phone, she went over and knelt in front of Evelyn, pulling her towards her in an embrace. At first, Evelyn acted much like an automaton, but as Isobelle's warm clasp permeated her shock, she responded by clutching Isobelle tightly back, the sobs beginning to rack her body.

"Why can't he just leave me alone?" she managed between the tears. "I never did anything to encourage him, because I never liked him. Why, Oh! Why can't he leave me be?"

Isobelle let her cry for a while, squeezing her every now and then to reassure her, before she got up and made her a sweetened tea.

"Drink this down, sweet pea. It will make you feel a little better." As Evelyn sipped, Isobelle suddenly fancied that she had found a pet name for Evelyn without consciously thinking about one - but what an inopportune time to do so. She felt a quick, but brief, flush of guilt sweep through her, but it was short-lived as she knew that any sign of support and affection was what Evelyn needed more than anything now.

"I'm so sorry that I have dragged you through all this," whispered Evelyn, the tears still running down her damp cheeks.

"Please don't say things like that, my love. I am so glad that I was here with you and I intend to help you through this. I love you, don't you see. What a shallow person I would be if I upped and walked at the first adversity." Isobelle back down beside Evelyn, lent over and delicately licked at her tears, gracefully kissing the path up to the corners of her blue eyes. She quietly quoted,

"Let there be such oneness between us, that when one cries, the other tastes salt. You know, when I was young, my mother loved her garden and she tried to teach me about the flowers that she grew. Being in the Middle East, many were exotic, like the sensual hibiscus (my favourite), with it's shape and form that can only be feminine; the frangipani with so

much passion in a name; the dancing lantana, with varied coloured florets so bright against the cool whites of the buildings. I wanted all these in my garden one day, but I could not afford a flat with a garden when I was looking to buy. However, one day I was in a garden centre and saw seeds for a plant which mesmerised me with its colour and I saw that I could grow it in a window box. It was a Morning Glory, and when it bloomed, the blue was like no other blue I'd ever seen. That was, until I saw your eyes. You have that intense, elegant blue hue which thins out at the edge of your iris into a subtle pinky-mauve. The sad thing about the Morning Glory is that they barely survive past the morning, before they curl up and die. Whereas in your eyes I see life and love everlasting."

She giggled, her face inches from Evelyn's. "I will water you daily and make sure you grow strong and healthy!"

"Tell me a little about your mother," asked Evelyn. She was not shaking quite so much.

"I will, but first let me take you to your bedroom, so that you can lie down and I can hold you properly." She was guided easily to her bed, where Isobelle removed both their shoes before lying down next to Evelyn, hugging her against her own body.

"I think my mother had been destined for another life, for she was very beautiful and intelligent, yet had an airy quality about her as if the world was rushing by her. But she was still stood in the pioneering days of the 1950's, where the ex patriots lived in huge houses with maids, child-minders and gardeners. Although not particularly strong in stature, she had a strength which propelled her through our postings from West Africa to the Middle East, organising everything from the packing to selecting schools for us. The thing that I found amazing about her was the way in which she found it incredibly hard to understand that there was bad in the world. She had this propensity to just switch off when troubles ventured beyond a certain point."

"How so?" asked Evelyn, intrigued.

"To give you an example…..let's see. Oh! Yes. My mother was mad about cats. She was like a pied piper going around collecting all the strays and waifs and putting out food for them, de-fleaing them, helping those that were hurt, caring for the pregnant ones - nothing was too much. Then I came out for a school holiday, bristling with anger at my recently foray into the world of animal abuse and vivisection. I regaled her with diatribes on man's disgusting treatment of animals, forcing one repellent picture after another under her nose. I truly thought that with her love of these strays, that she would understand my aversion to these loathsome molestation and why I simply had to become vegetarian. But no matter how much I created, I learned to recognise the glaze that slipped over her retinas signifying that she would be somewhere else. She could not begin to comprehend that people could treat animals cruelly and so, long before it registered she just changed channels in her mind. That was one occasion, but there were many of them on subjects like wars, school shootings and the like."

"I sort of envy her that," said Evelyn, "particularly with regard to this horrid man. How I wish I could change the channel on him!"

"Yes. Although it means that if you ignore it those around you have to deal with it for you. Ignorance can be bliss, but think of all the injustices in the world that would no doubt continue had it not been for those brave souls who stood up for a belief. We are lesbians and we can have certain rights because others before us did not switch off. I hate this Richard Bleach as much as you do, principally because of the hurt he has caused to you, but I am going to stand with you now and do my utmost to make sure that he cannot keep hounding you."

As Isobelle was speaking they became aware of police sirens in the middle distance, drawing ever louder as they neared the tower. It was comforting to hear, yet also unnerving, for they knew that for the next few hours, their lives would not be their own. Isobelle rose from the bed and watched as two patrol cars turned into the drive. She was also gratified to see that of the four members that got out of the cars, two were policewomen. She was sure that they could be just as hard-nosed in their line of questioning, but she would put money on them being more sensitive to the trauma. As she watched them heading towards the front door a line popped into her head, *'Ah! When will this long weary day have end, And lend me leave to come unto my love?'*

"I'll just go down and let them in," she said, taking Evelyn's hand in hers. "Will you be alright with the questions? I will answer as much as I can on your behalf, but some information they may need from you?"

"I will be alright now," she answered with an attempt at a smile. "And, Isobelle….thanks for giving me strength."

"That's what love is truly all about," replied Isobelle as she made for the stairs.

"Hello, I am Detective Jan Davies and this is my colleague, Sergeant Robson. We were contacted by Detective Keenan and filled in on the situation regarding Miss Hertford. Are you Miss Hertford or her friend?" asked one of the police women, a smallish, but sturdy looking woman.

"I am Evelyn's friend, Isobelle Swanson. I called Detective Keenan on Evelyn's behalf, as she was naturally quite upset.

"That is understandable if it relates to this stalker. Perhaps you can show us where the damage has occurred. If you do not mind these two will just have a look around outside." In saying this, she motioned towards the other police woman and policeman behind her.

"By all means," agreed Isobelle. "Would you care to follow me?"

She led the way up to the bedroom first, where she introduced them to Evelyn, before guiding them up to the lounge and the mess therein. Neither the detective nor her colleague entered the room, explaining that they were advised to leave it for Detective Keenan to investigate. Even as they spoke, the sound of another car could be heard entering the drive. Shortly after, voices could be heard downstairs, followed by someone athletically bounding up the circular stairs to where they were grouped on the landing.

"I hope you don't mind my coming up unannounced, but I thought you would prefer not to have to go up and down these stairs too often," he greeted with a boyish smile. He was a middle-aged man, but one that was fighting it all the way, for he had a figure that told of many hours in the gym. With blond hair and square, rugby-player's jaw, he must break many hearts, thought Isobelle. But jock with no brain he was not, for in his eyes there was an intelligence and compassion. It was strange, mused Isobelle. A few weeks ago I might have gone weak at the knees for such a man, whereas now I have eyes for no one but Evelyn.

"How is Evelyn?" he asked, genuine concern in his voice.

Isobelle told him how she seemed to fold when they had discovered the damage, fearful, no doubt that Richard Bleach was about to commence his persecution again.

"I'll pop down and see her in a minute, but first, let's establish whether it was this Mr Bleach or not."

"Can I make you a drink in the meantime?" asked Isobelle, not quite sure how to be of help.

"You're an angel sent from the heavens. I am parched!" beamed Detective David Keenan.

CHAPTER EIGHTEEN

Within an hour of his arrival, Detective Keenan knocked on the door of the bedroom where Isobelle and Evelyn were awaiting the result of the search upstairs.

"Can we just go into the kitchen and chat a moment?" he asked. Isobelle noticed that he had a more uncertain air about him that suggested that perhaps it was to do with Richard Bleach. Once they were seated, he looked over at Evelyn.

"I guess that you are still feeling pretty unsettled," he sympathised, "and what I have to say now will do little to comfort you; either of you." He turned towards Isobelle as if to reiterate the point.

"How do you mean?" asked Isobelle, confused.

"One of the rocks he used had a note wrapped around it. I want to show it to you and ask you whether it is true. I am asking, not because I am nosy but because it will mean that I need to review this case. Here…" He laid out a creased note on the table, encased in a plastic folder. It read:

"My God!" exclaimed Evelyn, "what have I got you into?" She appeared very close to tears again.

"Oh! Evelyn. This is none of your doing. How can you say that you have caused my involvement when this is the last thing you ever wanted. I am here for you and nothing he does will break that bond."

"I am sorry if I am reading this incorrectly, but from that remark, can I assume that you both are in a relationship?" interjected Detective Keenan.

"Yes," confirmed Isobelle. "How will this affect what your investigation, for presumably you will be trying to find him anyway."

"We will need to get this note to the lab and compare it to the others. However, what is really concerning here is the fact that he has made a threat on your life. Although he has made Evelyn's life pretty miserable, so far he has not threatened her or anyone close to her." He sighed as he gathered up the note. "What we will have to do is have a look at the security protection on your home."

Isobelle told him about the fact that her flat had a security door and that the residents were all aware of the dangers of letting in strangers following a recent talk from the community police as part of the Neighbourhood Watch scheme. "This is all new to me though; this stalking thing. Can you tell me more about it? Why is he doing what he's doing?"

Detective Keenan nodded. "To answer your question properly, I think it would be a good idea if I started by providing some history. Stalking has been going on for years, but it was only in January 2000 that the UK's first national anti-stalking unit was authorised by the Home Secretary. This was mainly the result of the growing incidence of stalking prosecutions under the Protection from Harassment Act in 1997. Statistics from the United States show that 1 in 12 women and 1 in 45 men will be stalked in their lifetimes. It can have a devastating effect on people's lives, as Evelyn can confirm, so it is certainly a crime to be taken very seriously.

Although stalking is a gender-neutral crime, most of the stalkers are men. They come from no specific socio-economic background, are mainly young to middle aged and have above average intelligence. As there is no particular psychological or behavioural profile for stalkers, nearly anyone can be a stalker and likewise, almost anyone can be a victim."

While he had been talking, Evelyn had made another cup of tea. After taking a generous mouthful, Keenan continued.

"There are a number of different typesets that stalkers can fall into, such as Intimate, Vengeful, Delusional, and Erotomaniac, but these are lumped into two main categories, namely Love Obsession and Simple Obsession stalkers. I myself think the names are a little confusing, for the Love Obsessive is one where the stalker has only had a slight acquaintance, if any, with the victim but for whom they develop deep fixations. The best examples here are stalkers of celebrities. Anyhow, these stalkers usually suffer from a history of mental illness such as schizophrenia or manic depression. They constitute about 20 - 25% of all stalking crimes.

Now Richard Bleach falls more into the Simple Obsession group. In this group there has been some previous personal or romantic relationship between stalker and victim, usually before the stalking activities began. We know that in Evelyn's case, Richard Bleach knew her at Manchester and that he had tried unsuccessfully to begin an affair with her. He fits the common personality traits in that he was emotionally insecure, very jealous when he could not seduce Evelyn and he probably suffered from low self-esteem. His arrogance was undoubtedly a cover for this. He followed all the typical behavioural patterns, for he began by sending notes when Evelyn did not show interest in him, using intimidation when he saw that she was spurning his advances. This intimidation lead to unacceptable jealous intrusion, which soon lead on to a persistent form of harassment. He wants to effectively have power and control over Evelyn and he has now seen that she has someone in her life, namely you, Isobelle, who is diminishing that control. In an effort to reassert his dominance he is escalating into threatening behaviour and this is what worries me, because this is moving rapidly up a stage to potential violence."

"So, what you are saying is that he is now targeting Isobelle rather than me?" asked Evelyn, horrified.

"No, he still wants you, but if he cannot have you he will not allow anyone else to have a close relationship with you. He sees Isobelle as a threat and he will act to re-establish his control over you. To be blunt, I'm afraid that these cases are not pretty, which is why I am grateful that I can try and help people such as yourselves who are caught up in something so out of your control."

They were all silent for a moment, absorbing this frightening information. The only sound over the ticking of the kitchen clock being the sound of the other police personnel crunching on glass in the lounge above. Isobelle shivered involuntarily.

"So," she asked, "where do we go from here?"

"For us - we need to get this back to the lab and see if we can get anything incriminating from it." He motioned towards the bagged note as he spoke. We will also carry out local enquiries to see if anyone noticed him about here recently. The only problem is that he has money through his family and he can change his vehicle regularly. We already know from the past that he rents so that he can move on quickly, making him very hard to locate. On my way over, I established that he had moved on from the last known address that we have, so we will have to try and locate him quickly. You are both going to have to be very careful, particularly you, Isobelle. It would be a good idea if you stayed together or had company with you as much as possible. Ideally, if you could get away on a holiday for a couple of weeks, all the better. If you ever see him, do not try to tackle him. Alert either the police or myself as soon as you can. He is too dangerous for you to approach. If you have mobile phones, all the better for contacting us quickly.

Now, we are almost done here, but I don't know what you wish to do tonight. Unfortunately, our resources are such that we cannot station a car outside, but what we can do is send a patrol car past the house every now and then. It would be best to stay elsewhere, but with the windows smashed, I can understand it if you do not want to leave the house."

"I would prefer to stay with the house - I do not want him in my house, ever. What do you think Isobelle? Do you mind staying here tonight?" Evelyn lifted her defiant blue eyes to Isobelle's green and Isobelle knew that she would stay forever, if that were what was required.

"Okay, that's settled then. I will go and see how the others are doing and arrange for a patrol car to swing by the house a few times in the night." He left, his body language both sheepish and apologetic for the fear that he had very necessarily instilled in them.

Once he had left the room, Evelyn reached out and covered Isobelle's hand with her own. She appeared to be struggling to find the right words, but eventually she whispered contritely, "I am so sorry that you have been exposed to this."

Isobelle felt a little rush of anger and tried to keep it from her voice. "Evelyn, enough! I am in this as a result of falling in love with you and if you think that he is going to drive a wedge in between us, then think again. Look upon this as the first test of our relationship, one that we will deal with together. So, please, no more apologies from you. How can you think of apologising for his actions when you have done nothing to encourage him. Let us not let him ruin our lives or he has what he wants....let us fight him with our love for one another. A potent weapon if ever I saw one!"

At long last, Detective Keenan came into the kitchen to announce that they were now ready to go and that he would contact them the following day.

"We have moved some of the heavier furniture away from the broken windows just in case it rains."

And with that, followed by slamming car doors, they were gone. Isobelle and Evelyn decided to survey the damage once again. Although nothing other than the windows was broken, the destruction seemed so excessive. Conversely, the evening was beautiful, the sun still bright and spreading a orange hue across the lounge floor which sparkled on the myriad of glass shards as if on a chandelier. Together they lifted, heaved and pushed items such as the electrical equipment, books and pictures to the wall furthest from the windows now open to the elements. Evelyn decided to telephone a 24 hour cleaning company to come and sort out the mess, as there were so many tiny splinters of glass over the chairs and in the carpet, that only an industrial vacuum would stand a chance of collecting them all. On the off chance, she also contacted the Specialist Company that supplied the windows and was pleasantly surprised to find the office still manned. Checking their files for details of the window dimensions, they confirmed that they could supply a rush order, but that it would be costly as a crane would be required. *So be it*, was Evelyn's reply, *the windows had to be repaired.*

CHAPTER NINETEEN

"If we have finished in here, can we just go into your garden for some fresh air and enjoy the evening?" asked Isobelle. Now that Evelyn was busying herself, she wanted to help keep her mind firmly off Richard.

"Why not," grinned Evelyn. "I have a bottle of wine still in the car and I feel that we deserve to open it while we stroll round the shrubbery."

They began by unloading the groceries that Evelyn had in the back of the Land Cruiser. Isobelle was intrigued to see that there was a small fridge in the back where the milk and perishables had been stored.

"I remembered that you are a vegetarian, so I went and picked up some things on the way down to London. It seems an age ago now. Still, I hope that you like spaghetti as I bought some vegetarian mince," she said.

"It is a good job you did remember, as I was so pleased to hear from you on the telephone that I totally forgot to remind you. And yes, spaghetti is ideal."

Glasses of a fruity red in hand, they wandered out, arm in arm, to the back garden. It was the type of garden that was designed for low maintenance, with plants and shrubs of varying colours and textures for year round enjoyment. The pride of place on this Spring evening was the cyanosis, a neon blue lighting up the surrounding greens. But in the field of fragrance, the prize had to go to the wisteria entwined around an arbour and cascading mauve bunches of flowers like grapes with a scent so sweetly heady as to leave the women almost inebriated.

"If I lived here, then I would definitely sit out here each evening and enjoy this piece of nature," longed Isobelle, her eyes drinking up the peaceful view from the patio.

"Then perhaps that is what we will do," agreed Evelyn, adding, "and I will enjoy this piece of nature!" As if to emphasise the piece she had in mind, she ran her fingers over Isobelle's cheek, an act which sent a jolt of pleasure through her whole face.

They walked through the garden, hand in hand, while they sipped at their wine and drank in the scenery. Nearby was a large well established pond partly shaded by some trees where there was a carved wooden bench. They sat down and watched the carp swim lazily in the water, an occasional splash the only indication of their ability to suddenly react at the unfortunate insects which crossed their basking path.

"How are you reacting to this threat?" asked Evelyn, her fingers clasping those of Isobelle tightly.

"I admit that it frightens me, but it angers me more so. How can this man create so much fear in your life for so long and get away with it? Now he threatens me as well. What have women got to do to feel safe? I just cannot believe that he can create so much unhappiness without either of us giving him any just cause other than not accept his crude advances and to love each other? Oh! I know he is probably mentally mal-adjusted, but that doesn't help us. If he does anything nasty, you can bet he will receive all the necessary treatment from our caring state and we will have to suffer the psychological hurt ourselves." It was an uncharacteristic outburst from Isobelle, but its intensity made Evelyn proud of her. She squeezed Isobelle's hand in support.

Just as quickly as she had flared up, Isobelle's demeanour switched to reflective. "When was the last time you had a holiday?" she queried.

"Eons ago, and even then it was largely spent with my parents. Somehow the thought of a holiday abroad as a single female has always seemed daunting to me. I presume you are thinking about David the canny detective's suggestion."

"Mmm! No flies on you! I don't imagine that you've taken a decent break for a long time and to get away from this horrible atmosphere for a while would do us both the world of good."

"I have to admit that the thought of a holiday with you does have an appeal. I hope you have something in mind where the only exercise was down to us," she replied mischievously.

"Evelyn Hertford, you are incorrigible!" Isobelle declared, ruffling Evelyn's hair playfully. "Actually I did have a suggestion as to a location, but it can only be forced out of me by a beautiful woman's kiss!"

Evelyn gave the appearance of peering left and right theatrically. "Well, darling, in the absence of that beautiful woman, I guess all that I can do is vainly try and unlock the secret myself. The things that I have to do for my country!" With that, she cupped Isobelle's cheek in her hand and guided her lips to Isobelle's waiting mouth, pressing long and softly before letting their lips gently part.

Isobelle assumed a pained expression, speaking through gritted teeth. "Arrh! Miss Bond, your methods are persuasive, but you will have to do better to get anything out of me!"

Evelyn smiled evilly. "Miss Goldfinger, I should warn you that I have only just begun. I am a civilised woman, but my methods can get cruder unless you reveal all. The wine, of course, was drugged. Now, the holiday destination, Miss Goldfinger?"

"My lips are firmly sealed, Miss Bond."

"In that case, I shall just have to unseal them!"

Setting down her wineglass, Evelyn slid her hands into Isobelle's silken hair and pulled her tenderly towards her. Running her tongue lightly over her lips, she then kissed Isobelle with small pecks, getting longer as she tasted the sweetness of the wine on her breath. She carefully edged her wet tongue onto Isobelle's bottom lip, running its tip slowly and seductively around the sensational curves of the mouth, every now and then temptingly dipping to slide under the inside of her lip against her teeth. A moan escaped from one of the girls, although neither knew from whom as their minds could only just about accept the surges of bliss that were as heady as the wisteria. Their tongues met and they too performed a dance of their own, curling and caressing, their tempo changing as the waves of desire pitched and ebbed. Even though they were seated, Isobelle's body was shaking, so much so, that she knew had she been standing, her knees would have certainly given way beneath her. As it was, she felt dizzy, a prickling running up the length of her arms. When their lips at last parted, she felt as floppy and light-headed as if she had drunk the whole bottle of wine herself.

"You win, Miss Bond," she managed to whisper, drowning in the turbulent sea blue eyes right before her. Evelyn began to kiss away the succulence around her lips, the evidence of her physical onslaught to obtain the vital information.

"Speak, Miss Goldfinger, or I will have to really try and I would not be able to vouch for your sanity afterwards!"

"The destination, Miss Bond, is….France."

As with all warm days that grace the shores of England during Spring, they have a tendency to turn chilly very quickly. This abrupt change in temperature soon drove Isobelle and Evelyn back into the warm confines of the tower, where, having bolted the front door securely, they began to prepare the evening's spaghetti.

"I do hope that you like yours spicy," quipped Evelyn suggestively.

"Mmm! The hotter the better, although I do get hiccups which can be rather embarrassing in a restaurant."

They avidly discussed the idea of a trip to France together; the more they deliberated, the better the venture appealed to them. Isobelle was convinced that if they were to go, it should be relatively soon, mainly to get Evelyn and herself away from any immediate threat from Richard Bleach, but also because of Fiona and Piers' impending wedding.

"You know that I mentioned my sister, Fiona, is marrying Piers in June? Well she has asked whether I wish to invite anyone as my guest. I am going to be seeing her on Monday for lunch and wandered if I could tell her that you would be my partner?"

"I would be honoured to go with you - we will have to go shopping together for outfits unless you already have bought something to wear. I like the thought of shopping with you, as I usually have to do it alone."

"I am not organised enough to have bought anything yet, so you and I will definitely have to make a day of it." She hesitated a minute before declaring, "I am going to tell Fiona about us on Monday."

Evelyn stopped stirring the spaghetti sauce and stared at her, a look of admiration and love coursed over her features. "Are you sure that you want to yet, darling? It is going to be a big step for you to take and I am more than aware of what you could potentially lose."

"Yes, I am very sure indeed that I love you deeply and I feel it is only fair to tell the other woman in my life whom I love dearly. I very much want her to hear it from me. As she and I are so close, she might feel hurt if she thought that I could not confide in her. With this stalker threat, I also want her to be aware in case he finds out my name and sends any spiteful notes about us to her. I'll see what she says about telling the rest of the family."

"Good for you, Isobelle, and thank you for you trust in me. I suppose we have already made our first confession to Detective Keenan….poor man, alone with two beautiful women and a handsome guy like him didn't have a look in!"

"He is good looking, not what you would expect of a policeman…more a male model. But not a pip on my fair Evelyn, that's for sure." She sealed the statement by nuzzling through Evelyn's hair from behind and planting a kiss on her nape.

Once they had dished out the spaghetti and opened another bottle of Italian red, they resumed their conversation on the holiday. Evelyn was fairly convinced that her boss would actually welcome her request for a holiday as she had been recommending that Evelyn take some time off for ages. Isobelle was going through a fairly quiet period at the office, as the annual budgeting process did not hot up until the end of July, so there was every chance that she would be able to take the time.

"Now all we need to decide is where in France and for how long," announced Evelyn brightly. "Have you any suggestions on that as I am not familiar with France?"

Isobelle smiled cheekily. "I have actually and I will give you this piece of information on credit! When I was a teen, we went on a school trip to the Lot region of France and I remember how impressed I was with it. I have always wanted to go back there. So I thought, if we could organise a lovely well-furnished cottage just for us with a decent swimming pool, then that would be the ideal. Does that sound tempting to you? Please do not let me steam-roller you into anything that you do not want to do."

"What you are suggesting sounds marvellous, all the more so as it will be with you. You cannot imagine how thrilled I am at the prospect of this. It's just that I have not had a holiday that I have really looked forward to for so long."

"Well, sweat pea, I am already there in my mind! Tell you what, once the cleaners have done here tomorrow, what say you and I pop into Hertford and pick up some brochures? Better still, if you have a laptop, we can call up some sites and see what is available. Now that we have started on our planning, I have become too excited to stop just yet."

"What we can do is get rid of these dishes, make some coffee and take it and the rest of that wine through to the bedroom. I will go and get the laptop from the lounge and then we can surf in comfort. I would not mind putting a wedge on the lounge door. I am sure that he could not ascend the outside of the tower, but I would rather not take the risk."

"Good idea," Isobelle agreed, helping to collect up the plates and loading them into the dishwasher.

CHAPTER TWENTY

Early evening found them both lying curled up on Evelyn's king sized bed, searching through sites and jotting down any interesting and potential cottages. Although the selection was extensive in the Dordogne, they held fast to their plan to find somewhere in the Lot, a beautiful area not quite so populated by the tourists. Their tenacity paid off, for they suddenly stumbled on a cottage that contained just what they required and more. A 350 year old, but luxuriously appointed farmhouse set in 10 acres of valley, surrounded by woodland and streams. It had a restored pigeonnier so traditional of the area and a 12 metre swimming pool. The bonus was a floodlit tennis court, although neither Isobelle nor Evelyn were serious players. It looked so perfect, perhaps the only drawback in that it was essentially for 6 - 8 people. That put the price up somewhat, but Evelyn insisted that she would be prepared to pay as it would make up for all the previous holidays missed.

"But Evelyn, my sweet, I cannot allow you to pay for it alone. I must pay my way too," complained Isobelle.

"Well I have a proposal. What if I pay for the cottage and you cover the cost of the ferries and hotels? We can share the food bills. Please let me do this. I really want to and the money is not a problem. Go on, pretty please!" she begged, grinning as she tickled Isobelle's ribs.

Isobelle squirmed out of tickling reach. "Okay, okay," she laughed. "It is not really fair, but if you insist."

"Yes, I do," she affirmed. Pointing at the laptop screen, which at that moment was displaying a picture of an historic C13th bridge spanning a tranquil River Lot, she continued, "With the nearest main town this lovely Villeneuve-sur-Lot and being surrounded by good vineyards and prune country, how on earth can we go wrong!"

They quickly made a fortnight's temporary booking for two weeks hence and, linking the dates into the ferry services there and back, also made provisional bookings on the ferries and overnight hotels at Caen.

"We will need to get you insured to drive the Land Cruiser and I can arrange the green card with the insurance brokers. "A sudden thought made Evelyn add, "I did not ask, but can you drive?"

"Yes," Isobelle tittered, "although you may have to let me have a practice in your Land Cruiser before we drive on the right hand side over there."

After an hour of conscientiously listing down and allotting all the tasks that they would need to do prior to the holiday, they felt very pleased with themselves, but also fairly weary. Isobelle had been dwelling in her mind about how to broach the night ahead now that the lounge and sofa were out of the question. This was partially solved by Evelyn, who in between a stifled yawn, managed to say, "I do not think we can really do any more tonight...I feel like relaxing in a bath. How about you?"

Isobelle managed to blush again, something she had hoped she was over now. Obviously not, she thought as she asked, "You mean together?"

"I do," replied Evelyn, "unless, of course, I am being too presumptuous. Did you not want to share one with me?"

"Of course I do," blushed Isobelle yet again. "Why do you always make me tongue-tied and blush?"

"Because you are devilishly in love with me and worship the very ground that I stand on!" cried Evelyn as she jumped off the bed and made quickly for the bathroom. A pillow flew by her, striking the wall, followed by some laughing curses from Isobelle. As Isobelle knelt on the bed staring after her, she reflected that, although said in jest, Evelyn's statement was not far from the truth.

She soon heard the reassuring sound of the bath running, sending a shiver of expectancy tingling down her spine. This would be a new step in their relationship, because for her, the act of making love to Evelyn would definitely mean a commitment. Despite the fact that their love for one another was bashfully young, it was such that Isobelle knew it not to be fanciful but steadfast and honest. She was not given to casual sex or sleeping around, so the fact that she very much wanted to make love to Evelyn further cemented in her mind her devotion for her. What is more, she knew in her soul that Evelyn was genuine, that she was not the kind of person to trifle with another's affections. No, Isobelle was as positive as she could possibly be that they complimented one another and that they could only get closer as time progressed.

Happily she hopped off the bed and wandered into the bathroom. The bath was steamily full and Evelyn was applying a bubble bath with the fragrance conjuring plump, purple dewberries. She crept up behind Evelyn, who was now bent stirring the foamy water, and grabbing her waist, playfully pushed as if to plunge her into the bath, pulling her back at the last instant. Crying out in surprise, Evelyn swung around, grasping Isobelle by the shoulders, amusement in her eyes.

"Why, you little vixen!" she exclaimed. "For that blatant act of insolence, I think that you will be the first one to test the water."

Once again, she characteristically cupped Isobelle's face as she guided her into a kiss, their dry lips meeting and pensively sticking, resisting slightly as they drew apart.

"We must try to keep our eyes open," whispered Evelyn, as she pressed her lips once more onto Isobelle's, her blue eyes pining Isobelle's greens in a hold too powerful to break. Wickedly, her tongue darted in tiny forays, licking at the corners of Isobelle's mouth before running along her teeth and teasing her own seeking tongue. Just as Isobelle felt her legs shimmer with the imminence of trembling, Evelyn broke off, her dreamy eyes drinking up the effect of her kiss on Isobelle's blood-filled lips. Her hands slipped once again onto Isobelle's shoulders, holding her just apart, but close enough to smell her desirable grape-red breath. Her eyes were still fixed firmly on Isobelle's, sending her signals of assurance and love, of warmth, compassion and friendship. Her fingers glided tenderly up Isobelle's slender neck, aimlessly meandering their path over the contours of her face, before halting near her mouth. As she ran her thumb delicately over Isobelle's lips, Isobelle opened them slightly, inviting the thumb, then running her tongue along its polished nail. Their eyes never left one another's.

"Time for your bath, young lady." Evelyn spoke to those eyes, her low voice husky with desire. Her fingers moved hesitantly from Isobelle's face, down to the top button on her silk blouse. She fumbled with the tiny button, her long fingers suddenly uncoordinated. Isobelle closed her hands over Evelyn's as if to steady them, then guided them with fleeting and reassuring touches of her fingers as they travelled down the buttons of her blouse. When she arrived at the waistband of Isobelle's trousers, her now more confident fingers dextrously undid the buttons and zip, allowing the blouse to pull free. Isobelle's eyes, warm green, soothing green, encouraging green, bore into Evelyn's as Evelyn slipped the blouse off her shoulders.

"Let it drop," sighed Isobelle. Evelyn allowed the silk to cascade from her fingers, pooling on the bathroom floor. For the first time in what seemed like a pleasurable age, Evelyn's eyes swept down over the smooth flesh of Isobelle's shoulders. As her eyes travelled, so her hands followed, both senses of sight and touch as erotic as each other in their passage. The fingertips traced across the swell of her smallish breasts, dipping to run tantalisingly along the lace cups of her pink bra, before following its supportive form under her arms and sweeping around to the hooks at the back. As these hooks parted and the material fell to join the blouse on the floor, Isobelle was conscious of Evelyn's gasp.

"Ohh! Isobelle, you are so beautiful," she purred as her fingers circled wondrously over Isobelle's large, but girlishly rose pink nipples, almost at one with the protruding areolae.

"I've not been gifted with large breasts, but nature made up for it by giving me these large nipples'" breathed Isobelle, half wanting to cover them in her shyness and half proud to expose them to Evelyn's admiring scrutiny. They were erect and sensitive beneath her doting gaze.

"You have glorious breasts, Isobelle. I adore them." As if to reinforce this declaration, she furled down and ran her moist lips over Isobelle's right nipple, her fingers still caressing the left. Her hungry lips closed over its puffy mound, licking slowly, then sucking as she played up its receptive length. Isobelle emitted a whimper of delight, her fingers tightening within Evelyn's silken hair. Evelyn relented only after she had grazed her teeth almost imperceptibly over each swollen bud. She smiled impishly at Isobelle as she knelt down seductively in front of her, leaning into Isobelle's stomach to brush her lips over the warm young swell, her tongue dancing into the dip of her navel. Drawing back, she began to lower Isobelle's muted gold trousers, teasing them over her hips and down her slender and athletic legs. Obediently, Isobelle stepped out of them, hardly trusting her balance with the power of the ardour coursing through her. Evelyn savoured the moment, her face just inches from the dusky pink of Isobelle's panties.

Above her, she could hear Isobelle's breathing, laboured as she tried to control her passion, waiting with senses on fire for Evelyn to strip away the last vestige of clothing to leave her naked before her love. Her limbs shivered with excitement as Evelyn's fingers delved under the lacy waist of her panties and began to slip them down her thighs. Inching them down so delicately that Isobelle had to steady herself by griping Evelyn's shoulders to stop herself collapsing to her knees. The sensation was so seethingly erotic. Never before had she experienced such a sense of vertigo as a consequence of her passion. And it was getting headier; more and more intense as Evelyn's darling lips followed the waistband's downward journey, gently kissing, each one with their own little current of electrifying bliss. For a second time she heard Evelyn's intake of breath, for she had lowered the flimsy material enough to realise that Isobelle was free of pubic hair, that it was a smooth, soothing slope down to her neat folds of womanhood. Evelyn could not help herself, desire and curiosity merged, blending into a potent cocktail, driving bashfulness to some distant corner of her being. She could smell Isobelle's excitement, she could almost taste it, so powerful was the imprint within her senses. Her fingers flew as her mind soared. Tenderly, but insistently she parted, dipped and stroked Isobelle's point of liquid desire, egging her on and on into a wet crescendo of ecstasy so fiery that her legs could no longer hold her as she crumpled naked and exhausted to the welcoming carpet beside Evelyn. Even as she lay, she continued to twitch and quiver with the aftershock of her orgasm.

"How many more surprises have you in store for me, young lady?" asked Evelyn, her voice thick with the influence of their lovemaking. Her eyes were flowing over the shapes, lines and curves that composed this woman she loved so dearly.

"Give me time to recover and hopefully I can show you one more," replied Isobelle, green eyes half closed and opaque, saturated with fulfilment. Evelyn could not believe that it was possible to be so sexually charged while still clothed. Isobelle's nakedness was so pure and absolute that it was all she could do not to rip off her clothes and curl round her, but she knew that, being their first time, this lovemaking, above all, should be the most memorable. She must let Isobelle lead as she had led, let her discover the joy of another woman's body, learn its messages as Evelyn had so learned.

Leaning over Isobelle, her fingers brushed to shape miscreant wisps of ruby hair that fell carelessly over her clouded eyes. Strands almost damp with the force of their exertions.

"Hello you," smiled Evelyn.

"I have been waiting for Evelyn Hertford from the moment my life began," Isobelle said quietly, staring up at this woman who had taken her so gloriously beyond any dimensions or boundaries she thought possible. Oh! she of captivating blue eyes and statuesque features. Her Evelyn. She liked the sound of it. Her mind played with it. Isobelle knew that she had changed now, that she had eased through some moment in time, some warp, which had opened her eyes to view the world anew. Her senses were alight. If this is love, and it could only be love, then she relished in it's diversity of emotions, all combining into this overwhelming wish to hold and protect this radiant blond before her.

She stirred from her crumpled tanglement, her arm snaking out as her fingers followed the pattern of Evelyn's profile. Her palm cupped round Evelyn's cheek as their lips covered the diminishing distance to meet in a lingering and eloquent kiss, one in which no words were spoken, yet so much communicated. Twisting around, Isobelle lowered Evelyn until she lay on the carpet, blond hair fanning out over the royal blue of the deep shag-pile. Straddling her, Isobelle gazed down searchingly into her encouraging eyes, begging tacit forgiveness in advance for any fumbled caress, muddled position or scrambled eagerness.

"Don't think about it," Evelyn consoled her. "Just follow your heart's desire and you will not go wrong."

Isobelle smiled so warmly in response, Evelyn almost felt the tears welling. How many times had she thanked the fates for arranging that train journey which would so alter her life. Isobelle shifted, her knees either side of Evelyn's face, her wetness hot against Evelyn's midriff. Lowering herself to her elbows on either side of Evelyn's face, Isobelle began to pepper her neck and face with tender sweet kisses, her fingers playing softly against her earlobes.

"I love you so much it hurts, poppet," breathed Isobelle into her slightly parted lips, before lowering her own lips, her tongue avidly searching, finding, melting in the softness of Evelyn's mouth. Isobelle's fingers rubbed and kneaded her arms, working their way up, up to her neckline, unbuttoning one, two buttons before ducking into her cleavage. Her hand covered the mound of a full breast, only a thin cotton between her palm and the firm, sensitive nipple eager for her touch. Isobelle's finger slithered between bra and breast to circle and slightly squeeze this throbbing bud, Evelyn trying unsuccessfully to hold her breath and allow Isobelle's fingers more room. She arched her back, her head thrown to one side, hair untamed, eyes closed in submissive abandon as Isobelle's hands slipped under her to release the constraints of her bra.

Quickly, with hands sure and certain, she undid the remainder of Evelyn's buttons, casting aside clothing in a flurry so that the only modesty afforded her were floral cotton panties. Isobelle let her own body sink to cover Evelyn, small firm breasts to fuller softer breasts, hip bone to hip bone, toes curled and legs entwined. Evelyn's body trembled as Isobelle descended to her breast, tracing it's fullness with her tongue in decreasing circles until, at last, the tip of her tongue teased and seduced the dusky rose-pink pinnacle. Evelyn moaned in pleasurable gratitude as Isobelle worked her magic over the other breast, her fingers keeping the first erect with delicate tweaks and flicks.

Onward she descended, her hands, mouth and tongue learning the language and complexities of Evelyn's body, it's textures and it's hues. Fingers almost imperceptibly mapped the route in from hip towards pelvis, fingertips clipping the elastic of her panties, to draw them down over contours and dips to an idyllic corner. Evelyn's hips rose to take her in, every nerve singing in her body as an electricity flowed to one point in her being, one spot where Isobelle's tongue and fingers wove their sorcery. Her body moved of its own intent and will, wetness and juices liquefied her insides in the moment of impending orgasm. A fantasia of light and sheer bursting of emotion left her suddenly exhilarated and sobbing and gasping for breath. Isobelle quickly slid up her, cradling Evelyn's head in her arm and salting away her tears with feather light kisses.

"What's wrong, darling? Did I do anything wrong?" she whispered into her ear.

"I'm not crying because I am sad," she replied through her tears, "I'm crying because I am so happy. I can safely say that you have just given me the most memorable moment of my life. How do I tell you what I feel for you when there are not the words to express the magnitude? You have taken me to heights and places that I have never been."

"And rest assured we will definitely go there again," comforted Isobelle.

"I cannot believe that I am so drained, Isobelle. Tell me you'll always love me. The thought of ever losing you is more than I could bear. I know you cannot predict what will happen in the future, but I do hope that we can ride everything together."

"I am not going anywhere but with you. We will make things work and I am sure we'll grow old together," Isobelle smiled.

CHAPTER TWENTY-ONE

Later found them soaking at either end of the bath, arms draped along the side and legs interlocked under the suds. Their eyes had hardly left one another, locked through the steam, doing all the talking that their bruised lips could not. Later saw them drying each other with fluffy towels, exulting in the feel of the sharing such a personal and usually mundane task. Later caught them slipping into Evelyn's bed, nuzzling and caressing into further crests of passion, long into the night until at last, they fell asleep, Isabelle curved around the natural symmetry of Evelyn's bath-warm body. And even in sleep they accompanied one another, inhaling hopes and exhaling the dreams of times to come.

When morning cast its slowly warming fingers of light across their bed, it was Isobelle who woke first, a smile greeting the sunshine of another day with its memories of last night. Adjusting her position carefully, she marvelled at Evelyn's beauty in the cocoon of sleep, the innocence of a child on her face. She lay on her front, hair spread over the pillow around, mouth slightly open as if in pout. Her unblemished shoulders hunched, hardly moving with her shallow breaths, with the stunning curvature of her spine flowing down to the beginnings of the eiderdown was almost as much as Isobelle could bear. *I have made love to this goddess*, she thought, *and I love her so intensely that when I look at her like this, it hurts, as I want her so much. To run my fingers over the tiny hairs of her arms would be so tempting. Yet it would wake her and I am enjoying watching her too much.* She knew that there was nothing that she would not do for Evelyn now. It was amazing that she thought that she knew the female body through her own, yet she realised she knew little. Evelyn's, although close in stature to hers, was so different. She adored every inch of it, but longed to know more; she ran her eyes over it, yet they did not see enough. It will take many exquisite hours of study and Isobelle was a thorough person, well up to the task. As she raised her gaze up to Evelyn's face, she saw that, through the rambling hair, Evelyn's eyes were open and watching her, lips curled in a knowing smile.

"Caught you!" she said with her husky voice.

"I confess," laughed Isobelle, "I could not help taking advantage of your helplessness to let my senses have their way with you!"

"Your senses, with one exception, are very, very naughty then," she grinned.

"Oh! And which one of them passes muster?"

"Taste, for you have excellent taste in loving me and I really want to experience taste again now," she said, leaning across to Isobelle and kissing her on her consummate lips.

With the exception of the time in which the cleaners arrived to clear the lounge of the glass, they remained together, comfortable in each other's company. They managed to rig up a heavy-duty plastic covering for the windows, which would suffice as long as the weather held clement. Other than that, they touched, kissed and often made love, surfacing occasionally in order to eat. But then, eating is a seduction and they responded as the lovers they were, sharing and feeding each other, laughing at dressings which were deliberately dribbled down chins, or ice-cream dabbed on a nose. But as the weekend progressed, so did their love. At individual times they both reflected how it was impossible to love the other more. Yet a casual turn of head, the act of sweeping a wayward hair off the face, a word, a touch, or just the inflection of voice; that was all it took for an additional surge of protectiveness. So at various times of the day, Evelyn would just walk up and embrace Isobelle, or Isobelle would come up behind Evelyn, locking her arms around her and resting her cheek in Evelyn's hair. Subconsciously, they followed each other with glazed eyes, never letting the other leave the periphery. When close, their hands sought each other and fingers interlocked, little squeezes of reassurance as to their love. For in a world of order and reason, these dalliances are understood although the emotions are generally not.

The spoken language has limited words for the longings, the reassurances, the needing, but the language of the body and of the eyes speaks multitudes, conveying in a look what one could struggle to say in an age. And yet, we still crave for those three words, said so often between lovers, although particular to each. We need them and draw strength from them. Without a whispered *'I love you'* we flounder and feel our love is incomplete. Not so with Isobelle and Evelyn. They made sure that they told each other regularly and, more often than not, reinforced the telling with action.

"I am going to miss you dearly tomorrow at work," said Isobelle during supper that evening. "What shall we do about meeting up during the week?"

"Regrettably I've got to take you home tonight so that you can sort yourself for work tomorrow. How about you pack some things for work, and tomorrow night instead of going home, get off at my station and stay here overnight?"

"Mmm! I just remembered that I am going to reveal all to Fiona tomorrow."

"Are you very worried about that? I suppose it must seem more difficult as it gets closer."

"Funnily enough," said Isobelle, "it feels a lot easier now. I really feel euphoric when I am with you. I know that this is right for us and it has given me the confidence to tell her. No, I don't think that I am worried about it. What I am concerned about is leaving you here alone at the moment, for in our happiness, we both know that there is this threat lurking and I must admit that I would feel so much better if we could stay together."

"Oh! Lord! You're right. Do you know that being with you this weekend has made me forget totally about it for the first time in ages. Even when we were mending the windows upstairs I was not really thinking about it. No, please stay. You are so right, we must stick together when not at work. Is your flat okay, or do you need to get back to it for any reason?"

"Apart from clothes, there is no reason to have to go back."

"Let's look in my wardrobe. Another advantage in our relationship is that with the exception of our busts, we are almost the same size. You can wash your underwear tonight and put it in the dryer. Hopefully I will have something you'll like."

"I am sure you will. And as for our busts…..," she said with roguish grin.

The time flew to her meeting with Fiona on the Monday lunchtime. She had hated leaving Evelyn at the station, but at least she would be seeing her again that evening. It had felt strange on the train, thinking back to their first meeting and the relationship that since developed. It seemed a lifetime ago. And what a lifetime it had been with such ups as she had experienced in their confirming their love for one another as against the downs in their fear over the vindictive Richard Bleach. She had not liked to admit to Evelyn how much the threat of potential violence had frightened her, but she now had an inkling of the kind of fear poor Evelyn must have suffered. It was no wonder that she seemed to crumple when the harassment raised its head again. Still, at least they had the holiday to look forward to. Hopefully during that time the police would locate him and warn him off, or ideally arrest him. Talking of which, as soon as she had arrived at work, she had checked with Paul about taking time off in two weeks. Surprisingly, he had appeared shy and kept breaking eye contact, an alien concept to Paul, as he was a rare breed of male who usually spoke with you rather than at you. Anyhow, he readily agreed to the time off, so she had not particularly dwelt on his evasive behaviour.

Fiona was pleased to see her as ever and, again as ever, was abundant with smiles and good humour. Isobelle envied those who worked with Fiona, as she considered that she must be such a source of inspiration. They chatted about the wedding and common friends en route, but once they were seated at the Thai restaurant, she could contain herself no longer.

"Right Issy, I have been thinking more about you over the weekend than my wedding and you know that the wedding preparations should be my sole purpose in life! So redeem yourself. Tell me about this someone you have met."

Isobelle could not help but grin at her sister's teasing and that made what she had to say so much easier.

"As I intimated, I have met someone very special and with whom I have fallen very much in love."

"Wonderful! In love! Even better," she exclaimed during mouthfuls of Gang Panang. "And does this special someone have a name?"

Isobelle closed her eyes and swallowed. Here we go, she thought. No turning back now.

"Yes, of course. Her name is Evelyn, Evelyn Hertford." She opened her eyes cautiously to see Fiona smiling at her.

"Did you find that hard, Issy?" she asked quietly.

"A little, but not as much as I thought. I am surprised at your reaction though. No pregnant pause, gasping, horrified intakes of breath. What have I got to do to shock you?"

"You forget, Issy. We know each other too well. Besides, when you arranged this lunch with me, you alluded to this person but were overly careful not to mention the gender - you said you were going to this friend's house rather than his house or so-and-so's house. It struck me over the weekend that it may be a woman. Just a hunch. So, although it was a little surprising, I had half guessed."

"No pulling the wool over your eyes, Fi. I did not consciously plan this; I did not previously have any lesbian tendencies. But somehow with Evelyn it just seemed so right and I have fallen in love with her as a person rather than for her gender. That said, I have found that I have experienced the most amazing physical relationship with her too. Will you let me bring her as my guest to your wedding?"

Fiona fished in her handbag for an instant, producing pen and paper. "Write down her name and address and I will send her an invite. Knowing how you feel about her, I would be insulted if she didn't come." She smiled again and reached over to take Isobelle's hand. "And now, from the beginning, tell me all."

Isobelle was in seventh heaven that evening as she climbed into Evelyn's Land Cruiser at Brookmans Park station. They gave each other a public-friendly peck before Evelyn drove off.

"You look like the cat that got the cream," she said. "What are you holding back in that beautiful head of yours?"

"Well, firstly, I managed to obtain the okay on our holiday." As she told Evelyn she recalled Paul's strange reaction that morning. "Although Paul appeared to be unusually cagey with me. I am sure that it was not to do with the holiday though."

"You don't think that he has a secret crush on you and detects that you have found someone. Perhaps he is jealous."

"No, he is very happily married, Miss Mischief!" she announced, playfully slapping Evelyn's arm. "No, it was something else. Anyhow, next piece of good news. I met Fiona today and she had already guessed. Didn't bat an eyelid. In fact she said she was very happy for me. She wants to meet you and has asked whether we would have supper with them on Saturday. How do you feel about that?"

Isobelle's enthusiasm was so infectious that Evelyn burst out laughing.

"I'm so pleased that she took it so well - I worried for you having to tell her today. And yes, of course we'll go to supper with them. I am looking forward to meeting this extraordinary sister of yours."

"Just do not like her too much!" warned Isobelle.

That evening they made a firm booking on their holiday and sent off all the relevant payments. That aside, they delved into Evelyn's wardrobe and discussed the clothing that they would take with them. When it came to swimming costumes, Isobelle insisted that Evelyn try each one on in front of her, knowing that it was exciting Evelyn to do so.

"No, not that one! Remove it this instant!" commanded Isobelle in mock horror. "Now that is much better," she announced, as Evelyn stood naked before her.

"You never know," responded Evelyn, "if we have enough privacy in our pool then I could wear this one occasionally."

"This holiday sounds better and better. Though I think that I need to get into the holiday spirit," she ventured as with bended finger, she beckoned Evelyn seductively towards her.

They lay entwined on the bed in the already darkening room. The sky outside the window, fiery red with tomorrow's promise of another sunny day, cast blends of cinnamon across the floor and over their limbs. Isobelle licked at a trickle of sweat that had traced its way down Evelyn's slender neck, tasting the salt, tasting Evelyn.

"What do you like most about my body?" she whispered into Evelyn's ear before nibbling delicately on the lobe.

Evelyn considered. "To be honest, most of it. When I kiss your lips, I love them. When I run my fingers through your hair, I adore the sensation. When I caress your breasts, I worship them. When I taste you, I am ecstatic. It is difficult as I am in love with the whole package. I do have a special affection for these erotically protruding nipples of yours; they have a strangely aromatic flavour that I cannot describe, but I will keep on trying to pin-point it!" She began to nuzzle and suck at the objects of her appreciation, nipping teasingly. Before long their pink glowing post-climax lethargy had been replaced with a renewed urgency as their education of each other's body progressed with yet another lesson.

And while they gambolled and frolicked through the evening, falling fat with love and satisfaction into sleep, those Fates smiled down, boyishly jealous at their happiness and eager to impose themselves in some gangly inept way. Their wish for attention so child-like that it often manifested itself in a negative manner.

CHAPTER TWENTY-TWO

The following day as Isobelle arrived for work, she could immediately sense that something was wrong. None of the managers were present in the department and some of the employees were packing up their belongings with an air of disbelief on their faces.

"What is up?" Isobelle asked of Meyra.

"They are making people redundant," said a fearful Meyra. "So far they have called up four people. Paul's up there with the other finance managers and the CAO."

Isobelle felt cold fingers run down her spine. Was that why Paul could not look her in the eye? It was beginning to fall into place now, or was it? No use speculating, but nevertheless she began to sort through her desk looking for all her personal items, placing them into a bag. In the past, she had seen too many people so stunned by the news that they forgot to take home things of value. As she was popping a collection of tiny metal aeroplanes (a reminder of her boarding school days, flying between London and the Middle East) into the bag, Meyra received her phone call.

"They've asked me to go up to the main meeting room," she said, her voice aquiver. Isobelle quickly got up and gave her a hug.

"Hang in there, Meyra. Do not give them the satisfaction of seeing you cry."

Meyra nodded, wiping the accumulating tears from her eyes as she made for the door. Most of Finance had their heads down, but they still watched her go. Isobelle knew that she would be next and, because she knew it, she could not stand the wait for the phone call. Nowadays there was supposed to be no stigma attached to redundancy (or the new catchword, restructuring), but that was of no immediate consequence to someone in that unfortunate position. Isobelle already felt that she had failed somewhere, had made some mistakes, even though she knew full well she had not. *Don't think that way,* she told herself. *Be aware of what they say to you as it is easy to miss important points if you are upset.*

Within minutes her phone rang. Isobelle could see her colleagues looking around, trying to identify the direction in which the bad news was headed. Taking a deep breath, she picked up the phone.

"Isobelle, could you come up to the Manager's Meeting Room?" asked Paul with a neutral voice.

"Certainly," replied Isobelle, equally neutrally. Let them wait for me, she thought as she composed herself. After a few minutes, she got up and walked towards the door. As with all such impersonal occasions, it was a painful process to go through. She understood the role that Paul had to adopt, but it was still upsetting that the man she had so respected was now so formal and almost cold. Much as she felt like crying, she was able to prevent herself by digging her nails into her hand. Contrary to her mood, she had to admit to herself that the package she was to receive was very generous. However, she was loath to let them know and remained stony-faced through most of the ordeal.

Finally, she was asked top clear her desk, say her farewells and leave the premises as soon as possible. At least there was not the indignity of an escort, but she still felt tainted as she returned back to her desk. For five years she had spent so much of her life in this department, worked conscientiously for the company and now, because of a merger with a larger concern, she was no longer required. Naturally she was angry and was eager to leave as quickly as possible. However, she had made a fair number of friends around the company, who, once they heard the news on the furiously efficient grapevine, came down to sympathise and wish her well. This was by far the hardest part to handle and more than once she had to quell the tears fermenting at their kind wishes. Before she left, she elected to call Evelyn.

"Hello Isobelle darling. Are you alright? You sound distinctly sad."

Just the tenor of Evelyn's voice was such a comfort and Isobelle longed to be with her immediately.

"I rang to make sure you were home," she said with lamentable voice. "I have just been made redundant and really need some of your TLC."

"Make your way home now and you will have all you need and more. How dare they lay off my love! At least I know that they will be the worse for it. Hurry home and I'll meet you at the station."

As the almost deserted train clattered its therapeutic way out of London and into the country, Isobelle could only think on how much a catastrophe it would have been if she had been made redundant a few weeks earlier. She and Evelyn would never have been thrown together and she would never have received the comfort and support she knew would be afforded by Evelyn. Her family would no doubt have rallied round, but she would have been alone too much, allowing it to fester. And her faith in Evelyn proved worthy, for although she maintained her composure when she met Evelyn at the station, once they were in the house and Evelyn had taken her into her arms, all the anger and frustration flooded out of her, her body wracked with sobs. Evelyn held her comfortingly, whispering soothingly in her ear, but otherwise letting her get it all out of her system.

When Isobelle had finally calmed down, leaving her with red swollen eyes to fringe her green irises, Evelyn led her to the bathroom and delicately washed her face.

"What I suggest," she said as she dabbed Isobelle's face with a towel, "is that we drive over to your flat, make sure that everything is alright there and pick up anything that you might need for this week. Then you can stay here with me. I am working largely from home this week anyhow, so we can keep each other company".

"I've got to consider getting another job," said Isobelle half-heartedly.

"No. Worst thing you can do now is look for a job. You are too upset and may compromise your skills for a lesser job just to be employed. Why don't you wait until we've been on holiday. You will be refreshed and in a better state of mind."

Isobelle beamed, lighting up her freshly washed and post-tearful pink face. "I knew you would do and say the right things. Who said that *'Arguments out of a pretty mouth are unanswerable?'*"

"Well you were the one to help me when I was shaken up by this stalker business on Friday. I am sure we will both be a strength for one another for a long time to come," she replied, squeezing Isobelle's hand. "Let's have a bite to eat and go to your flat."

CHAPTER TWENTY-THREE

Evelyn had not been into Isobelle's flat, so while Isobelle was sorting and packing, she was more than content to wander the rooms, curious about all the nick-knacks and dressings of Isobelle's life. She was interested to see the Veronica Lake poster, but as with most people confronted with their likeness, she was not able to see the similarities that captivated Isobelle. She was particularly impressed with Isobelle's statues.

"Are these the Tom Greenshields statues that you told me about in the train?"

Isobelle poked her head out of the bedroom. "Yes. Are they not the most graceful figurines you have ever seen?"

"They are certainly the most graceful," agreed Evelyn, adding quietly to Isobelle's retreating form, "but not the most beautiful. That honour is reserved for you."

With enough clothing to last until the weekend, Evelyn helped her to load it into the Land Cruiser.

"You are definitely into Celtic music, judging by your CD collection," observed Evelyn. "Can you select a few good ones and bring them along? I need something new to listen to."

"What did you think when you first saw me on the train?" asked Isobelle on the return trip to Evelyn's. Strains of Enigma's overtly sexual MCMXC AD floated dreamily through the vehicle.

"But I told you when you first came over to the tower," she protested.

"I know you did, but humour me. Tell me again. P-l-e-a-s-e," she begged, fluttering her eyelashes in mock film heroine fashion.

"To tell you the truth, I could not think for a minute. You know how you look at some people and think he's handsome or she's pretty, but then you look closely and see things you are not so fond of; dirty fingernails, coughing without covering the mouth, filthy shoes, weird clothes - often trivial things. But with you, when I saw you it was almost as if I knew that I would fall in love with you. There was no doubt, no indecision, nothing. For a moment I forgot to even breathe. I just knew there and then that my heart would belong to you. I could not drag my eyes away from you and, in a strange sort of way, I wanted you to notice."

"What would you have done if you had not seen me again on the train?"

"I would have had no hesitation in catching that same train time and time again until I did. Intuition made me believe that it was not a one-off trip for you."

Isobelle leaned over and kissed her on the cheek. "My lady in shimmering ivory come to rescue me on her white mare!" she smiled.

The week passed by blissfully. While Evelyn worked on her designs, Isobelle read from her extensive range of books, including 'The Village Affair' which she had meant to borrow from Evelyn on their first date. Unfortunately, the ending was one that left her saddened although determined to harbour Evelyn's love and not let outside influences split them. She found that she could pretend to be reading and study Evelyn for ages over the top of her book. Several times she had been caught with a delicious smile, but she had tried hard not to distract Evelyn too much. As she was the one working, Isobelle made herself useful by fetching drinks, making meals and massaging her tired neck. On the second evening of this assumed role, she sneaked up behind Evelyn in only a sheer night-dress and seductive perfume, whispering through her golden tresses into her ear, "Your supper is ready and so is your waitress." Evelyn devoured both, but not in that order.

Friday was taken up entirely by the delivery of the replacement windows. As a crane was required to install them, the noise and interruptions made it impossible for Evelyn to do any work. To escape, they packed a picnic and went for a walk, enjoying the unseasonable sunshine whilst it was favouring England with its embrace. Evelyn led them to a pond in a haven of tranquillity, a glade where sunlight refracted through the tender new green leaves of the surrounding trees. Tiny flies skimmed lazily over the surface of the pond, but otherwise there was a total air of stillness.

"This is idyllic," raved Isobelle. "Is this still part of your property?"

"Yes." answered Evelyn. "It is my private spot. My father was not one for walks, so I think I am the only human that comes here. Once, when I had been sitting here for ages, a Monkjack deer wandered into the glade. The moment was ephemeral, but it made me feel a part of something very special. Now you can share it with me."

"It is breathtaking. Thank-you for bringing me here."

They sat on a grassy bank eating the sandwiches they had brought, watching with amusement the arrival of a family of noisy starlings. The fledglings, now as big as their parents, stood flapping and chirping, still expecting to be fed by their tired parents. When this did not happen, they sulkily marched around pecking at the ground and vocally showing their disapproval. While stifling their laughter at these antics, a sudden crack of a snapped branch sent the panicked starlings careering into the sanctity of the forest and the girls, alarmed, to their feet. Each of them scanned the area, suddenly frightened by their seclusion so welcome moments ago.

"Do you think it is one of the workmen come to find us for something?" asked Isobelle. She could sense the hairs erect on her arms.

"No. They would not know to come down here. Quickly, let's get back. Grab those things."

Picking up one of the baskets, Isobelle followed closely in Evelyn's footsteps as they cautiously, hesitantly made their way back to the tower. Isobelle was positive that her thumping heart was so loud it would be audible to anyone within the vicinity. It was at that instant, when sufficiently away from the glade and beginning to think that they had been spooked by nature itself, that Richard Bleach stepped out from behind the cover of some rhododendron bushes, blocking the narrow path ahead.

"Why hello, Evie. Long time no see...well, at least up this close anyhow." His voice had a belligerent timbre that scared Isobelle. It became worse when he turned his gaze to her. She had once seen the eyes of a rabid dog hiding under a parked car in the Middle East and the eyes boring into her sizzled with the same violence and hatred. "And you. You must be the queer that is sullying Evie with your filthy perversions. Why did you have to come along and spoil things? Evie doesn't need your sort of slime. She needs me to get you out of the picture so that I can look after her."

In the time it took for him to spit out this vitriolic threat, Isobelle perceived that her mind, in its terror, had slipped into a slow motion. Everything seemed to be said and enacted in real time, but she seemed to have so much time to observe the events taking place. She had never seen this Richard before, but knew immediately it was him from Evelyn's past description. In another place or time, he would be considered attractive, with the kind of confident looks normally associated with tennis stars or football icons. But not here. Here his menace oozed from odium-filled pores, his calmly swinging arm clutching a large section of branch making his whole appearance malevolent and so incongruous in this beautiful setting. She noticed Evelyn move forward, arms outstretched to placate, open hands on view to demonstrate her lack of threat. Her husky voice was particularly calm and soothing.

"Leave her, Richard. This is between you and me. Let's go back to the tower and sort this out. Please, I am sure that both you and I can resolve this without anyone getting hurt."

As she got nearer to Richard she put a hand behind her back, so that Isobelle would see her hand gesture indicating that she should retreat and flee the scene. Either way it could not have worked, for Isobelle would never have left Evelyn to face him alone; but anyhow, he had anticipated their collusion and acted in a burst of aggression. Before Evelyn could respond, he had sent her crashing to the path beyond him, stunning her with a back-fist to her chin. Then, springing agilely over the gap between them, he swung the branch in an arc at Isobelle. She felt a searing pain in her protective arm and guessed that he had broken it, but her defiance was such that she managed to ignore it as she sent a kick into his exposed groin. Unfortunately, his anger was enough to send a second swing of the branch into the side of her head. As she felt herself blacking out, her last conscious thought was of Evelyn, beyond Richard's back, staggering away down the path in escape. At least he won't get her, at least she's safe......

Isobelle's recollections over the following couple of days were distinctly sketchy. She had moments during which she was convinced she was watching a soap opera in which she was the star, in a hospital bed surrounded by Evelyn and her family, all of them peering intently at her, awaiting a signal that she was going to pull out of her coma. But I am here, she would call. I can see you all - look up here. But they would not look up and soon she found herself sliding once again into that netherland of jumbled dreams and flashes of childhood incidents normally long forgotten. Sometimes she could see part of Evelyn, just the eyes of Morning Glory blue, but her mind was too scrambled to offer her the comfort of features or delineation. However, those eyes helped her, for the blue radiated a warmth and well being in which she mollycoddled. She begged the eyes to stay on her and searched through the kaleidoscope of mind patterns to locate them if they ever dissipated. Occasionally, she felt her body being moved and knew of the subsequent pain that came with it, but although she tried to fight her discomfort, she was vaguely aware that she could not move and that her mind was more active than her body.

It was the evening of the second day that her eyes flicked open and, after much blinking, was able to assess her immediate surroundings. She immediately recognised the room was in a hospital. In a chair to her right, uncomfortably scrunched in sleep, was Fiona. Piers was seated on her left reading a newspaper by the limited light eking in from the corridor. What is going on, she worried, why am I here? Piers must have perceived a subtle change in the room, for he glanced up at that point. For a second it did not register and his eyes were about to sweep back to the paper when he noticed that she was looking at him.

"Isobelle, can you hear me?" he asked anxiously, quietly.

Isobelle's mouth was so dry that she had difficulty in forming the response. It felt as though she was having to learn how to speak all over again.

"Yes. Why am I here, Piers?"

The sound of her rasping voice was enough to stir Fiona, who quickly shook off her sleep.

"Issy, darling, how are you feeling? We've all been so worried for you."

"I think that I'm alright, Fi. My arm is so painful and my whole body feels incredibly sore, but otherwise I am okay. What am I doing here? Where is Evelyn?"

Fiona and Piers exchanged glances.

"Can't you remember how you came to be here?" Fiona gently asked.

"No. My head thumps if I think too hard. Where is Evelyn?"

"Evelyn's asleep. She has not had any sleep since you came in, so mum drove her home. She is not very well herself, so mum is keeping an eye on her."

"Not well? What's wrong with her? God, Fi, I feel so confused."

Isobelle found that her eyes had become so heavy and that a weariness had suddenly assailed her. Fiona noticed how her eyes were flickering, trying to keep awake.

"She's going to be fine. I promise, Issy. And so are you now, darling. Go to sleep and we'll talk again later."

CHAPTER TWENTY-FOUR

Early next morning she was awakened by the arrival of the nurses to wash her down and change her bedding.

"Ah! So you're awake at last. You had us all a bit worried, you know. The doctor will be along to see you shortly."

While they had been administering to Isobelle, Fiona and Piers had temporarily left the room. However, as soon as they had finished, Fiona rushed back to her side.

"Hello again, Issy. Feeling a bit better?"

"Yes, I think so. You look very tired though. Have you been here long?"

She smiled. "Don't you concern yourself about me. I'll be as bright as a button after a shower. Mum and Evelyn should be coming in shortly to relieve Piers and me."

Isobelle was very pleased to hear Evelyn would soon be with her, but she was still frustrated at not knowing what was going on. "I cannot remember much, Fi. I know I am in a hospital, but which one and why is a mystery."

"You are in Royal County Hospital, Issy. As for the why, though, it is probably better if Evelyn tells you as she was the one who was with you at the time. She acted brilliantly and we owe her a great deal for seeing you safely to hospital." Fiona clasped Isobelle's hand tightly at this point. "Issy, I told both Piers and mum about your relationship with Evelyn. Under the circumstances, it seemed to be the right thing to do. They had to realise how close you both were and why Richard was prepared to attack you as he did."

The attack! The words triggered off a trickle of memories; the pond, the thrushes, the snapping branch. Each image began to blend in her mind, getting faster and faster until she was whisked into the fear and anger as the log crashed against her head. So vivid was the image that she actually jolted in the bed. She remembered seeing Evelyn stagger off down the path while Richard's attention had been on herself. So Evelyn must have escaped him and managed to somehow transport her here. She could not wait for Evelyn to arrive so that she could thank her and find out what had happened.

"I'm beginning to remember it all," she told Fiona. "I recall how he reminded me of a rabid dog, but he was so much more terrifying. I will wait for Evelyn to tell me what happened."

"I could tell from your eyes that you were starting to remember. One thing that I pray heartily about is that that horrid man will trouble neither of you again. Evelyn told us that you had been made redundant at work. I heard that some people had been laid off, but as I did not hear from you, I assumed you were not one of them."

Isobelle groaned. The redundancy seemed so long ago. "I'm so sorry, Fi. I did mean to tell you all, but I was not quite ready. It hurt me quite bit and I wanted time to adjust. I was staying with Evelyn and she was helping me through it. Unfortunately, with the mental hurt it appears that I also had to endure the physical hurt." A thought suddenly occurred to her as she was talking. "Did you say that you had told mother?"

"Yes, I did. I am sorry, but the whole episode would have been too difficult to explain otherwise. Evelyn agreed that it was the best course to take, as she would have needed to know at some point."

"Oh! Fi, I am not blaming you at all. I could not recall if you had told me or whether I had imagined you telling me. No, you were right to let her know. How did she take it? Was she shocked?"

Fiona smiled, an act that made the tired edges evaporate from her face. "Issy, you thought that I took it well. Now mother, she did not bat an eyelid. In fact she said, good, it's about time she found someone special! And what is more, she has really taken Evelyn to her heart, as we all have. Evelyn refused to let anyone look at her wounds until you were taken care of. While we kept vigil, we were all very taken with her obvious love for you. She told us a great deal about herself and the torment she had to suffer through this stalker. Poor girl." Fiona broke off, hesitating slightly as if not sure about continuing. Seeing Isobelle pleading expression, she carried on.

"She was devastated at first, especially when the results of your injuries were not apparent. She kept blaming herself, saying that she should never have bought that hateful man into your life."

"But I have told her that I love her. He was not as a result of anything she did. She keeps going on about it to me because she feels so guilty," stated Isobelle sadly.

"Well, she did not reckon on mother!" Fiona assumed her mother's bossy tone. "That's enough of that, she said, you didn't ask this man to stalk you, in fact you did everything you could to deter him. And presumably you have no regrets about falling in love with my daughter. So please, no guilt. If it was not for you she might now be dead; let us all be thankful that she is alive. Now, if I am not going to get grandchildren from Isobelle, then at least I want to have gained a happy new daughter. So, young lady, let's see you smile."

"Mother said that!" exclaimed Isobelle laughing. Although this was a characteristic outburst from her mother, her laughter was pure relief that her mother had accepted her lover so readily and that she would not have to go through the trials of having to tell her.

"More or less. I think I covered the gist of it," said Fiona with a grin.

"Now if Evelyn gave mother the same smile she gave me, then no wander she was bowled over by her."

"She bowled us all over. We all like her very much and I think she will fit into our crazy family very comfortably. What do you think, Piers?"

"Issy, if I can fit in, anyone can," he replied jokingly.

"Well I believe that we could not have had two nicer people join our family than yourself and Evelyn," confirmed Isobelle, "and I am truly grateful to you both for staying with me. Hospitals are not exactly the most salubrious places to hang out."

It was at this point a kindly, neat middle aged man walking in wearing the obligatory white coat, stethoscope and an assortment of pens and pencils in his top pocket.

"Hello, my dear," he announced, glancing at Isobelle over the top of tiny bifocals. "I am Dr. Phelps and I am looking after you. I heard that you were awake. So, how do you feel today?"

"If the truth be known, I ache all over and my left arm is particularly painful. Can you tell me what injuries I have sustained?"

"Well, let's see" he replied consulting the notes in a folder at the end of her bed. "Mmm! You certainly took a beating from this despicable person. We have treated you for two broken ribs on your right side, a broken wrist and arm on your left and severe bruising all over your trunk. However, they will heal. What concerned us most were the blows to your head. Fortunately they appear not to have caused any damage that we can see, but we want to keep an eye on you for a few days just to make absolutely sure. I think you may have headaches and be in discomfort for a couple of weeks."

"Dr. Phelps, my friend and I have booked to go to France on holiday in about 10 days time. Do you think that it will still be possible?" she asked hopefully.

"As long as I am satisfied that you have no serious head injury, I do not see why not. However, I would advocate a quiet, peaceful holiday so that you can recover from this ordeal. If you were planning hand-gliding or bungee jumping, I would reconsider." He tittered happily at his own humour and Isobelle had to smile, despite the pain it caused her. "Now, can I have a bit of privacy so that I can examine this young lady?" he added with a pointed grin at Piers and Isobelle.

No sooner had the examination finished and Dr. Phelps left the room, then Evelyn came bursting in, her joy at Isobelle's recovery so evident on her radiant face. Just seeing her again was a tonic, for as Isobelle had slipped into unconsciousness following the attack on her, there had been the real possibility that they may never see each other again. With that knowledge in mind, neither of them felt inclined to spare the sensibilities of those present as they kissed each other long in celebration. When at last they parted, if only to see each other's faces clearly, Evelyn moved aside to let Isobelle's mother get to her.

"I can see that you two have a lot of catching up to do," she said, her face serious but eyes a twinkle. "Fiona has told me all about the injuries, but it sounds as though you were very lucky not to have suffered brain damage.

Thank goodness Evelyn managed to get help or who knows what that thug might have done to you."

It was while her mother was talking that Isobelle dragged her eyes from Evelyn's and noticed the scar running down her chin. Reaching out, she delicately ran her finger over it. "Is this where he hit you?" she asked.

"It looks somewhat worse than it feels," replied Evelyn, "but at the time all I could see were stars and my legs just turned to jelly. It was only my fear of what he would do to you that helped to motivate me to get help."

At this point Isobelle's mother interrupted. "Isobelle, sorry, but Fiona and Piers should go now and get some sleep. I will go down with them and get a cup of tea at the canteen. That will give you two time to catch up."

"Of course," said Isobelle, "I'm sorry, Fi, I should have thought. Thanks very much to you all for your support over the last couple of days, both to Evelyn and me. I really do appreciate it."

"That's quite alright, Issy," replied Fiona as both she and Piers kissed Isobelle on the cheek. "I know you would do the same for me. We will try and pop in this evening if we get the chance."

She waved to them with her good arm, thanking them again as they disappeared.

"I am so glad that I have got such a lovely family," she sighed contentedly.

"And so am I," agreed Evelyn. "They have been fantastic to me. I must admit that I did not care too much initially how your mother would take it, as I was so wrapped up in my concern over you, but as I began to get tired, I really appreciated their help and acceptance. I can see why you are so close to your sister as she is a total sweetie, but I love your mother's quirkiness and Piers' calmness. Yes, you do have a lovely family and I consider myself very fortunate that they have taken to me."

"Who couldn't," said Isobelle with a grin. "Now, while we have the chance, kiss me and then tell me what happened after I blacked out." Evelyn leant in close and, with gently luscious lips, kissed Isobelle daintily, but insistently. Isobelle luxuriated in the soft velvet touch of her mouth. It was hard to credit, but every kiss she had from Evelyn melted her insides and she found herself convinced that it could never be surpassed. Then come the next kiss, away flew that theory! For this moment, this second chance that had been given to them, it was a kiss of renewal, a kiss of remembering and one that was too precious to rush.

"That was some kiss, Miss Hertford. Fancy taking advantage of a young girl bound so in plaster and unable to defend her honour and dignity. You should be ashamed."

"And you thought that my face was flushed with lust, Miss Swanson? But no, with embarrassment at my brazenness. My bosom heaves with the audacity with which I avail myself of you."

"Then know, Miss Hertford, that you will only find solace by enlightening me of the events that took place, for I have awaited patiently your arrival." They both laughed at their vain attempts to emulate 'Wuthering Heights' in a modern hospital. Taking a more serious tone, Evelyn began.

"Although I was pretty dazed from his strike, I was aware enough to know that unless I got help, he was going to kill you. I hated leaving you, but fortunately for me, the men installing the window saw me staggering along the path shouting and quickly came to help me. As they were calling out to each other, Richard must have heard them and he took off through the wood towards the road. It was a pity that they did not catch him, but at least he did not have the chance to inflict the damage he could have done had those men not been there. I made sure your heart was still beating and then rang the police and ambulance. I did not dare move you for fear of making things worse, but it was all I could do to stop myself from hugging you. The time it took for the police and ambulance to get there was an eternity in my frantic state, yet in reality it was quick. Because I knew Fiona's name, the police were able to contact her and, she in turn called your mother. Piers drove down to the Cotswolds to pick her up. Ultimately, we all ended up here where I had to fill the police and your family in on what happened."

"So what about Richard? Did they catch him?" asked Isobelle nervously. The thought of him on the loose was not very comforting.

"No, I'm afraid not and that does frighten me now that he has resorted to this violence. The police have allocated someone to watch over the tower, supposedly as protection for me, but I suspect more to entrap him should he return. I do not feel safe there at all. I hope you don't mind, but your mother and I ended up using your flat last night. We borrowed the keys from your bag."

"Don't be silly. Of course I do not mind. In fact, I would feel better knowing that you are safe. What about the hospital, though? Do you think he would dare come here?" In her present state it was a worrying prospect.

"I would guess that he does not know you are in hospital yet as he is probably more concerned with trying to avoid the police. Even if he does follow the news stories, the hospital has been instructed not to comment on your presence. Hopefully, he will assume you are in the nearer Queen Elizabeth Hospital in Welwyn Garden City." Evelyn looked thoughtful for a minute. "Still, you have a point. I will talk to Detective Keenan about it, for I don't want anything else to happen to you."

"I wish they had caught him. I do not usually hate anyone, but I am really beginning to hate him," said Isobelle. Shrugging, as if to throw off his memory, she changed the subject. "Oh! I asked the doctor about the holiday and he said it would be alright if no injuries to my head become evident. I would have been so upset to have to cancel that after the horrid things that have happened of late. I cannot wait to spend time with you all to myself. Selfish woman that I am."

"I have almost forgotten what a holiday is and the expectation of two weeks with you is enough to make my toes curl. So, I guess that makes me pretty selfish too!"

"Pretty, but not selfish," retorted Isobelle.

"Do you know how long you will need to be in here?" asked Evelyn.

"The doctor intimated about two days. They want to ensure that I have not had damage to my brain. After that, can I come and stay with you again?"

"Either that or I come to your flat. Where would you prefer or feel safer?"

"Well, I've got clothes at you place and I do prefer it there. If there is a policeman watching out for us, we should be okay. We'll just have to be careful if we go out."

"That's fine. I think I will use your flat until you are released if that is okay. I cannot say that I want to stay at the tower alone."

"By all means. My flat is nearer, so you can stay and keep me company for longer. That will be a pleasure for you!" She gave Evelyn a wry grin.

"Actually, it will be a mutual pleasure. I can read to you all the things I like and you will not be able to stop me, trapped in your bed and your plaster."

CHAPTER TWENTY-FIVE

Isobelle remained in hospital for a further two days, which alternated between pleasant and frustrating. She longed for the hours that Evelyn spent with her, reading to her, puzzling over crosswords and blending in so readily when Fiona, Piers and her mother visited. Her mother was staying with Fiona, so they all tended to arrive together and the time spent on family reminiscences were warm and cosy to Isobelle, as well as being amusing. What she predominantly enjoyed were the times when Evelyn was alone with her and would divulge little gold nuggets of information about her youth. After most of these snippets and stories, Isobelle would just want to take her in her arms and hug her. For although Evelyn related them factually as they had occurred to her, Isobelle saw beyond the stories to the young girl largely ignored by her parents, certainly starved of proper affection. It was not that they had been intentionally cruel or neglectful, but had been caught up in a class and time where there was a distinct wedge between parents and children of the privileged. Evelyn's relating tended to mention nannies with more frequency than her mother or father. She must have been a lonely girl, thought Isobelle, which was why she had become so strong in herself and so studious. Knowing this, it became more and more heart-warming to see how well she integrated with Fiona and their mother. Isobelle could tell that for Evelyn, there was an air of simple delight and contentment when she was with them.

The frustration was that the room was not very private and various orderlies, nurses and doctors traipsed in during the course of the day and night making it absolutely impossible to have much physical contact with Evelyn. Oftentimes as Evelyn read to her, she would study her features, marvelling at the grateful curve of her cheekbone as it lent an arced line towards the corner of her mouth. And that mouth. When Isobelle watched her lips, glossy and shiny with lipstick, she could feel herself become aroused. She would find herself unable to stem the dampness between her legs and the tingling that would sensitise her clitoris like a persistent itch that screamed for scratching. Yet she could do nothing but squeeze her legs tightly together and hope that her flushed face was not too much of a give-away. Once, when Isobelle had been admiring the plunge of Evelyn's cleavage, Evelyn glanced up from the poem she had been reading and caught Isobelle's look of lust and obvious restlessness as she tried to deal with her rising excitement. Moving her chair closer to Isobelle's bed, Evelyn burrowed a surreptitious hand under the sheets and sought out the point of Isobelle's erotic discomfort. However, no sooner had Evelyn's glorious fingers begun their ministrations, then the tea orderly burst through the door.

"Hello, dears," she announced, oblivious to the sexual tension that charged between these two dears! "Would you like a cup of tea?"

She must have noticed Isobelle's heightened colour, for she added, "Sorry dear, did I wake you?"

"No, that's okay," said a husky Isobelle, "Evelyn here was just rousing me as you walked in." It was all Evelyn could do to stop herself bursting into laughter.

And then the morning of her release arrived and Evelyn appeared with a big box of chocolates. "I thought you may like to give these to the nurses," she said as she helped gather up Isobelle's possessions into a small case.

"Was that dress I bought okay?"

Isobelle had asked Evelyn to bring in a floaty poppy-print dress, as she did not want anything to tight against her body, as the bruising was still very tender.

"Excellent choice. Of course you realise that you are going to need to help me dress and undress for a while!"

"Well, the undressing part should not be a problem!"

Isobelle had worried how she would cope with going back to the tower, whether it would open wounds in her mind or not. However, as they neared it she found herself strangely excited. It was Evelyn's home and she supposed that as it held so much of Evelyn in it, that its obvious benefits outweighed the bad incidents that had taken place there. Besides, it was a unique and very comfortable place to live. Most people would give their right arm to stay in such a well-designed and exclusive property, so she was damned if she was going to let Richard taint it for her. Her only tiny complaint was the stairs, for in her present fragile condition, it was painful going. However, on reaching the lounge, the numerous vases of decorative flowers made it all worthwhile.

"Welcome home!" beamed Evelyn. "I hope that you don't suffer from hay fever!"

"Oh! Evelyn. They are stunning. Thank-you so much. Let me give you that lingering kiss I have been dreaming about for the last two days."

"As long as the tea lady doesn't decide to drop in!"

A little later found Isobelle stretched out on the settee, banked by plump cushions and with her head in Evelyn's lap.

"It's a shame that we never got to have that meal with Fiona and Piers. On the positive side though, at least you have met them and I do know they like you, especially Fiona."

"And I really like her. Your family is lovely and they have been so kind to me. Anyhow, we won't miss the meal…as you would find it tricky to go there, I have invited them all here for supper tomorrow. I meant to mention it earlier, but with one thing and another, I forgot. I'm sorry, darling. I was not sure if they were vegetarian like you, so I elected to make a cheese pasta bake. We can have tomato and mozzarella slices with pesto to start and Jamaica rum cake with orange sauce to finish. How does that sound?" As she spoke, she was stroking Isobelle's hair idly.

"My goodness, that sounds lovely," exclaimed Isobelle. "I am salivating already!"

"In that case, come and keep me company while I cook us something. I'll carry some cushions down for you to protect that desirable body!"

The following evening, subdued lighting, candles and hearty cuisine made for a very successful supper. The weather played fair and maintained the calm, mild temperatures that had surprised the country of late and which meant that Evelyn could open some of the huge windows. Sherry, wine and a cointreau eased the conversation and by the end of the evening Evelyn had been firmly adopted by Isobelle's family. Any potential awkwardness at the passing displays of affection between Isobelle and Evelyn were soon swept away in the ambience of the occasion. On the drive home later, Fiona commented to Piers as to how she was amazed to find that she considered their relationship as natural as their own. "They are so comfortable together. It is strange that in a couple of weeks an affair that I'm sure I would have been confused about has become so perfectly right."

Their mother was more straightforward about it. "I had a lovely evening and I really like Evelyn. I don't really care about what they get up to in private, but I am glad that Isobelle is with someone so sensible and caring. It is obvious they are in love and that is all that matters to me."

Piers and Fiona in the front of the car exchanged a secret look of mock incredulity and amusement.

CHAPTER TWENTY-SIX

As spring flowed effortlessly towards summer and hot coloured blooms emerged in the gardens, Isobelle's body and mind began to heal, revived by warm, lazy days and lashings of love. Evelyn proved to be every bit an attentive and responsive nurse to Isobelle, although gracing her with additional services that even the most private of patients could only dream about.

"My treatment is holistic," she would counsel, "it's all about curing the whole body and mind!" Isobelle was not overly sure about the theory, but was quite prepared to let Evelyn's therapeutic fingers do their work.

Unfortunately, despite the warm climes that tempted them to go out, they were fairly housebound by their fear. The tower offered sanctuary, but even though the garden tugged at their senses with perfumed jasmine and vibrant red poppies, they could not feel safe with Richard still on the loose. Detective Keenan had telephoned regularly, but the confidence of an early apprehension that he tried to instil into them dwindled as each day passed and Richard failed to surface. Not that they complained, as the lounge was a veritable sun-trap in which they languished, Isobelle carefully ensuring all aspects of the holiday were covered and listed, while Evelyn dealt with her structural drawings for work.

Midweek, Evelyn had to make a trip into the office in town and Isobelle readily agreed to accompany her. Evelyn's colleagues, having been informed of the events that had taken place both by the police and Evelyn to ensure security in the workplace, were very sympathetic and eager to fuss over Isobelle in her plaster. It was while at the office that Evelyn sprung another pleasant surprise. She had left Isobelle at her desk for a moment while she went to see her manager, Irene Jessup. However, after a short time it was both of them that returned. Irene was a kindly, yet efficient looking lady, her silver hair and well-applied make-up showing her to be very attractive in middle age. Add to this her beautifully tailored and probably very expensive suit, and you knew you were in the company

126

of a woman of substance. Isobelle could see why Evelyn liked her so much - she was the kind of woman that you could not fail to like or admire.

"Hello, Isobelle. It is nice to meet you at last. Evelyn has told me a great deal about you," she greeted, her voice soft, yet sure.

"And she has told me about how you are her confidant. Now that I have met you, I can see why," returned Isobelle, shaking Irene's small hand.

"I see that you were treated rather despicably by that Richard character. How are you feeling now?"

"Still a mite sore in places, but what with this excellent nurse and the impending holiday, my spirits are soaring very high."

"I meant to thank-you for that. I knew that you must be someone very special when Evelyn requested some holiday. I have been nagging her in vain for years to have a decent break. I was beginning to think that she had forgotten how to relax."

Evelyn was blushing on being spoken about so, a frailty that Isobelle had not previously seen - she was the blusher of the two of them after all. She wished she could grab her hand in support, but instead seemed to make it worse as she replied, "Don't worry. I shall do everything I can to ensure that she relaxes."

Irene appeared to hesitate a brief moment before speaking again. "Isobelle, tell me if you think that this is none of my business, but Evelyn told me that you had been made redundant. Well, I was thinking; we have a largish finance section here, so if you are amenable, why don't you send a resume to me and I will see that it finds its way to them. I cannot promise anything, but we are always on the lookout for intelligent and friendly staff."

Isobelle beamed with obvious delight "No, I don't mind you knowing about my redundancy. Your offer is very much appreciated and I certainly will be sure to send you my curriculum vitae. Thank-you so much."

"I am happy to help anyone who is close to Evelyn. We have been fortunate in that although we work together, we are also great friends. I look forward to being friends with you too." She glanced down at her watch. "Oops! I have a meeting that I must dash off to now. I do hope you heal up soon and do have a lovely holiday together."

127

As they watched her glide out of the Evelyn's office, Isobelle reached over and gave Evelyn's curvaceous bottom a pretend slap. "I've got you to thank for all this. When have you been hatching up all this about the job? And what is the great deal that you've told her about me, you devil?"

"I make a point of calling her each day when I am not in the office, just to keep tabs on any developments and to let Irene know how I am doing. Naturally, we natter about this and that as well. As she said, we're friends, but in many ways she is the mother to me that my mother is not. Did you like her?"

"She is gorgeous. Sophistication itself. Is that where you get your amazing clothes sense?"

"I suppose so. When I was new and insecure, and with Richard still around, she took me under her wing. Shopping was one of the fields of training that she took me through!"

As the holiday got closer, so did their excitement. For both of them it was novel in that they would be spending it with each other, neither having been on holiday with a partner in a relationship before. For Evelyn, there was the almost childish euphoria of actually having a holiday of substance, rather than time with her parents or at home. And there was the shopping. From Isobelle's carefully constructed lists there were the food and household items from the supermarket, followed by the more entertaining and fulfilling items of clothing. The latter required a few trips to London's West End department stores with return trips loaded with bags of items, some of which were integral to the holiday, many not. But that is the joy of a holiday, accumulating those items that have been on the wish list under the pretext of being so necessary. Because of Isobelle's plaster cast on her arm, she had to have Evelyn assist her in the changing rooms, a task that had them in fits of giggles on a number of occasions. However, as if by some unwritten, but tacit agreement, they refined their displays of affection for each other in public to occasionally holding hands. There was the sneaky kiss where they felt that they were private, but neither felt the desire to arouse unwanted public curiosity or resentment about something so precious to each of them.

Before they knew it the eve of their departure was upon them. However, orderly women that they were, they were prepared, packed and eager to depart. Ideally they would have loaded the Land Cruiser that night in readiness for an early start, but the niggling fear of Richard's presence somewhere out there was too much of a deterrent. So instead, they had all the boxes and bags arranged by the front door. It was fortunate that the back seats of the Land Cruiser could fold down, as once all together, it appeared more like a house-move than a holiday. That evening they went to bed early as Evelyn would be doing the driving over the next few days and Isobelle fussed about her having her beauty sleep.

"Once we are there we can relax and do all the things we have wanted to do together for a while," said Isobelle.

"Mmm! Gives me something to think about while driving!" purred Evelyn.

"I know France is the country of romance, but I don't think their gendarmerie will accept the excuse of your weaving over the road due to erotic thoughts!"

"They would when they see you!" Evelyn retorted.

CHAPTER TWENTY-SEVEN

The fates were either feeling sorry for them or up to mischief elsewhere, for the following morning was clear and warm, ideal for the six-hour ferry crossing from Portsmouth to Caen. They were in buoyant mood and, following family traditions of holiday entertainment, they sang enthusiastically down the motorway to the ferry terminal. On such occasions, especially when the sun is shining, it is as if Pleasantville has materialised, for as they neared the coast and the chalk downs, wild flowers dotted the verges and people seemed to be smiling more. They made good time and, because they were near the front of the queue, they were soon loaded and installed in their cabin. Having deposited the bags they bought with them, they went and stood at the railings, watching Portsmouth and England slip away as they scythed out into the Channel. After watching the light refracted off the dip and swell of the waves, broken only by swooping gulls as they followed the passage of the ferry, Evelyn broke their silent reverie.

"Shall we go and have something to eat before it gets too busy? Then we can stroll around the ship or lie down in the cabin for a while."

"Sounds like a splendid idea. I do feel a little peckish."

The dining room had yet to fill up, as everyone seemed to be exploring the ship or else booked into the cinema, which was just about to begin screening a popular science fiction film. The cuisine was a strange mixture of French and English, a diet to please the multitude of cross Channel travellers. The girls both joked about how the French fries were actually English chips and that the English beef was probably French following the foot and mouth scares over the last few years. Both had the vegetarian lasagne option.

"I guess that if you are a vegetarian, then I am going to have to get used to it," Evelyn pointed out. ''Still, it will do me good to have a proper diet for a change."

"Have you ever driven on the right hand side of the road before?" asked Isobelle as they ate.

"No. I must admit that although I have done a fair amount of driving around the UK in the course of work, the prospect of driving on the right is filling me with dread." She pulled an appropriate face to illustrate that dread.

Isobelle laughed. "Don't worry, darling, I will help you with the map reading. It is strange. After passing my test, some friends of mine all decided to come over to France for the day. As I was the only driver, I had to take the bit between my teeth, but funnily enough, as many of the French roads are dual carriageways, it was not as bad as I had envisaged. I actually found it trickier when we got back to the UK for some unknown reason."

"I expect that after a while I will get used to it, but for goodness sake remind me which way to go at any crossroads or roundabouts."

After a drawn out lunch, they made their way around the decks, collecting tourist information on the best routes to take, visiting the duty free and the newsagents. Apart from a bottle of peach schnapps for the holiday, neither of them was tempted by the perfumes and accessories. Isobelle nodded towards one of the display windows.

"When I was a young girl and flying to and from the Middle East was considered a two day trip, the BOAC hostesses used to wheel trolleys through the aircraft with such items for sale. This is one aspect of the world that has never changed - I bet they still sell the same things. I'm sure that if we looked, there would be the ubiquitous Muelhens 4711 perfume, Hermes scarves with scenes of London and jars of gentlemen's relish on one of the shelves!" joked Isobelle.

"You may jest, but I can see the 4711 and the Hermes scarves from here," laughed Evelyn. "Shall we go back to our cabin, or would you prefer to walk around some more."

"No, let's go back now. I could do with a lie down."

The cabins were functional with two bunk-like beds and a small bathroom with shower. To avoid creasing their clothes, both stripped down to their underwear before stretching out on their bunks.

"I actually feel quite tired," yawned Evelyn, "but I cannot possibly fall asleep without having you snuggle up to me. Come and share my bunk, shipmate."

"I thought that you'd never ask, skipper," complained Isobelle, easing off her bunk and hunkering down beside Evelyn, her plaster cast bound arm resting against the cabin wall. Evelyn curled at her side, wrapping a leg over Isobelle's and an arm over her stomach. Her head rested in the crook of Isobelle's fit arm, Evelyn's soft breath settling into a rhythm over Isobelle's chest. Before long, she was asleep, her face in sleep relaxed and radiant. Isobelle was positive she would never discover all the glories of this exceptional woman, but it was going to be enjoyable locating every freckle, finding every foible that composed her make up. She studied Evelyn's arm, with its tiny golden hairs and pink creamy complexion, which curved down to a delicate wrist and swept on to long fingers. Those fingers had the magic to master an artistic pencil with the same care and dedicated attention that they used when they trailed tantalisingly over Isobelle's own architecture, moulding her knotted muscle into pliant flesh. Then still further, the pliant flesh turning into a rippling liquid that pitched her senses to a crest which she would arc and strain to surmount.

As the monotonous vibrating hum of the ferry's engines changed almost imperceptibly in pitch, Evelyn stirred slightly, her flaxen French plat slipping over Isobelle's shoulder. She could smell the shampoo-fresh aroma of Evelyn's hair and let her lips plant a swift kiss in its midst. She let her eyes linger on the undulation of Evelyn's smooth breasts, calmly rising and falling against the white cotton of her bra. She was in awe of Evelyn's breasts. She could understand why men were so fascinated by breasts having enjoyed her time spent with Evelyn's. Her ideal was when they lay together, one on top of the other so that the respective parts of their bodies matched and their breasts pressed together. She would hold Evelyn tightly as if by doing so she could become a part of her, let her experience some of the intensity of the love for Evelyn that coursed through her being. Turning her head slightly, she rested her cheek against Evelyn's hair and, before long, her eyes growing heavy with the lull of the ship, she drifted into sleep with her images of Evelyn.

The sudden noise of voices passing by the cabin first roused Evelyn. She carefully lifted her arm to check her watch. Time to get a coffee and a Danish pastry before they arrived in Ouistreham. Unaware of the fact that she had been scrutinised by Isobelle earlier, she allowed her eyes to meander over her innocently defenceless lover. Isobelle's skin, like many women with red hair, had a very pale alabaster hue, adding to the delicate air she had about her. Her powder blue bra was in compliment, creating an almost Wedgwood appearance of fragility and beauty. Evelyn could see that Isobelle's delightful nipples strained hard against the flimsy material, even when not erect. Mischievously, she blew lightly at the nearest one to see if she could enlarge it. When that did not seem to work, using the nail of her middle finger, she teased it over the material, feeling the nipple below soon begin to swell.

"What are you up to, you wicked woman?" Isobelle's voice was the throaty of the freshly wakened.

"Ascending Everest without a sherpa," replied Evelyn with a cheeky grin.

"Just so long as you left your crampons behind," Isobelle retorted. "Besides, with my nipples, I probably resemble the Eiger more than Everest."

"Whatever summit, they are always a pleasure to climb!"

Having had a coffee and a bite to eat, they stood together on the deck and watched the approach to Ouistreham. Although Isobelle had been through the far quicker Channel Tunnel, she much preferred the option of the ferry. She felt that she had actually journeyed to another country when she travelled by sea. There was a certain thrill in watching one country slip away and another appear. With the Tunnel, without the view of the sea, it was difficult to envisage the same sense of transition. Regarding the peaceful town and the clean sweep of beach, it was challenging to imagine the scenes of carnage that had taken place along the shores as the allies landed during D-Day. Isobelle had seen some of the veteran soldiers in their be-medalled uniforms at Portsmouth, obviously making the pilgrimage to spots they were probably happy to no longer recognise. After all, many of their colleagues had fallen for this better place, this better life.

CHAPTER TWENTY - EIGHT

Despite Evelyn's reservations on driving in France, after an initial hiccup and a few trips around a roundabout, she gained confidence and they found their hotel relatively easily. The sea air had obviously lived up to the old wives' tale, for both of them were tired again by the time that they checked in. So after a quick meal and a bath too small to share, they selected the most comfortable of the two beds and cuddled up. Isobelle had calculated that it would take about 10-12 hours to reach Villeneuve-sur-Lot from Caen, so they made sure that they were up early for a prompt start.

A clear blue sky met them as they left the hotel and, with an air of contentment, they motored their way down the left side of France on reasonably empty toll roads. Like most long car journeys, they tend to pass in a protracted blur of songs, detours, toilet stops and the occasional distraction. This was so with Isobelle and Evelyn, their distractions being the distant sight of the imposing Mont St. Michel, the terrifyingly high bridge at Nantes, the stunning fields of crowded sunflowers near Niort and the regimental rows of vines by Bordeaux. Close to their cottage, they found, to their amazement, a Prune Museum and vowed that they would visit it for the novelty factor alone.

As they approached the cottage, their weary spirits rose, for it was so picturesque - the type of cottage that would grace a chocolate box or jigsaw puzzle. Behind the property was the swimming pool, most inviting after being seated for so long, with a stunning view from the patio down a tranquil valley. It's height ensured its privacy and Isobelle and Evelyn exchanged knowing looks behind the owner's back. The owner, Mrs. Martins, was English for which they were both grateful. They were too washed out to grapple with the ins and outs of the pool filter system in pigeon French, so it was a blessing to go through the hand-over period with relative ease. Mrs Martins had the orderly look of a retired ambassador's wife; crisp, efficient and with a hint of eccentricity. She dutifully ticked off all her points as she marched them round the premises. The largest bedroom looked over the pool and the valley beyond. It would catch the morning sun for sure.

"We'll sleep in this room," declared Isobelle as soon as she saw it.

"But won't you want your own separate rooms, gals?" Mrs. Martins questioned over the top of her spectacles.

"Yes, of course," blustered Isobelle, realising her error. "We'll fight it out later."

Evelyn was staring pointedly out of the window, but Isobelle knew she was laughing by the way her shoulders were shaking.

"My husband and I live a mile up the road. Keep bees, you know. Must have passed it on your way here. Any problems, drop by. Cheerio!" With the clipped sentences no sooner out of her mouth, she hopped onto an ancient relic of a bicycle and peddled furiously up the gentle slope of a drive to the road.

The girls watched her pumping legs disappear out of view before collapsing into fits of laughter.

"Come on, gal. Grab a bag. Empty the car. Things to do. Keep bees, you know," imitated Isobelle through her giggles.

"So, which bedroom are you having?" teased Evelyn, holding her sides which were aching.

"She's probably MI5 and has got all the rooms bugged," declared Isobelle, wiping laughter tears from her eyes.

"In that case, she is going to have plenty to report," chuckled Evelyn.

Distributing their bags and boxes in vaguely the right rooms, they decided that they would unpack the following day.

"Let's have a float around in the pool and then have a salad with a bottle of wine," suggested Evelyn. "I could do with just unwinding if that is alright with you."

"You must have read my mind. After all that driving you deserve a good rest. I'll probably paddle for a bit and then I will make the salad while you take in this lovely view."

Evelyn came up behind Isobelle and put her arms carefully around her. "Which lovely view would that be then?" she murmured into Isobelle's ear.

"I'm surprised you even had to ask. Why me, of course." She pretended to sound perplexed. "Oh! Evelyn, you didn't think I meant the scenery, did you?"

Evelyn began to unbutton Isobelle's blouse. "Come on, sex kitten, let's get you into a swimsuit. You obviously need to cool down that ardour!"

Evelyn had a bold red bikini that made her look devastating. Isobelle wished that she had the confidence to wear one, but hers tended to be functional one-piece sporty suits. She had learned that for her speed swimming, they were the most practical, particularly when performing tumble-turns.

"It should be me admiring the view, Evelyn. You look good enough to eat in that bikini. I feel positively frumpy beside you." She was sitting on the steps of the pool, her body immersed to her waist and her plaster cast resting on an inflatable ring.

"Ah! But you don't need a bikini to show off your wonderful figure," said Evelyn as she set off up the pool. Not being an advanced swimmer, she tended to stick to a breaststroke and keep her head above the water. With the sun beginning its downward dip into early evening, the water in the pool was cool, but pleasant enough to ease her joints and muscles after the journey. Isobelle watched her swimming up and down, feeling as happy as she had ever been. *Two weeks of this would be tantamount to heaven,* she thought. Her only regret was not being able to swim herself, what with her broken arm. It would have been nice to have given Evelyn some swimming lessons.

After a little while of inactivity, the cold water chilled her, driving her inside where, one-handedly, she managed to present a reasonable supper for them both at the poolside. Once they had eaten, they poured over the tourist brochures that Mrs. Martins had left in a folder on the dining room table, sipping wine and dividing venues into a 'Yes, let's go there, gals' pile or a "Good grief! Not on your life' pile.

"Isobelle, look! Here's one for that prune museum that we passed - le Musee du Pruneau. Makes it sound so exotic when said in French. Mind you, it does seem well worth a visit. Shall we go tomorrow after we unpack?"

"Okay by me, darling," agreed Isobelle. "This one is interesting. All this week Monflanquin, a 13th Century bastide town has medieval days with music, jousting, crafts and theatre. The whole town takes part, dressing up in medieval garb. Sounds brilliant. Would you like to go?"

"Definitely. It is something a bit different. Woe betide any roving knight that tries to win your favour though!"

They had a relatively early night and slept in the following morning. As Isobelle awoke, she found the whole room bathed in a cornflower blue as the sunlight filtered its way through the thin cotton curtains. She felt a tingle of delight run through her and could not resist leaning over and excitedly kissing Evelyn's ear.

"Good morning, poppet. Just look at this glorious morning. I swear that the sunlight has penetrated through to my heart for I feel so happy today."

With that, she clambered out of bed and drew back the curtain allowing the sunshine unfettered access. From Evelyn's position in bed, Isobelle's naked body was silhouetted, her athletically fit figure sharply defined by the light.

"Come back to bed, you sexy thing," commanded Evelyn, opening her arms in invitation.

Isobelle's body, cooler now that she had been up, carefully lay down against the bed-warm fullness of Evelyn. Grinning, Isobelle rubbed her small freckly nose against Evelyn's, before showering her lips with quick, wet kisses.

"Tell me how much you love me," she enquired, "and it had better be more than your work or I'll leave you for the desirable Mrs. Martins!"

Evelyn laughed. "But how on earth can I compete with her bees! You're too cruel!"

"Come on. You have got your lovely secret glade at home to counter her bees. So, win my heart forever and tell me how much you love me."

The mention of the glade by Evelyn's tower only sought to remind her of the frightening run in with Richard. "Well, my darling. When I saw how Richard had attacked you and how you did not come out of the coma, I was petrified that I had just lost the one person who had come to mean the world to me so soon after our meeting each other. I could not believe it at first. Once I had time to take it in I was almost frantic. To be honest, if you had not come round, I do not know if I would have had the will to carry on any more. In the short time I have known you, you have changed me so much inside. My work used to be my all before, whereas now it is a distraction from time spent with you. I find that I cannot get enough of you. I want to know all there is to know about you, to touch you as much as I can, be with you for as long as I can. That is how much I love you."

Isobelle seemed to weigh this up. "Mmm! Let's see. I think that about tops Mrs. Martins," she teased.

"Young lady, remember that you have a bad arm which will soon become worse if you continue to taunt me so! Now it's your turn. Tell me about your love for me."

Isobelle became more thoughtful. "I'll be honest in that I was taken aback at how strongly I felt as regards you, even before I knew that much about you. I had some unsettling fantasies in which you featured that I tried vainly to suppress at first. But something about your impression on me was too powerful. I found that I could not stop thinking about you. I hated it when I thought I might not see you or communicate with you. And now; well now I find that my soul yearns for you each waking hour. I know it sounds corny, but it is true. Do you ever have this strange feeling that you want someone so much you wish you could almost become them, you want to be so close?"

"Yes, I suppose that is what I was trying to explain somewhat inarticulately."

"That's how I feel with you. I adore your company so much that I would not want to ever be parted from you for long. And, I cannot resist your gorgeous body. In a way, for me that is the strangest part of our relationship. I don't think that I have ever really considered a sexual attraction to girls before. I have never even had female crushes. Yet along you come and I almost immediately experience a sexual fantasy and now I find that making love with you is so blissfully natural and enjoyable."

"Now I am interested in this sexual fantasy. What was that all about," asked Evelyn, clearly intrigued.

Isobelle blushed slightly. "It was the first day that I saw you on the train. That evening, I was in the shower and remembering your smile, how luring and sexy it was, when before I knew it I was playing with myself."

"How?" questioned Evelyn huskily. "Show me what you were doing."

"What now?" asked Isobelle, knowing the answer and the game they were already playing, but clearly embarrassed about beginning.

"Yes now, my love," crooned Evelyn. Her low voice was even lower and more sensual.

Isobelle moved her good arm and began to stroke her breasts and play with her nipples. Her initial embarrassment began to ebb away as it was replaced with a growing feeling of comforting excitement. As her fingers moved she found that she was so stimulated by Evelyn's watching her, that she happily continued past the point of caring and into the lap of desire.

"I was stroking myself," she panted, "when suddenly I thought of your lovely red glossy lips covering my nipple."

"Keep on going exactly as you are," instructed Evelyn. Isobelle watched her through sex-glazed half-open eyes as Evelyn eased from the bed and selected her lipstick from off the dressing table. Soon she was back, her lips as bright as her eyes. Isobelle moaned as Evelyn knelt beside her on the bed and lowered her lips to Isobelle's now swollen and eager nipple. Isobelle savoured the moist warmth of Evelyn's mouth as it ran up and down the length of her large nipple and areola, sucking and gently tweaking at it with her teeth.

Swapping over, she then followed on with Isobelle's other nipple until Isobelle thought they would burst with their rigidity and heat. Seeking Evelyn's hand, she guided it down and pressed it between her legs, Evelyn's fingers immediately slippery with Isobelle's juices. Isobelle sensed Evelyn move, but dared not open her eyes in case she lost this pitch of exhilaration that was causing her body to strain on the outside, yet turning her liquid within. Just when she thought her senses had reached their pinnacle, Evelyn's tongue flicked over her clitoris, sending a voltage of undiluted pleasure through her. Her breath came in frenzied rasps as Evelyn's tongue and touch carried her into an ephemeral higher plain, her body convulsing with shudder after involuntary shudder.

Muscles relaxing, her form sank wearily and quenched into the mattress, mussed red hair cascading over a careless pillow and exhausted little mews emitting from her throat.

"You are delicious," purred Evelyn, settling beside her once again, her fingers stroking Isobelle's arm soothingly. She raised her other hand and kissed at Isobelle's musk, sticky on her fingers. "That's how much I love you," she said. "There is nothing that would not do for you."

CHAPTER TWENTY - NINE

These heady, eternal days were the bedrock of their love from which they would begin to lay the bricks of the friendship and trust. They were the days in which the mind's camera clicked away, cataloguing precious moments to be pulled out time and time again in the future. For these were carefree days of seemingly limitless time together, sunshine and wine. It was a hermetically sealed existence away from the everyday considerations of home. After the tribulations of the previous weeks, it was certainly a tonic for both of them.

They visited the Prune Museum and found it a surprisingly enjoyable afternoon, the highlight being the tasting later that included some prune chocolates and liqueurs. The moist warm smell of the prunes being heat dried pervaded the museum with an agreeably intoxicating aroma. By the time they reached the gift shop, confiseries aux pruneau were definitely on the list of presents to take home for the family. There was, strangely enough, also a maize maze in which they got helplessly lost. They found that they could allay their potential panic with playful petting until 'rescued' by tagging on to the end of a group of passing schoolgirls.

They ate when they liked, swam and lazed in the sun. Habitually, they walked the quiet lanes in the early evening, seeking out wildflowers and orchids that dotted the roadside verges. They discovered that there was so little traffic and so few people encountered on these walks that they felt safe to hold hands as they sauntered along. They were walking along as such one evening when they were startled by Mrs Martins' voice. She had been sitting quietly on a shooting stick, tucked away in a field entrance. Because they had been watching the antics of a buzzard as it launched itself off a nearby telegraph pole to circle gracefully on the air currents, they had not noticed her presence. Quickly they unclasped their hands as she spoke to them, her voice carrying in the still of the evening.

"Been watching him for ages," she said, nodding at the buzzard. "Loves that perch. Always there around this time. Enjoying your holiday, gals?"

Isobelle thought that perhaps she had not noticed their handholding. "So far it has been absolutely wonderful, thank you Mrs Martins. This is such a beautiful spot."

"Call me Henrietta. Love this place. Came here twenty-five years ago. The Colonel and I fell in love with it. Bought our house and later the farm. No looking back. Plenty of privacy here, y'know." When she said this, Isobelle visibly coloured. She must have seen us after all, she thought. There did seem to be an inflection at the mention of privacy. For the first time since they had met her, Henrietta smiled. "Don't mind me. Woman of the world. Seen it all. You two lovely things look happy together. All that matters. Too much misery around without trying to create more. Good luck to you is what I say."

"Thank-you. We appreciate your sentiments," replied Evelyn with feeling. Had a little chink appeared in Mrs. Martins' armour, Isobelle speculated.

"Must get back. Got the Colonel's tea to make. Enjoy your walk, me dears!" She gave a curt nod and began to stride off down the road, her sensible walking shoes slapping against the tarmac. The girls watched her disappear around a corner, although her footfall was audible for some time after.

"She appears so gruff and militaristic, yet underneath I think she is probably a very warm and lonely woman," pondered Isobelle.

"Don't say I have more than her keeping bees to contend with now!" chuckled Evelyn as she took Isobelle's hand again.

One morning, while sitting by the pool after a croissant breakfast, Evelyn brought up the subject that they had avoided, the taboo.

"Isobelle, one thing we will have to face when we return is rat face Richard. If the police do not capture him, he is going to be a constant threat. Because it is you he wants to hurt, I am worried sick about what he might do. We have to think about this."

"I have thought about it a fair bit since the attack," Isobelle replied. She did not want his unwelcome ghost to intrude on their holiday, but she knew that Evelyn was being level-headed in bringing the matter up. They had to discuss it at some point before their return. After a pause, she continued.

"I think that I am as frightened of him as you have no doubt been ever since college. But the difference now is that you are not alone and neither am I. Sure he attacked us both before, but I still maintain we stand a better chance together than alone. Now that I have not got a job, I suppose that I could stay with Fiona or my mother, but I don't want to be away from you. We must also be responsible and not include anyone else, especially family, as he may see that by hurting them he can hurt us. Also, I know that Detective Keenan said that he probably would not harm you, but I could not accept that risk. I would be as worried about you as you would be about me if we were apart."

"Oh! Isobelle, I am so glad that's what you thought. I was going to ask if you would move in with me or vice versa once we got back. I was half afraid you would decide to go to Fiona's though."

"Now I am disappointed in you," replied Isobelle crossly. "How could you think that I would do such a thing. I definitely could not leave you in any potential danger by yourself. Who do you take me for?"

Evelyn looked shame-faced. "I am sorry, darling. I didn't mean it disrespectfully. I did hope you would stay with me, which is why I mentioned your situation to my boss, Irene. If we both worked in the same company, there would be less time in which were alone and vulnerable."

Isobelle could not be annoyed with her for long. She looked so forlorn and apologetic. "Now I am sorry, Evelyn. I bit your head off for no reason. Will you forgive me?"

"Of course I will. What do you think we should do? Would you wish to move into the tower for now, or would you prefer not to? After all, he knows about the tower, but I think your place is still unknown to him."

"If you don't mind, I think that I would prefer the tower. My head tells me that my place would be safer with more people living around, but my heart says that I love your home and, once inside, I feel like we are protected in a fortress. Besides, the police are more aware of the dangers around the tower and will hopefully keep up the patrols."

"That settles it then," agreed Evelyn with a smile. "When we get back we will move all the things you need and we will stay together in the tower. So enough about rat face Richard. Are you coming in for a dip?"

CHAPTER THIRTY

Undoubtedly the highlight of their holiday was the trip to Monflanquin, about an hour's drive from the cottage. Monflanquin, built in 1252 by Alphonse de Poitiers, was one of the many walled towns, or bastides, in this area of France. Fought over by the French and English through medieval times, its protected stance covering a hill in the middle of a vast agricultural plain must have made it a formidable challenge. It has now become one of the most beautiful towns in France. As Evelyn drove over the level countryside towards it, the armies of sunflowers gave it the appearance of emerging on an isle surrounded by a sea of nodding yellow. Colour was in abundance that day, for once they arrived at the town, they found streets bedecked with standards and ensigns of the medieval lords, armoured knights on horseback with shields bearing vivid coats of arms, and vibrant troops of musicians with accompanying fools.

They followed the winding street up the hill to the main square. With hardly a cloud in the sky, the sun was free to beat down remorselessly. Fortunately, as the streets were narrow, the shadow from the buildings offered a welcome shade. People's spirits were up as nationalities that had fought each other so viciously in the 100 Years War now laughed and joked together in the modern day re-enactments. Restaurants on two sides of the square had tables outside so diners would not miss the spectacles taking place. On the other two sides were crafts and jewellery. In the middle of the square, costumed vignettes were performed, while the troubadours and trouveres enthusiastically danced and played the authentic instruments of the period. Streets leading onto the square offered stone carving, archery, horse-riding displays, calligraphy and children's entertainment. Although the air was busy with mixed melodies and multi-lingual voices, it did not have the claustrophobia of slow moving crowds in packed spaces.

As soon as they reached the square, the girls were immediately collared by two peasant women in a dancing troupe, joining them in their twirling and spinning, imitating their exaggerated movements of the head, hair swishing to and fro. The music from the pipes was mesmerising, as if working their limbs with invisible strings in time with its roaming lilts. As the troubadours moved on with cries of "Magnifique!", Isobelle and Evelyn fell temporarily exhausted into each other's arms, laughing at their daring in dancing so wildly in front of strangers.

"My goodness! I am boiling after that," gasped Evelyn. "We must find some drinks."

"I don't know how those women dance for so long in those outfits," sympathised Isobelle. "Poor things must be absolutely melting."

As the restaurants were only just starting to fill, they decided to eat there and then, so that they could enjoy the rest of the day without having to worry about queuing for food later. In the afternoon they were almost teenagers again. Having watched an amazing display of bareback horse riding, Evelyn found a passion for archery, having go after go. As Isobelle could only use one arm, archery was out of the question, but she was equally happy sitting on a straw bale observing Evelyn have her fun.

"Isobelle, once your arm has healed, we must both have a go at that. I know your arms will be strong from all your swimming."

"I would certainly like to have a go. If you've finished the archery now, let's go and watch the stone carving. You can join in with the children and carve one specially for me!"

As they strolled down one of the quieter streets, they came upon a studio where the photographer would take your picture in medieval costume. As it was a digital camera, he could show the image on the computer and print it up on quality paper there and then.

"You know, we have not had a photograph taken together yet," said Evelyn eyeing a young couple in flamboyant court outfits having their image captured. "Shall we have a go? I'll help you with your dress."

"Why not, but it must be one together, not separate."

"I'm sure he will be agreeable to that, darling. You'll have to do the talking though as my French is not up to that."

Isobelle gave it her best shot. "Est-ce que vous pourriez nous prendre en photo, s'il vous plaît?" As it happened, the photographer could speak good

English, although with endearingly odd expressions. After pointing at the Lady Guinevere-style outfits and explaining that they wanted to pose together in the picture, the photographer seemed to grasp the situation very quickly. They disappeared into an accompanying changing room where they slipped on the long fluted-sleeve dresses. The dresses were of a velvety material and both were grateful of the fan working overtime in the room. Donning long ornate belts and assorted costume jewellery, they returned to the studio room.

"Now I am having an idea," said the photographer, as he brandished a length of silken material. Turning to Isobelle, he draped the cloth over her shoulder as if a cape, letting it fall casually over her arm and so cover the give-away plaster cast.

"Voila, it is good?" he asked, obviously pleased with his ingenuity.

"C'est bon!" replied Isobelle with a laugh.

"How do you want your picture?" he asked, indicating to a number of options based upon photographs pined to a notice board.

Isobelle gave one of her naughty smirks to Evelyn before replying. "We want to pose like the man and the woman before us." They had stood side by side, with the man holding the woman's hand as if about to bring it to his lips and kiss it.

"Vraiment. Okay. It is no problem. Please…" he indicated where they should stand, then taking Evelyn's hand, placed it in Isobelle's. "Now you wish to look to each other's eyes or to the camera?" he asked. They elected to go with one of each since it was a special occasion.

After each photograph, he let them both see the result on the computer screen prior to printing them off. They were both stunned to see how easily they transformed into the role, particularly Isobelle with her long flowing red hair and chaste sensuality. She could easily have been a potential model for a Rossetti painting. The photographer was obviously impressed with the pictures too as he offered an additional free if they wanted, provided he could retain a copy of one for his demonstration board.

"You are both too beautiful, no? It is good for me to have beautiful femmes for the advertissement of my studio, comprennez?"

"Oui. Yes, of course," smiled Isobelle, lightening the embarrassment the photographer noticeably felt at asking them for the picture.

"I am seulement having this one, if you are saying yes. I show you then that I am stopping them on the camera if you are afraid," he blustered.

"Tres bon. Nous sommes content," replied Isobelle. The one he had selected was where both of them were looking at the camera. For their complimentary one, they assumed the positions they had for their previous photograph, but then Isobelle, still holding Evelyn's hand, leaned forward so that her lips just touched those of Evelyn. The camera clicked before Evelyn had time to show her shock.

"Isobelle. You're a rascal! You'll embarrass this poor man," she protested weakly.

"Nonsense. He would have picked this picture to keep if he'd had half a chance," whispered Isobelle.

The picture was excellent, exonerating Isobelle for her cheekiness. The photographer tried to act nonchalantly as he cleared the pictures from the camera in their presence. Isobelle noticed his hands shook slightly as he carefully packaged their prints for them. By the time they had removed their costumes, he had re-arranged his notice board, their picture taking pride of place in the centre.

"Voila, Mademoiselles! Thank-you for coming to my shop," he beamed.

"C'est rien. Au revoir et merci, monsieur," replied Isobelle.

"Au revoir," echoed Evelyn, still shy at using her limited French phrases.

The heat was not quite so stifling as they emerged from the studio and headed back towards the square. A fool came bouncing up to them, mouthing French far too quickly for Isobelle to pick up. Seeing her puzzled expression, he asked, "English?" Grinning at their nods, he continued, "There is a show wiz the ah.....oiseaux...."

"Birds?" offered Isobelle.

"Yes, birds," he confirmed, "mais, not little birds, les grands birds."

"Oh! You mean birds of prey!" exclaimed Evelyn, pleased to have been able to participate in the conversation.

"Yes, mademoiselles. Birds of prey. Voila. The show is soon, there." he pointed towards the arena where they had watched the horses earlier.

"Thank-you. Merci," said Evelyn.

With a hugely exaggerated bow, the fool continued on his way, no doubt broadcasting the forthcoming show. Stopping to buy bottled water, they joined the throng to the arena.

Although entertaining, the arena was not covered and the heat was intense after a while, more so with the proximity of so many people. As they emerged, they were relieved to be able to find refuge under the shade of a tree in the main square. A troupe of jongleurs were singing love ballads nearby, so they enjoyed the meandering tunes as they watched children taking turns at going in the stocks while others threw wet sponges at them.

"I could do with going in the stocks myself if it meant you throwing wet sponges at me. It is boiling today," groaned Isobelle.

"Don't you dare," threatened Evelyn, slapping her playfully on the arm. "You've already embarrassed me once today."

Isobelle poked her tongue out. "Have you enjoyed today though?"

Evelyn squeezed her good arm in reply. "I have loved it. Thank-you for suggesting it."

By the end of the first week, they had established a routine. The afternoons were proving too hot to be doing much but lie in lethargic bliss beside the pool. Mornings, after a dip, were reserved for sightseeing and the still, drawn-out evenings for walks, followed by a bottle of wine on the patio as they chatted through the continually astounding sinking sun. And so they slid into their second week, familiar with their routine and relieved that the issue regarding their immediate future once they returned home had been resolved.

Whoever said that familiarity breeds contempt must never have found a sincere love in their life, for as each day passed, the girl's love for one another broadened and deepened. They enjoyed the familiarity of each other's company, but that did not imply that neither had their individuality to bring to the relationship. Similar in so many traits, the girls were quite different in personalities, which had emerged in the course of their affiliation, but these differences were like opposite fields of a magnet; once close, they clamed together forcefully and remained bonded.

Evelyn lay on a sun bed, one afternoon, her back almost visibly bronzing under the sun's rays. Isobelle was seated under the shade of a parasol. Her pale skin and ruby hair were not conducive to direct sunlight, she burned blotchy and painfully sore far too easily. Also, she found she sweated so in the plaster cast. To stop it reeking, she had to devise a method using a chopstick and cologne wipe to try and keep her arm clean and smelling sweet. The thought of any part of her reeking was discomforting enough to cause further sweating! As usual with her, she had been admiring Evelyn, her eyes working over the fluidity of Evelyn's hypnotic back. She wanted to learn it's contoured lay, it's textures, in the same way a soldier learns to read an ordinance survey map. While she learned, she also wrote:

> *She reclines....*
> *Glazed with heavy oils, and*
> *placed carefully under hot grill,*
> *She sizzles....*
> *Shifts, ensuring even browning,*
> *Toasted golden finish.*
> *And I watch, eyes*
> *protected behind dark glasses*
> *as the subtle silky breezes*
> *coolly caress her body,*
> *fingers erecting downy hairs.*
> *And I am hungry.....*

And once she wrote, she plotted her route. Quietly standing, she tiptoed over to Evelyn's sun bed and sank carefully to her knees beside her. Then, inclining over Evelyn's shoulder-blade, she let her tongue follow it's natural path down and along her spine, collecting up the beads of sweat as she went, tasting Evelyn's saltiness. She vaguely heard a moan of languorous satisfaction escape from Evelyn's lips as her tongue trailed enticingly down to her bikini bottoms. Undeterred by this lycra obstacle, Isobelle one-handed eased the material down, Evelyn twisting her hips to accommodate. The obstruction now removed, Isobelle's tongue once again claimed it's right of passage, lapping at the dip in Evelyn's lower back, before ascending the rise to her incredible bottom. Over these curves her tongue and mouth continued, unrelenting, and Isobelle could feel Evelyn's legs tightening as her as mounting desire gripped her muscles. Sucking, licking and lapping, Isobelle's path dropped into that natural cleft leading to Evelyn's treasures, her tongue tracing small circles around each nook, using all the senses of taste, touch and smell, before darting the tip of her moist tongue in and out. As her fingers explored within Evelyn, her lips found and drew on Evelyn's throbbing clitoris, inhaling her, drinking her as the sweat-tossed Evelyn flailed and writhed in a rhapsodic intoxication of impending orgasm. As Isobelle's fingers delved deeper and faster, so Evelyn's urgencies soared and flew until, her ecstasy on a par with a wire taut with stress, she burst into a plethora of moans and juices.

Isobelle moved up to kneel so that she could see Evelyn's eyes, luxuriating in the sex-fat dreamy look that they held before filling with love as they turned slowly towards her.

"Isobelle. That was out of this world, so you must be my angel. How I love you"

Isobelle did not reply, but smiled her joy at Evelyn's evident satisfaction. She brushed her lips with her own swollen mouth, a tingle of excitement making her own legs squeeze together as she realised that Evelyn was tasting her own syrupy passion along with Isobelle as they kissed.

CHAPTER THIRTY-ONE

"Penny for your thoughts," asked Evelyn as they sat outside in candlelight, listening to the strange sounds of the night wildlife rebounding within the valley.

"Don't be cross," Isobelle replied quietly," but I do worry about the fact that financially I am not giving a great deal to our relationship. Now that I have not got a job, I have no income. I really want us to be on an equal basis, although I realise I will never command the salary that you have. I don't want to be dependent on you. Do you understand?"

"But I do understand," replied Evelyn. "To partly corrupt George Fox's quote '*Don't walk in front of me, I may not follow. Don't walk behind me, I may not lead. Just walk beside me and be my lover forever*'. However, very few relationships are built on an equal financial basis and I am positive that it will not be long before you are in a job again, especially if Irene has anything to do with it. Also, if you do decide to move in with me permanently, it would not be worth keeping on your flat, so you will be contributing the proceeds of that to our relationship. I do not see that as a paltry contribution. Please don't get hung up about such an issue, darling, as our relationship is much more than financial."

Isobelle was quiet for a moment. "You are right. I wasn't thinking this out properly. I should get a good price for the flat as the market has rocketed since I bought it. However, are you sure that you have thought through me being with you permanently. It is still early days and you might find that after having the run of the place for so long, I might have habits that irritate you."

"You have been at my place for a while, so I think those irritating habits would have surfaced by now. As to my being used to having the run of the place - I am not naturally a loner. In fact I rather hate being alone, but Richard has messed my life up so that I did not trust many people. I have immersed myself in my work, but I do get very lonely. So I couldn't ask for more, having such a beautiful woman share my love and my house with me. Besides, this could work both ways. You have lived alone for some time now, so you might find it hard to adapt to life with me," replied Evelyn.

"I cannot think of anything that I would like to do more than move in with you and be with you permanently. I have loved the time spent with you before the holiday, during the holiday and the thought that it will not end after the holiday is bliss."

"I think though, that I would like to show you a level of my commitment. If you are putting the proceeds of your home into our finances, then my commitment will be to change the deeds of the tower into both our names. I would feel much better about that."

"Oh! Evelyn. That is very sweet of you. Are you sure that you would want to do it so readily though. I know that you love me as I do you, but it is a big commitment to make. Do you want to give our relationship some time so that you feel sure?" Isobelle could not help but reach out and squeeze her hand in gratitude at her faith.

Evelyn looked fixed in her determination. "No, I feel as sure about us now as I have ever been about anything. If, heaven forbid, anything happens to the one of us, then the other should never go begging. I want to share my life with you and that includes my worldly goods, Isobelle Swanson, so there's an end to it!"

"Evelyn, you are a sweetie! So if that is the case, then we can open up a joint high interest account and the money from my flat will go into it. I do actually like the idea of sharing with you. It is actually amazing that we are about the same size, so we can even share our clothes. Mind you, I would never look as good as you in that red bikini."

"That is because of your colouring. Which is why it is nice that we are individual in our clothing. You can wear colours that would look terrible on me and visa versa. With your sea green eyes, you can do things with green that I can only dream about. In fact, I get so jealous about how good they look on you that it is a pleasure taking them off you!" she purred naughtily.

For a moment they listened to the sound of an owl as it called out it's warning to the scurrying mammals from somewhere nearby. The darkness around edged around them, drawing their visibility to only the pool of light from the flickering candles.

"Talking of clothes, have you had any thoughts about what you are going to wear for the wedding?" questioned Evelyn. "I was actually quite surprised that you were not going to be a bridesmaid."

"My goodness, no!" exclaimed Isobelle. "I am not cut out to be a bridesmaid although Fiona did ask me. I prefer to do the watching; far more fun. Besides, there are so many young cousins champing at the bit to be bridesmaids that I couldn't possibly have ruined their dreams for them. I am not even sure I will be out of plaster by then, but either way, it would also have proved awkward with my arm as it is."

"Mmm! I can see your point, although you would have looked endearingly cute as a bridesmaid, herding up all those little ones!" laughed Evelyn.

"I assure you that if I had had to have been one, I would have made sure that you would have joined me. I would have bribed Fiona, and then we could have looked endearingly cute together!"

"Poor Fiona. Two giggling lesbians following her up the aisle would be all she needed on her big day!" joked Evelyn. They both could not help laughing at the image.

"You still have not answered my original question about what you are going to wear," reminded Evelyn.

"In truth, I was stalling for time as I hadn't given it much thought recently. I think we'll have to shop in earnest when we get back. Unless we go into Villeneuve and see what the shops there have to offer. The brochure claimed that it was very chic in the centre of town."

"Good idea," agreed Evelyn. "Shall we go tomorrow? I don't think we had anything specific planned."

"That's settled then. What about you? Did you have any thoughts about your outfit?"

"Well, my colouring does suit red, but that might be inappropriate for a wedding, so I was considering a black or deep purple. Sort of depends on what hat I find as well."

Isobelle clapped her hands together as if to accentuate Evelyn's good choice.

"Yes, sweetheart. Purple would probably suit you fine. You have that lovely violet bardot top that looks gorgeous on you, so I would imagine that purple would be sensational."

"Mind you, what you imagine and what you actually end up with are not often one and the same thing. Still, I'm sure that we'll find something suitable. With your background, you ought to wear a tartan."

"Don't. Mother went on and on about that at one point. My brother, Gordon, has been persuaded to wear a kilt and she thought it would look the occasion if I had a long dress in the matching tartan. Much as I am proud of my Scottish heritage, I don't like the way so many weddings now are swathed in tartans because it is fashionable to do so. No, definitely no tartan for me," announced Isobelle vehemently.

"I suppose you cannot blame people for wanting their wedding to be special and you must admit, tartan kilts do look the bees knees. Anyhow, I am pleased to hear that I will eventually get to meet this elusive brother of yours. Tell me more about him."

"Gordon is definitely a Swanson, but unlike Fiona and me, he never inherited the red hair and freckles. He had very light hair which has almost gone bleached with all the time he spends in the sun. You know he works in the United Arab Emirates, but I'm not sure if I have told you what he does. Well, he and a few Arab friends of his set up an adventure tours business, taking tourists on desert trips, archaeological tours, wildlife trips, etc. Because he loves meeting people, he usually always drives one of the Land Cruisers, so he is exposed to the elements a great deal. Consequently he is always very brown. You would sort of imagine him to be well built, but he is slight in figure and quite tall, about six foot I think."

"Sounds like he would break a few girl's hearts. How do you get on with him?" asked Evelyn.

"I think he probably does break a few hearts. He is not one for commitment. A soon as he feels that his girlfriend is becoming too homely or too comfortable, he leaves her and looks for another. Personally, I think he likes the idea of falling in love and the novelty of it, but beyond that it is too much bother for him. As for Gordon and I…we appear close when we are together, but we do not really know a great deal about one another. Being girls growing up together and going to the same schools, Fiona and I were naturally closer. As a brother, I do love him, but I don't know that I would otherwise. He and I have very different personalities and our priorities in life are very dissimilar. I'd say we are chalk and cheese."

"How do you think he will react to us?" enquired Evelyn.

"I could have an educated guess and I am sure that I would not be a million miles off. I would imagine that he would not be in the least bit phased at our relationship, but once he sees how beautiful you are, he will think nothing of trying to seduce you. He would not regard it as an insult to me, as he does not really think sensitively. He would just class you as fair game and it would be his right to try and claim you, if you see what I mean." Evelyn could read between the lines and she could tell that the thought perturbed Isobelle.

She reached over and laid a comforting hand on Isobelle's arm. "Don't you worry, my darling. My undying love only extends to one member of the Swanson family and she knows full well who she is. If we are done out here, let's go up to bed and I will illustrate to the said Swanson just what I mean!"

CHAPTER THIRTY-TWO

Villeneuve-sur-Lot proved to be a treasure-trove for the girls, particularly a bight and cheerful clothes shop off the Rue Des Cieutats, which was ironically called 'Ma Cherie'. During their introductions, it turned out that the proprietress, Mlle. Gervais, had spent some years working in a selection of London department stores prior to returning to Villeneuve and starting her own shop. This not only gave her a command of English, to the girl's great relief, but also an eye for well-tailored classic clothes, ideal for formal occasions. Evelyn propelled Isobelle forward, her hands firmly guiding her by the hips.

"Mlle. Gervais, if you could deal with Isobelle first. We had thought perhaps a green to match her eyes."

"Vert. Yes, a green would go very well with her eyes and, I think, also her hair. I have just such a dress." Moving to a rack of dresses at the back of the boutique, she produced a fuchsia leaf embellished chambray dress and presented it to Isobelle with a flourish.

"Oh! Evelyn, that is beautiful!" exclaimed Isobelle . "What do you think of it?"

"I agree. It's lovely. I do like the fact that it is not all green, only the leaves. Quick, let me help you try it on."

Once on, it appeared as if made for Isobelle's lithe figure. With the white background it also meant that it would be easier to find a hat and bag to compliment it. Mlle. Gervais, meanwhile, was thinking ahead and appeared at the dressing room with a long royal blue cotton-mix dress and matching jacket.

"I think maybe it is for you," she said offering it up to Evelyn. "I think that the colour is good for your skin and your blond hair."

"Mlle. Gervais, you are a wonder!" announced Isobelle. "That should look spectacular on you, Evelyn. Go on, your turn to strip off!"

Isobelle pirouetted around admiring her dress while Evelyn carefully slipped into the suit. Isobelle was right, it did look spectacular and it was very comfortable. "Isobelle, you know I think that something's not quite right," said Evelyn. "I can never go into a shop and find an outfit just like that, never mind two, counting yours. We haven't had to toil, sweat or curse at all!"

"I know what you mean, but if you care to glance at the price tag, you will definitely have your chance to curse," whispered Isobelle.

Evelyn glimpsed at the tag on her suit. "Wow! I see what you mean. Still, if we can get them sorted out now, we can concentrate more on our moving when we get home. Hopefully, buying outfits here in France will avoid bumping into someone in the same dress on the day. I will definitely pay to avoid that embarrassment."

They were paying for their outrageously priced, but stunning outfits when Mlle. Gervais asked, "Is it that you will be needing a hat for the occasion of this wedding?"

"Yes, I think we could both do with one, especially if it is hot," answered Evelyn.

"Then I may be of help, Mademoiselles," beamed Mlle. Gervais. "I have a friend nearby who has a hat shop, I think you say milliner in English. I can take you there now if you wish."

"That would be very kind," thanked Evelyn.

"She also has the bags to go with them. You will see."

Indeed they did. Locking up her shop, she escorted them through a few historical narrow streets to emerge on another main road, the Boulevard de la Republique. The hat shop sat incongruously between a number of street cafes, but nevertheless certainly looked well stocked.

"This must be her sister, Madeleine's shop," whispered Isobelle cheekily to Evelyn as Mlle. Gervais greeted the hat shop proprietress. "Her cousin, Adele, owns the shoe shop and niece, Giselle, the lingerie boutique!"

Evelyn nudged her. "Shush! You are incorrigible at times!"

"All part of my unique service," grinned Isobelle. Just then a hat caught her eye. "Oooh! Love, look at this! I have always wanted one of these ever since I saw the Great Gatsby." She had dragged Evelyn across to a 1920's style hat near the counter.

"That would be very beautiful with your dress," said Mlle. Gervais from behind them. "The white will match the background of the dress, and the green leaves of the flower are also suitable." She spoke in rapid French to her friend. "This is my friend, Madame Dupres. She does not speak English, so I will tell you what she is saying."

Again they uttered a staccato of French between them.

"She is saying that this is a parisisol straw cloche with a double fold brim and creased crown. The crushed velvet band and flower have been dyed to match the hat straw and then the leaves coloured. Would you care to try it, please?"

Before she could agree to, Madam Dupres intervened with a few more sentences at break-neck speed. They saw Mlle. Gervais nodding as she turned back to them.

"My friend is suggesting that you can change if you are wishing to, so that you can see the whole effect together."

"That's very kind of her," offered Isobelle as they were guided to a dressing room at the back of the shop. "Sorry, Evelyn. You must be getting fed up undressing and dressing me."

"I'll never get fed up undressing you," teased Evelyn, "but having to look at that body of yours and then dress you again without any hanky-panky is so hard for a poor tempted girl such as myself."

"Be a good girl and I will see what hanky-panky you can get up to later," giggled Isobelle. Lowering her voice, she added, "You may be lucky. Mlle. Gervais will probably find some matching camisole knickers that we'll have to try on later!"

Once they had changed into their wedding attire once again, Madam Dupres made Isobelle stand in front of a full-length mirror while she arranged the cloche hat over her malleable red hair. Evelyn almost gasped to herself as she watched. Isobelle was breathtaking. As she drank in the sight of this radiant sylph-like young lady, she found it hard to believe that Isobelle was her lover, her very own. It suddenly made her warm inside and it was all she could do to prevent the whelm of emotion from sending tears of gratitude streaming down her face. The stifled sound of her restrained sob must have reached Isobelle, for her joyous countenance quickly changed to one of concern as she swivelled round to face Evelyn.

"Darling, what's wrong? Are you okay?" she asked anxiously.

"It's nothing....I'm just being silly," replied Evelyn, trying to muster a reassuring smile. Isobelle used the pad of her thumb to delicately brush away the few tears that had eked past Evelyn's defences, glistening her eyes.

"Do tell me. What's troubling you, poppet? Have I done something to upset you?" Isobelle's voice was kindly and consoling.

"Oh! I'm sorry, sweetheart. It was seeing you there so resplendently beautiful and then thinking how I could have so easily lost you after the attack. It just suddenly slammed home. I know I couldn't ever bear to lose you," confided Evelyn, her speech slightly a-tremble.

"Well now, you dry those pretty blue eyes because I have no intention of leaving you. I am your loveable limpet! I take it from your reaction that you approve of my hat," she said, twirling like a model especially for Evelyn.

"I love your hat and I love you in your hat," she replied, mustering a smile.

"Good, then let's sort something out for you, so I can shed some tears over how captivating you look."

Mlle. Gervais and Madam Dupres had not been idle in their duties. During the girl's discourse, they had been scouting the shop for a bag for Isobelle and a hat and bag for Evelyn. Clearly they took their job seriously, for the items they presented to the girls were ideal. There was a discreet white bag with a long strap, just big enough to hold essential make-up and obligatory camera. For Evelyn, there was a similar bag in royal blue, but the piece-deresistance was the hat. Again, in a royal blue that matched perfectly with her suit, it had a high flat crown, large dupioni silk bows, a draped band and cotton gardenia accent. When madam Dupres placed it over Evelyn's head, everyone knew that there was no need to look any further for hats.

Isobelle came and stood beside her, interlocking her fingers through Evelyn's as they stared into the mirror together.

"I wish it was our wedding," sighed Isobelle. "We are made for each other. Who could not look at us here and think anything otherwise. Could we not pretend to marry each other someday?"

"Hopefully we won't have to pretend at all. I was reading in the paper during our ferry crossing that the Government are at last going to introduce a bill in the near future making it legal for same sex couples to hold a ceremony and obtain a certificate from a registry office. This is so that they receive the same rights as a heterosexual couple. So, dear, we may not have to wait for too long."

"That would be fantastic. To marry you would be the icing on my cake, for sure," grinned Isobelle.

Evelyn turned to the patient Mlle. Gervais and Madam Dupres, awaiting their decisions eagerly. "Ladies, you are marvels. We wish to take them all," she declared, indicating the hats and bags. "I don't suppose you know a good shoe shop nearby?"

One morning, Evelyn drove out to the local village to collect some milk, eggs and fresh croissants. On her return, she was puzzled to find an envelope pined to the front door with her name on it. Recognising Isobelle's writing on it, she quickly opened it up, a slightly apprehensive feeling in her stomach. Inside was what emerged to be a ferry ticket, much the same as those used for airlines. This is peculiar, she thought, as she distractedly turned the front page. Within, instead of the travel details, there was a note:-

TO THE BEARER OF THIS TICKET

This ticket entitles the bearer to free passage into this residence. Once inside the premises, the bearer should deposit her baggage in the appropriate compartment and make her way immediately to her cabin. She should go directly, avoiding any distractions on route. This is not a drill.

Chuckling to herself, Evelyn followed the instructions, depositing the milk and eggs in the fridge before making her way towards the stairs and their bedroom. It was then that she realised what the 'distractions' referred to were. All the way up the stairs were Isobelle's clothes, beginning with a blouse top and ending with a slinky bra draped over the top banister. By now, Evelyn was fairly melting at the prospect of Isobelle's game, and, with trembling hand, she slowly turned the door knob to the bedroom and eased open the door. Expecting to see Isobelle seductively adorning the bed, she was surprised to see the bed made and another note propped up against the pillow. Evelyn broke into a huge grin as she read:-

In the interests of hygiene, the management requests that the ticket holder remove all items of clothing. She will then make her way to our sauna suit (bathroom) and present her boarding card to the attendant. She will then receive a complimentary pampering by one of our trained beauticians. This is for the cardholder only. It cannot be traded or sold by the holder, particularly to one, Mrs. Martins.

Excitedly, Evelyn quickly slipped out of her clothes and, taking up her 'boarding pass', she headed towards the en suite bathroom.

Stopping at the door, she knocked gently. "Hello, this is passenger Evelyn Hertford reporting for her complimentary pampering," she giggled. The door edged open and Isobelle's hand extended out, followed by her imitation Eastern European voice.

"Please. You haf you boarding pass for inspection?" The fingers on her extended hand clicked with impatience. "Please hurry. Vulgar Volga Tours will be leafing soon and wish all passengers to be totally relaxed and comfortable." Evelyn placed her boarding pass in Isobelle's hand, which quickly withdrew. In a few seconds, the door opened fully, Isobelle standing in her mint green bathrobe facing her.

"Your boarding pass seems to be in order, madam, but I am required by the KGB, I mean Vulgar Volga Tours to ensure that you haf no secret cameras hidden on your person. Management protects the secret of the complimentary pampering very seriously."

"But where could I possibly hide a camera?" Evelyn asked innocently, pointing out her nakedness with an encompassing sweep of her hand.

"Our competitors haf ways, Miss Hertford. Please, if you lie on these towels, I will conduct a thorough search. As I haf broken one arm defending the Motherland, the search will be one-handed. It will be no problem for a professional such as myself."

Evelyn lay face up on the plump towels laid out on the floor. "Please do your worst, Olga. I am ready," surrendered Evelyn.

Isobelle's eyes lit up. "Ahh! Miss Hertford. You are maybe, how you say, blowing your cover. How did you know that I am Olga unless you are a spy? I can see that I must use my most persuasive means to extract a confession!"

Standing over Evelyn with one foot on either side of her hips, Isobelle suggestively undid her bathrobe before letting it fall into a crumpled heap beside the bath.

She then eased herself on top of Evelyn, separating her thighs with her knee so that she could rest intimately on Evelyn.

"I think that I shall haf to investigate your mouth first for any hidden cyanide capsules," she said huskily. Pressing herself firmly against Evelyn, she leaned into Evelyn's sensitive mouth, running her tongue gently along her lower lip. Isobelle's ruby hair fell like a thin curtain around their faces, as Isobelle, raised on her good elbow, held Evelyn's face securely in her hands. For some time, she peered deep into those loving, trusting morning glory blue eyes, before she sank onto Evelyn's moist reaching lips, her tongue probing and teasing between Evelyn's lips. Evelyn tilted her face up to Isobelle, chasing her lips before meeting in a frenzied kiss. Pulling away, Isobelle peppered her neck and throat with kisses, both hearing and feeling the moan that escaped from Evelyn. Lowering herself onto Evelyn's full breasts, Isobelle took an erect nipple into her mouth, bathing it with her fondling tongue as Evelyn whimpered, arching her back to push her turgid nipple deeper into Isobelle's mouth. She felt it harden in desire against the smooth strokes of her tongue. Savouring each nipple, Isobelle relished the intense pleasure, which she knew Evelyn was experiencing.

Kneeling between her parted legs, Isobelle leaned forward, her warm tongue trailing between Evelyn's saliva-wet breasts and down over her gently curving belly, tracing an outline around her sweet belly button. As she did so, Isobelle could feel her own breasts brushing against Evelyn's mound, the sensation tingling her protruding nipples. Following its brief foray in Evelyn's belly button, Isobelle's tongue moved on, gliding down over Evelyn's fair pubic mound and along the inside of her thigh. Evelyn's hands reached down and her fingers ran through Isobelle's hair, pulling Isobelle in towards her as she separated her legs still further. Nuzzling against Evelyn's blond mound of hair, Isobelle looked up at her with an ecstatic smile. "I am afraid that I haf to check here very, very thoroughly," she said, her voice throaty and hoarse.

Running her tongue ever so lightly along her thighs, Isobelle glided her fingers into her nest of fair curls, caressing between her glistening folds and then on, deep into her pool of wetness. Evelyn arched with anticipation as Isobelle moved lower between her legs, inhaling her incredible womanly scent. Breathing it in, she guided her tongue onto Evelyn's clitoris, luxuriating in the wetness and taste as her tongue snaked back and forth over the sensitive gland. Evelyn's body swayed with the rhythm of Isobelle's probing tongue that flicked and whirled, lapped and tasted. As Evelyn's senses began to blur into a mindless passion, so her body began to spasm and jolt with each gilded thrust of fingers, with each feathered touch of dancing tongue. Suddenly, Evelyn's fingers clenched in Isobelle's hair and her thighs tightened around Isobelle's shoulders, tensing, then releasing, jerking one final time against Isobelle's mouth before an explosive shudder sent spasms of hypersensitive orgasm cascading through her body like a tidal boar. As Isobelle rode her orgasm with her, she heard her repeating, "Oh! Isobelle, my love! Oh! Isobelle!"

Kissing Evelyn's glistening mound, Isobelle eased up the towels to lie beside the exhausted Evelyn, teasing the damp strands of fair hair from her forehead. Evelyn's eyes slowly opened, her warm smile lighting up her flushed face as she stared doe eyed into the absinthe green of Isobelle's eyes.

"Oh! Isobelle. That has to be the most passionate moment in my whole life. Thank-you, darling, for all of this. I do love you so." Evelyn's smile caressed Isobelle's heart as she guided her face closer and kissed her swollen lips delicately.

"I think, Miss Hertford, that you haf a very powerful secret weapon. I haf no answer for it, but to defect to your side. However, as a last act of courtesy for the Motherland, the bath is full and hot if you are ready for the complimentary pampering."

CHAPTER THIRTY-THREE

All too soon, these carefree moments of joyous abandon gave way to a nervous tension as the holiday grew to a close. For Isobelle, going back was not painful as now that they had a plan and purpose, she knew that she was not going to be parted from Evelyn and she was looking forward to Fiona's wedding. Evelyn, fairly unused to holidays, was sad inside, for she had found this time with her lover better than she could ever have imagined. She could not help but feel low that this protective cocoon that they were in was now going to open up to potential dangers. Having said that, the thought that Isobelle was going to live with her and had even talked of a marriage between the two of them was exhilarating. *If only there was not the almost choking threat of Richard overshadowing all their future plans and happiness,* she wished, *then I would go home without a qualm. We will definitely come on more holidays like this together.*

On their last evening, they invited Colonel and Mrs. Martins over for a drink. Unfortunately it turned out that the Colonel was not able to get out much, suffering from a severe shortness of breath as a consequence of years of smoking cheap and cheerful tobacco on his many oversees tours. However, Mrs. Martins was only too pleased to accept, starved of much company by her husband's illness. The girls were more or less packed up except for the overnight requirements when she peddled down the drive that evening.

"Evening gals. Enjoyed your holiday?" she barked, accepting a glass of wine from Evelyn.

"It has been absolutely heavenly," replied Evelyn. "We have thoroughly enjoyed ourselves here. This region is so lovely. We can see why you like living here so much." They guided her to the patio where they had laid out an assortment of nibbles on cocktail sticks.

"Have a seat, Henrietta, and do help yourself. How is the Colonel?" enquired Isobelle.

"Thank-you, dear," she said reaching for some olives. "I'm afraid the Colonel will never fully recover. One of the reasons we are still here is that he is better in the warmer weather, but his breathing will always be laboured and he often finds the most basic jobs very difficult. Unfortunately, he requires round-the-clock attention, which I don't mind doing, but what if something happens to me. Causes me a few sleepless nights."

"Do you have many friends around here?" asked Isobelle.

"Catch 22, dear. Not many people live nearby, but when there is something on, festivities or what have you, it is not always easy to get along to it without the Colonel. The people here are very kind and understanding, but they have been here most of their lives. We are still relatively new here and it will take time to be fully accepted."

"Do you have family to turn to at all?" asked Evelyn.

"One son. In the army. A Red Beret. He's currently on manoeuvres in Oman. He hasn't married yet, but if he does decide to settle down, I don't know whether he will be interested in living here. We hold the cottage in case, and it is a good source of income in the meantime. For me, it is something to keep me busy and a means to meet people."

"Well I don't see how he could not like it here," smiled Isobelle, "We have enjoyed every minute here. I am sure that it would be a lovely place to raise a family. Does he speak French?"

"Yes, fluently. Also speaks Spanish and Arabic. Seems to have a knack for languages."

"In that case, I am sure that this will be a huge temptation for him, especially if he can find work nearby," assured Evelyn.

Later that evening, as they lay together in bed, they felt a strong sense of sorrow for Mrs. Martins. Hers was a future trapped in a beautiful location, but a slave to loneliness. They both hoped for her sake that her son would one day return to take up this house, but Evelyn thought that unless he struck up a relationship with a local girl, bringing in a wife from elsewhere might raise it's own difficulties, particularly with regards to the isolation. Whilst on holiday, it was one thing, but to be so remote day in, day out, would be asking too much of many people.

The sun rose early with them the next morning and having loaded the Land Cruiser, tidied up the last bits and bobs in the cottage, they drove up to Mrs. Martins to deposit the keys.

"I have enjoyed having you around, gals, so anytime you feel like returning, let me know," she offered, an almost pleading look in her eye. "And I hope all goes well with your sister's wedding. You two are lovely girls, so look after each other."

"Of that you can be assured, Henrietta. You take care now and, if you don't mind, we'll drop you a line every now and then," replied Evelyn. It was one thing she and Isobelle had resolved to do for this lonely woman.

"Love to hear from you whenever you have time. Now you've got a long journey ahead, so be off with you and take care." They each kissed her cheek before climbing back into the Land Cruiser. She looked so forlorn as they drove off that for some time they did not speak, wrapped in their sympathy for her.

"I would hate it if you were made so lonely because I was virtually an invalid," said Isobelle after some miles on the road.

"But that is something that I would do out of love for you, darling, just as Mrs. Martins is doing. She obviously loves the Colonel. I suppose that it is the sad part of life that so many compromises and sacrifices have to be made. That is the mark of a true love though, enduring the difficult times as well as the good. If you had been brain damaged by Richard following the attack, there is absolutely no way that I would have walked away from you. In our relatively short time together, you gave me something very dear - your love. And I gave you mine. That can never be taken away or reversed. We loved each other and that would be through thick and thin."

"Oh! Evelyn, I agree! Don't get me wrong. I feel exactly the same about you. No, what I meant was that if I was conscious that I was locking you into such a lonely existence, it would make me so sad. I suppose that would end up as a vicious circle, everyone being sad. Life is so unfair at times," Isobelle replied morosely.

"It can be unfair. I felt that it was very unfair at college when Richard was making my life hell, but I managed to make it into a good job and, best of all, I met you. That has more that made up for it. Perhaps Mrs. Martins son will take up the cottage with relish, raise a family there and Mrs. Martins will end up with grandchildren running all over the place."

"You're a wise woman, Evelyn Hertford. Yet another reason why I love you," announced Isobelle, brushing a kiss on her cheek.

The whole journey back was much the same as it had been on the way down. The weather was equally as bright, the hotel as comfortable and the ferry trip as calm. Following their initial melancholy over Mrs. Martins, they resolved to live out the rest of the holiday and enjoy themselves. Consequently, on the ferry they decided to form their own private club, seeing as they could not possibly be a part of the Mile High Club. They called it the Sea-sore Club and declared it only open to females who were passionate enough to make love with another on a ferry. They joked about starting a website; producing T-shirts with double entendres about the Channel Tunnel; issuing a newsletter called 'Making Waves', all of which helped them to keep their spirits up and pass the time. However, once they were back on English shores, the practicalities began to creep in.

"What I suggest is that we go back to my place tonight, and then tomorrow drive over to yours. We can pack up as many of your things as possible and perhaps get your flat ready so that we can go to an estate agent next week. That is providing you are still keen on the idea of selling up," suggested Evelyn.

"Yes I am," affirmed Isobelle. "Since we discussed it last week, I am more than happy to sell it and move in with you. To be honest, I don't think it would take a great deal of time to pack my things together. I haven't really accumulated a great deal."

"You'll be surprised," countered Evelyn, "It is amazing how much you tend to collect over the years. I bet it will take much longer than you think. Mind you, at least you have the time now. Have you considered Irene's job proposal?"

"I have. It was a very kind offer by Irene and I will definitely take it up. I thought that I would get the move and the wedding out of the way first though, but I do intend to contact her about it," Isobelle replied.

"That would be perfect. You're sensible to wait for a few weeks. Moving while you are working can be pretty stressful, although as you are purely a chain-free seller, hopefully your property will sell quickly," agreed Evelyn.

That night they sat in the lounge in the tower, windows thrown wide open to allow what little breeze there was to air the stuffiness of the long empty room. They had decided to unpack and sort out straight away, knowing full well that if they had relaxed even a jot, they would never have had the energy or inclination to motivate themselves again. Weary now, they sat cross-legged, facing each other from either end of the settee with a cold glass of Chardonnay, staring at each other as if it was their first night together.

"Are you sorry to be back?" asked Evelyn.

"I suppose I was a little at first," replied Isobelle, "especially after having such a great time together. But now that we are back, I feel happy again, for this is just the beginning. We are young and can do so much together. Knowing that I am going to be living here with you from now on makes me feel really excited inside. I used to hate it when you had to drive me home."

"I used to hate having to drop you off. You know, I am quite pleased to be home again. Holidays are lovely, especially this one, but they are escapism, a kind of fantasy, so it is good to be back in reality and to know that the bubble has not burst."

"We must not let our guards down though. Try and be vigilant everywhere that you go as I don't believe that we've seen the last of Richard. Next time I want to be sure that we are ready for him and that he cannot hurt us."

"I wonder if there will ever be a time when I don't have to be afraid any more," said Evelyn with a small voice.

"There will be, my love. He cannot hide forever," reassured Isobelle.

They were quiet for a moment as they considered a possible future without threat. Surreptitiously, Isobelle continued to study Evelyn's face, mesmerised by its gracefulness and flawless elegance. As she was looking, Evelyn suddenly turned towards her, those exquisite features framed by her loose blond hair. Isobelle thought that she seemed totally oblivious of herself as she focused her whole attention on Isobelle as if she was the only person in the world.

"Sometimes when you look at me, the way I see you looking at me, I think that you must be looking at someone over my shoulder. I cannot believe that it is me, that I could be so fortunate to have your attention so." She said this in a low tone, so sultry, that Isobelle felt herself melt.

"I cannot help but stare at you," she said quietly, "you are so beautiful that I want to hold every feature of your face in my mind. I never want to forget the map of your features, ever. I will take it with me. I love you so much and will do so until I die."

Evelyn plumped up the cushions on the settee behind her before spreading out along its generous length. She patted the space beside her. "Here, come and lie down beside me," she said.

Isobelle moved up and stretched out along the length of Evelyn's body, entwining her fingers through Evelyn's and resting her head on her shoulder. Evelyn put an arm round Isobelle's neck, her lips close to Isobelle's ear. "Don't talk of death, darling. We have a lifetime to live yet."

Isobelle nodded, and glanced up at Evelyn. Their eyes met and held, something flaring between them. Something embryonic and very intense. Isobelle tried to put her finger on it, to describe the emotion, but she could not speak. Instead, she felt her face turn hot; she was suffused with a wave of such tender love for Evelyn that she gripped her firmly, expelling a gasp from Evelyn in its fervency.

"What was that, my love?" she whispered.

"My declaration of passion," replied Isobelle.

There were no more words between them, no more were needed. They curled together in the gradually darkening room, Isobelle moulding herself around Evelyn's back, her hand cupping one of Evelyn's breasts. *I feel so tired but I don't think I will be able to sleep*, thought Isobelle, but almost as she thought it, she was exhaling dreams, her breath a warm and comforting rhythm on Evelyn's neck.

CHAPTER THIRTY-FOUR

"Evelyn, you have a beautiful and most unusual house here," enthused Fiona a week after their return. They were walking in the garden, having shown Fiona fully around the tower. When she and Piers had come for the meal after Isobelle's release from hospital, it had been too dark to fully take in its grandeur.

"It's now actually our house as opposed to mine," replied Evelyn as she took Isobelle's hand with a smile. She had arranged for her solicitors to implement the change the day after their return. At first, Isobelle tried to advise that she wait until she was sure, but Evelyn was adamant, so she decided to rejoice in it rather than worry. After all, it was Evelyn's declaration of her trust in her and her belief in their future and that should not be thrown back in her face for any petty concerns.

"Yes," confirmed Isobelle. "We have already cleared out my flat, cleaned it up and employed an estate agent. It is going on the market tomorrow. I am now living full time with Evelyn."

"Good for you both," declared Fiona. "I could tell that you were both made for each other when I saw you together. I'm pleased it is all working out so well."

"We are so happy together, that's for sure," agreed Isobelle. "Anyhow, that's enough about us for the moment. What about all your news and arrangements?"

Fiona's face lit up. "Not that I have to do much of the hard work. I decide something, ring the organisers and they get it done. I must admit that it is a sheer luxury not to have to panic over everything. The wedding itself is running to plan at Middleton Hall, the dress is ready, the bridesmaids all excited, but fortunately kitted out and mother has scoured the stores of Cheltenham and finally found something that she feels is suitable. Piers is pretty quiet about it all, letting me get on with it and obediently signing the cheques!"

The girls all laughed. "Poor Piers, does he know what he is letting himself in for?" asked Isobelle.

"I should ask exactly the same of Evelyn," she retorted. "Evelyn, we'll have to get together, you and I and compare notes on my naughty little sister!"

"Ooh! I can't wait," grinned Evelyn. "I suppose I should be thankful that I do not have a sister to divulge all my secrets!"

"What about your outfits? Have you both had a chance to get out and look?" asked Fiona.

"Now that's our secret. You shouldn't be fishing," said Isobelle in a motherly voice.

"Go on, put her out of her misery," said Evelyn. "Tell Fiona about our French experience while I go and put together a few bits for lunch. I will give a call when it is ready." Isobelle blew a kiss at her and both she and Fiona followed her with their eyes as she breezed her way inside.

"She is a lovely girl," mused Fiona. "I can see why you are smitten with her."

"I am so pleased you like her. It would have been so awkward if you had not got on, or been repulsed by our affair."

"I love you dearly, Issy, and nothing you can do that makes you happy could ever repulse me. No, I really do mean it when I say that I am happy for you and also when I say that I really like Evelyn. We both do, and you will always be welcome at our house."

Isobelle reached over and took her sister's hands in hers, squeezing them gently.

"You are an angel, a priceless angel," she replied, her voice strained with the love she felt for Fi. They were silent a moment, basking in that close sisterly affection that pulsed between them. Isobelle could almost perceive an almost tangible flow passing through their connected fingers.

"Has there been any further news on that stalker?" asked Fiona quietly, as if diffident about bringing up the subject.

"No. Evelyn rang the detective after we got back for an update, but no joy. It seems he has gone to ground. The police are hoping that he has been frightened off, but I have to admit that for both Evelyn and my sake, I am not prepared to rest easy while he is on the loose out there."

"I don't blame you. I feel frightened for both of you too, especially after what he did to you. I cannot believe that he has not been found though."

"Trouble is, the police are stretched tight and I suppose that in the scheme of things, in their books this is a low priority. I don't know. I suppose that I am annoyed that it doesn't seem to be going anywhere. It's like there is inertia over following it through. If he had killed me, I bet there would have been no expense spared to find him, but a mere attack does not warrant a proper investigation." She sounded a bit bitter, but this quickly evaporated as she added, "I am sure that they are looking for him, but I do wish they would just find him and lock him away. It would be nice for Evelyn especially not to have to go through a large chunk of her life in a perpetual state of fear."

Fiona squeezed her hand. "He'll be found. Now tell me about your outfits. It sounds as if there is an amusing story behind them and I think we could do with a laugh."

Isobelle had just finished telling her when Evelyn called down from the balcony of the tower to announce that lunch was ready. They both made their way up to join Evelyn in the lounge, still laughing over the potential Villeneuve family connection in completely outfitting a woman from scratch.

"It appears you were very lucky to find your hats and dresses in Villeneuve in one excursion," she said to Evelyn.

"Yes, I couldn't believe how lucky we were. I thought we would be shopping for weeks. Still, I guess the proof as to whether we were successful will be at your wedding. I don't think we'll disappoint you though."

"I can't believe for a minute that either of you would. Incidentally, you will be sitting on the top table with mother, Gordon and his girlfriend, Rebecca, Piers parents and his best man."

"Who is his best man? Is it someone I know?" asked Isobelle.

"No, I don't think so. He is a childhood friend of Piers named Nigel. He's a surgeon at Guys Hospital. He is quite similar to Piers in temperament, so I can understand how they hit it off."

"So Gordon is bringing a girlfriend…did mother try and get her to wear a matching kilt?" joked Isobelle.

"You may well laugh, but she actually did suggest it. Fortunately I think it fell on deaf ears!"

They ate a lunch of couscous, pitta bread and a variety of dips and crudités, all washed down with a chilled Californian rose. The conversation jumped back and forth between the wedding and the holiday. They showed her some of the photographs and told her all about Mrs. Martins.

"We sent her a letter yesterday to thank her for the cottage and also to update her with all our news. We've promised to send a couple of photographs from the wedding, so hopefully that will cheer her up a little."

"That reminds me, we are going to have those little disposal cameras on all the tables so that if anyone forgets to bring their own, then they need not fret. The number of times I have forgotten mine and cursed myself," said Fiona.

"That's a great idea, Fi. We can use one for Mrs. Martins, poor soul."

When Piers arrived to collect Fiona that evening, he found them all getting on famously. From the relaxed manner of conversation, an outsider would have thought that they all had known each other for ages. They were on their second bottle of wine and urged Piers to join them for a glass before he and Fiona had to depart.

"How are you feeling about the wedding?" Isobelle asked him once he was settled.

"Excited, apprehensive, ecstatic, nervous, and sometimes all of those at the same time," he announced with a smile.

"I hope the apprehensive part is not as a result of my beautiful sister," teased Isobelle.

"Gracious me, no," he quickly confirmed, "No, I'm apprehensive about everything going well. A wedding leaves such a big imprint on the memory, so I suppose everyone prays that theirs will go well."

"I'm sure it will," agreed Isobelle and kissed him on his cheek to seal the irrefutability of it.

"What about you two?" he asked, hesitating at his boldness, as if suddenly shy. "Will you both ever have the chance to marry? I am pretty ignorant when it comes to lesbian issues, I'm afraid."

"Well I suppose that unless you are exposed to lesbian issues you probably would not know," said Evelyn, trying to lessen his obvious embarrassment at raising the question. She went on to tell him about the proposed new bill the Government were due to bring out in the near future.

"That will be brilliant!" exclaimed Fiona. "It would be marvellous if you could be married as well." Realising that she had presumed that they would, she added, "Would you want to get married?"

Evelyn and Isobelle answered together, "Of course!", causing them to burst into fits of giggles. Fiona soon joined in, although Piers kept his down to a wide smile.

Later when they were leaving, Fiona pulled Isobelle aside, and, with the pretence of kissing her goodbye, whispered in her ear, "She is gorgeous! If you don't marry her, let me know and I will divorce Piers and marry her myself!"

"You are terrible!" laughed Isobelle, swatting her on her backside. "Piers, take this wicked girl home now!"

Isobelle and Evelyn watched the car disappear down the road. Next time they would see Fiona, it would be as a bride. Isobelle linked her arm through Evelyn's and hugged her tight. "Fi is very much taken by you."

"And I very much like her. She is definitely your sister, but that said, I am only taken by you!"

"Semantics!" exclaimed Isobelle, tickling her. "Guide me inside and take me then, you vixen!"

CHAPTER THIRTY-FIVE

The day of the wedding boded well, for the girls were woken early by the light that flooded their bedroom, washing over their entwined bodies with waves of implied warmth, seeping brightness through their eyelids and urging them to awaken and worship it's brilliance. Isobelle threw an arm around Evelyn, drawing her close so that she could plant a kiss on her lips.

"Hello, you," she greeted. She was always in awe of Evelyn in the morning. She could awake and look as fresh as a daisy, her hair framing a face that never appeared to show the ravages of the night. She reached over and sifted her fingers again and again through the silk of Evelyn's tresses, before pressing her cheek against her hair, breathing in that familiar smell of the hibiscus shampoo that was enough to start the desire within Isobelle whenever she smelt it. She could not help but find Evelyn's lips, giving her mouth of exquisite velvet an unhurried, long and eloquent kiss. Evelyn returned the kiss deeply, melting in the softness of Isobelle's full lips, a moan of pleasure escaping from her powerless mouth.

"Your lips are the apple of temptation," murmured Evelyn, "and I am your Eve. I am naked, but with you I know no shame."

"Then taste of my lips," replied Isobelle. "All of them," she added impishly.

Evelyn responded by moving down Isobelle's body, feather light kisses tracing the swiftly beating pulse in her throat, her mouth flowing over her body with the same impunity as her eyes, her blond strands of hair brushing over breasts and stomach as she inched towards her goal. Isobelle writhed with purpose beneath her, legs opening in an urgent invitation as each electrified nerve quivered with anticipation of Evelyn's touch. Evelyn nipped her shaven thighs before gliding unswervingly to that spot which made Isobelle sigh aloud with unbridled indulgence. Evelyn slipped several of her long fingers inside Isobelle, as Isobelle's body arched, her hips rising to meet them as Evelyn plunged deep, her tongue stroking and swirling inside and over Isobelle's lubricious opening. Evelyn smelled the sweetness and tasted the musky nectar as her tongue fluttered relentlessly, seeking out Isobelle's fat swollen clitoris and sucking as her fingers increased their ministrations. Isobelle, covered in a light film of sweat, tried to grind her body into Evelyn, her fingers digging into the perfumed bed as her muscles contracted around Evelyn's fingers, clasping them tight within her. With the impending orgasm, Isobelle lost herself to an extremity, tongue and touch propelling her closer and closer to that sensual boundary where her only thought was Evelyn's name and a release so overpowering as to send her body into uncontrolled palpitations. Crying out, fingers in Evelyn's hair, Isobelle pulled her firmly against her shuddering thighs, slippery wet with the makings of her desire.

"Oh! Evelyn…oh! Darling," she gasped through spent lips, her body limp, damp and glorious as it splayed out across the rumpled bed. Evelyn moved up to lie next to her, planting a light kiss on Isobelle's mouth. Isobelle kissed her back, tasting herself on Evelyn's lips and smelling that unmistakable aroma of ecstasy.

"Are you back on this planet," whispered Evelyn with lips damp and hovering, into her pretty ear.

"I feel like a feather, circling round and round as it flutters back to earth," replied Isobelle in a raspy voice.

"We had best have a shower and get ourselves sorted out," said Evelyn. "We can hardly tell Fiona that we were late as a result of excessive lovemaking on her special day!"

"That is probably the one excuse she would understand. I feel bad that I am not doing the same for you, my love."

"Well don't feel too bad, darling, because you can rest assured that I will expect full appeasement after the wedding. So make sure you hang onto to some of that youthful energy! Come on, for a start you can soap down my back in the shower." She offered her hand, pulling Isobelle up off the bed and leading her into the shower.

Somehow, they managed to soap each other down and wash each other's hair without it leading on to further lovemaking, but then they were excited at the prospect of the day ahead. This would be their first big function together as lovers and even though it was a little nerve wracking, they were so buoyant at the occasion that any reservations or negative thoughts were pushed far to the back of their minds. However, that said, out of courtesy to Isobelle, Evelyn felt that she had to ask the inevitable.

"Isobelle, would you rather that we did not hold hands or show any signs of romantic affection at the wedding? I don't want to make anything difficult for either you or your family."

Isobelle was quiet for a short span. However, Evelyn did notice a momentary flash of anger tinge her green eyes. It departed almost as quickly as it had arrived, but Evelyn felt that she quickly ought to add, "Not that I want to change how we react with one another. I just wanted to save you any potential embarrassment in front of your family and friends."

Isobelle recognised that Evelyn was offering for all the right reasons and not because she was ashamed of a public relationship with her, so she broke into a smile. "I am hoping that my mother's impressively efficient network has been humming with the news of our relationship while we were away. That would give everyone time to get it out of their systems, so that come the wedding today, most of them will have come to terms with the situation one way or another. Today we shall act like any other couple in love, okay? Deal?"

"Okay, deal," replied Evelyn laughing.

Once they had donned their outfits, they stood side-by-side in front of the huge mirror in the bedroom, each gazing at one another with a mixture of adoration and pride.

"Evelyn, you are simply gorgeous," purred Isobelle. "How could anybody ever object to me showing any sign of affection to such a beauty? I think they would berate me if I didn't!" To emphasise the point, she found Evelyn's hand in the reflection and interlocked fingers, lifting them up and softly kissing their tips.

"You are pretty breath-taking yourself," replied Evelyn. "I will always be proud as punch to have you on my arm, even if you are young and impetuous!"

"Impetuous! Moi!" exclaimed Isobelle in mock horror. "Well, I guess it is a very good job I have got this Ice Maiden to keep me firmly disciplined!"

"Come on you, let's get a quick bite to eat and be off," said Evelyn, patting her on her shapely bottom.

Because Isobelle was the first person Fiona had consulted after accepting Piers's proposal of marriage, she had had the benefit of time over which she could consider what to buy them for a present. Also, she was well aware of Fiona's likes and dislikes, so it was armed with this knowledge that she had made her decision. Fiona had been given a diner collection of Poole 'Wild Clematis' by their mother and father when she had first left home. She adored it, but Poole had long since stopped making this Studio Collection and pieces were extremely hard to come by. Isobelle had trawled the Internet auction sites for months, as well as registering with a search and replacement service. However, her tenacity had paid off, for she had managed to find some diner plates, a couple of side plates and a gravy boat. It had been expensive, but she knew that it would give Fi a great deal of pleasure and it would be very individual. Since Isobelle and Evelyn would now be giving something together, Evelyn had augmented the gift with an embroidered Egyptian cotton tablecloth and napkins in the green of the clematis on the plates. They were sure that Fiona would love it and that Piers would grow to love it with Fiona's insistence.

With the present carefully loaded into the back of the Land Cruiser, they set off for Middleton Hall, where the service was to take place in the vaulted chapel attached to the stately home.

"Do you know how many are coming?" asked Evelyn as she drove through the country lanes, oblivious of the red hatchback car that pulled out of a lay-by and was following at a discreet distance.

"Fi mentioned that about forty were coming to the chapel and about one hundred and fifty to the reception. The reception is not in the house itself, but in a huge self-contained marquee. Apparently the gardens are beautiful there and guests can wander freely around them."

"Sounds marvellous. I am getting quite excited about it all. Where are your brother, Gordon, and your mother staying?"

"Fi said that Gordon flew in two days ago and that he and his girl friend were staying at a friend's place in Chelsea. Mother was using the guestroom at Piers' house in Highgate and Fiona decided it was easier to stay overnight at Middleton Hall. A bit like musical chairs."

"Did Fiona not have a hen night then?"

"I know she went out for a meal with some girlfriends from work, but she is not the hen night type. An enjoyable meal with some good friends is what she wanted."

"I don't blame her," commented Evelyn. "I always think it's a shame that some people get so drunk that they don't enjoy what must be one of the most precious days of their life, all due to a screaming hangover. When we get married, I want to recall every single minute of it."

"You said when. When we get married. That sends a lovely tingle up and down my insides. Mind you, for us it will be a case of us both being on the same hen night together, so we'd have to make a pact to be sure to keep an eye on one another."

"I'd have my eye on you anyway," grinned Evelyn, "being the old romantic that I am."

"What's with the old? You make it sound as if you'll be wrapping wedding decoration around your zimmer frame!"

"With all the sexual Olympics you put me through, I'll probably need a wheelchair by then," she laughed.

CHAPTER THIRTY-SIX

Middleton Hall was an impressive Elizabethan house adorned with herringbone brickwork and delightful pepperpot chimneys. A drive guided them through an assortment of rhododendron, which then swept them out around a lone cedar of Lebanon, and past the front of the prodigious house. A car park sign pointed onto a lane running beyond the house which curved up into a small wood, cleverly hiding the car park from the rest of the property. Climbing out, they followed yet a further sign to 'Mr. and Mrs. P. Adamson's Wedding and Reception', Isobelle carrying their clutch bags, while Evelyn carried the present. The path twisted around a copse before expelling them onto the start of a huge lawn, the house to the right and a large marquee to the left. They could see Isobelle's mother near the entrance to the marquee, so made their way towards her. She was speaking to one of the caterers, but when she glanced up and noticed them, she finished her conversation and quickly made her way towards them.

"My! Fiona and Piers will have to watch that you two don't steal the show. You both look so beautiful. It's good to see you looking so well." She gave them both a hug and a kiss on the cheek.

"You are looking the glamour puss too, mother," said Isobelle proudly. Her mother carried her age very well and still had her lovely red hair.

"Get on with you," she said, obviously thrilled, but pretending she was nonplussed.

"No seriously, you do look very attractive in that," agreed Evelyn.

"Bless you both," she teased. "You're only trying to make an old woman feel good. Now, are you going to walk me over to the chapel. Gordon and Rebecca are there and I know they are keen to meet Evelyn. You must tell me about your holiday, but first, do you want to deposit your present with the others in the marquee?"

"Yes please," begged Evelyn, "I think my arms have grown an extra two inches."

One of the waiters, seeing Evelyn heading towards the marquee, quickly came and relieved her of the present, carrying it to a long table just inside the entrance where other presents were arranged, all splendidly wrapped. Looking around, they could see about fifteen large round tables, each of which could seat about a dozen people. There were floral bouquets on each table, whites and greens, and silver settings with salmon pink linen napkins. It was very impressive.

"What do you think?" asked Mrs. Swanson.

"I would be over the moon if this was mine," replied Evelyn.

Mrs. Swanson patted her hand. "I'll take that as a positive then," she laughed.

As they neared the chapel they could see a cluster of people all milling around the door, obviously waiting for the brides mother to lead them in. As Gordon spotted them, he said something to the woman beside him and they both began to walk over to meet them.

"Hello, Gordon," greeted Isobelle with a hug, "and you must be Rebecca. I'm Isobelle and this is my partner, Evelyn. It's nice to meet anyone who can meet the challenge of my brother's terrible dress sense! However, you must be winning as he looks particularly dashing today!"

"I confess that it has been an uphill battle," she laughed, "but I am not sure that I can say that I am winning yet."

Rebecca was a small, slightly leading onto dumpy, but with a very open and childishly pretty face. She had long chestnut coloured hair that tumbled down to rest over an ample chest. Isobelle could see why she would have attracted Gordon, as she had a vulnerable look about her and he was one for taking the lead in all situations. He was not one for independent freethinking women. Isobelle wandered if that was as a consequence of growing up with two such sisters in the household.

"Pleased to meet you Evelyn," he said, politely shaking her hand, although Evelyn was conscious of his badly disguised appraisal of her body as he did so. *Probably lamenting the waste of a good body on another woman,* she thought.

"And you," she responded automatically, although she found herself amazed at how out of synch he was with all the women of the family. Isobelle, Fiona and their mother were all so sincere, yet she sensed an underlying aggression in him that she found rather off-putting. She did not know if Richard tainted her whole perspective as regards men, namely those who were like him and those who were not. Unfortunately, with his bleached-blond hair, good looks and almost arrogant manner, Gordon was too alike Richard and she instantly found herself extremely uncomfortable in his presence. She was thankful that he lived abroad and that he would not be in the habit of visiting them too often. So, after the perfunctory pleasantries were exchanged, she was glad when Isobelle led her off to say hello to Piers, his best man, Nigel, and Piers parents.

"Wow!" teased Piers, "Fiona's going to have to come up with something special to top you two. You both look fantastic."

"Only the best for my sister and her husband-to-be," replied Isobelle. "How are you feeling today?"

"A tad nervous would be an understatement," he said, a strained smile locked on his lips.

"Don't you worry, Piers. She will look stunning and once you see her you will forget all those nerves," encouraged Evelyn, squeezing his arm.

"Yes, how can you not feel perfectly at ease under the spell of us Swanson girls?" joked Isobelle.

"Works for me," quipped Evelyn and Piers burst out laughing.

"Thanks, girls. You are a tonic. How could I be worried when the two most beautiful girls here are chatting to me and my jealous wife is about to turn up! So let me be a good host and introduce you to Nigel, my best man."

Both the girls took instantly to Nigel, a serious man who was often funny without necessarily realising it. He had one of those boyishly charming faces that probably had so many of the nurses wanting to mother him. But he was very polite and interesting to talk to as he had travelled extensively in the course of his work. It was obvious that he was aware of their relationship, as were Piers' parents, but neither of them treated the girls with anything other than kindness and respect.

"You must get that son of mine to make sure he brings you both over to see us sometime as we are not that far away and we do like to have company. You beautiful young things would bring our house to life," offered Piers mother.

"We would certainly love to come over with Piers and Fiona," said Evelyn, "but I don't believe that your house does not have life. Not after the way I see Piers and yourselves conversing…there is a lot of family love there."

"Oh! You must definitely come, and often," laughed Piers' father, clapping his hands together with delight at her reply.

At this point one of the ushers came over and whispered into Piers' ear. Once he departed, Piers came over and joined them. "It seems that my future wife is being gracious or worried about missing out on any gossip, as she has decided not to keep us waiting long. So, if you care to make your way into the chapel, hopefully everyone else will follow."

Isobelle hooked her arm through Evelyn's and entered the chapel behind Piers' parents. Inside it was lovely…secretly, Isobelle would have called it sweet, but she didn't think that other people would understand her interpretation. It was small, probably capable of seating about 45 - 50 people, but gave the appearance of being larger because of the light. The walls were painted white and the windows were tall.

Although they contained stained glass, it was not overpowering, so that the light could pour in, sending rays at oblique angles across the aisle. Although Isobelle was not religious, she felt awed by the scene, as if nature had especially created these arches of sunlight under which Fiona would float on her way to the step by the font.

"That is mystical," said Evelyn in a low voice. "I almost expect to see a unicorn standing in the nave!"

"Yes, and little elves and pixies peeking over the top of the choir stalls," returned Isobelle with a hushed giggle.

An usher asked their names and then guided them to the front row where Rebecca and Mrs. Swanson later joined them. In place of their father, it was Gordon who would be giving away the bride. The pews behind quickly filled up with relations and friends.

Isobelle waved to a few, filling in Evelyn as to who they were. *There is nothing like a good wedding for making you feel romantic*, she thought, taking up Evelyn's hand in hers. Evelyn must have been thinking similarly, for she gave Isobelle one of her smiles that was guaranteed to turn Isobelle's heart to a jelly. Lost in her love, she did not notice that the chapel had filled and so visibly jumped at the sound of the Trumpet Voluntary announcing Fiona's entrance. For a brief instant, the music was drowned by the collective noise of the people rising as one, all turning to catch a glimpse of the bride as she was escorted by Gordon past their row. When Isobelle saw her, she breathed in sharply. She knew her sister was a very attractive woman, but never had she seen her looking as beautiful as she was in her wedding dress. Isobelle thought her heart might stop, she was so proud of her. As Fiona came adjacent to her pew, she caught Isobelle's eye and gave her a private wink. Isobelle threw her a kiss in return.

"She looks absolutely incredible," Evelyn breathed in her ear.

"She does, but not too incredible I hope. Remember it is this Swanson that you love so deeply!" breathed back Isobelle.

"How could I ever forget!" teased Evelyn, rolling her eyes.

The dress was based upon a simple, but elegant medieval Celtic design. Made from beautiful pure silk crepe de chine, the low square neckline, the edges of the full flared sleeves and the belt were trimmed with gold thread in a Celtic knot work embroidery. The dress was laced up at the back with gold ribbon. The belt, falling long at the front, was positioned low on Fiona's hips. She could have just stepped out of the pages of Camelot, the effect with the refracted light in the chapel was magical. Behind her came four young bridesmaids, each wearing the pinks and whites of fragrant sweet peas in a similar, but slightly simpler design. For Evelyn, the setting could not have been better choreographed. After all, she had grown up with the Flower Fairy books, and this is the type of scene that would have sat comfortably within the pages.

"Did Fiona tell you what dress she was going to wear?" Evelyn whispered.

"No. She wanted it to be a surprise and, to be honest, I wanted it to be a surprise too. I'm glad I did. In this setting it is enchanting."

The service was not overly long, but because she was enjoying it so much and was so attentive to every detail, it seemed to flash by. In no time at all everyone was emerging into the harsh midday sun to the strains of Bach's Toccata. As they filtered out of the chapel, Fiona, who had been greeting people at the door, virtually threw herself into their arms. Within seconds, all three of them were in tears, trying to all speak at once.

"What did you think of the bridesmaids?"

"Fi, you're stunning!"

"That service was mystical."

"Where did you get that exquisite dress?"

And so it went on until the photographer felt obliged to pull Fiona away for the official photographs. "Don't go far you two," called Fiona. "I want you both in the family photographs."

Evelyn had been a little worried about what to do when it came to the pictures, which included the immediate family, but she need not have worried. When she urged Isobelle off to join the group, both Piers and Fiona motioned for her to come over with them. Fiona grabbed her hand and planted her firmly beside Isobelle, adding, "You are part of our family now, Evelyn." Evelyn found that moment to be one of the most profound in her life. Isobelle's family had accepted her without reservation, showing her more love and affection in the short time that they had known her than she'd ever received from her own parents. As the pictures were taken, it was all she could do to stop herself crying with the overwhelming realisation of it. As soon as the photographs had been taken, Isobelle and Evelyn made sure that they shot a few of their own before Fiona came rushing back over to them on a wave of adrenaline.

"I can see that I'm going to have to go to Villeneuve if I ever want a special outfit. You two are putting me to shame!"

"Nonsense," laughed Isobelle. "Besides, none of the Villeneuve sisters, cousins, or aunts were able to provide a designer matching plaster cast for my arm, so it has rather let the side down."

"No wander none of the society magazines offered to pay for the exclusive pictures. All down to my darling sister and her 'oh! so yesterdays' plaster cast!"

Mrs. Swanson and Piers joined them at this point, just catching the tail end of the conversation. "How is your arm now, dear?" asked her mother.

"Healing nicely, thank you. Hopefully the plaster will be off soon, but I will have to take it easy in my swimming for a while. Definitely no housework allowed though," she said, grinning at Evelyn.

"That's what she thinks," countered Evelyn. "As soon as that plaster is off, I'll have her cleaning and scrubbing until her hands and knees are red raw!"

With feigned horror, Isobelle retreated behind her mother's back, peering round her at Evelyn. "Help, mother! Save me from this evil taskmistress. She keeps me locked up in her tower and now she's threatening despicable torture.....cleaning!"

"Get off with your bother!" laughed Mrs. Swanson, giving her a hug.

CHAPTER THIRTY-SEVEN

The groups made their way haltingly across to the marquee, splitting and merging with the new arrivals for the reception. Waiters wove in and out of these islands of people with cold sparkling wines and orange juice, dodging the children who had managed to stay presentable for an average of ten minutes before shirt tails came loose and grass stains appeared as they dashed around the copious gardens. Evelyn spotted the bridesmaids; the little dainty sweet pea fairies now were transformed into sweaty, chasing and tagging girls, tripping and tumbling over long hems. But they had performed to the threats and cajoling of their parents, so now they had every right to enjoy themselves in the way they liked best. *Good for them*, she thought. *Let the girls have fun. After all, this girl is*. And the colours; summery powder blues and aquamarines, elegant lemons and mouth-watering oranges, serene cerise and daring reds, all merging into a splendid cocktail stirred and blended as groups mixed, touched with a dab of tartan here and there.

"This has to be the best wedding that I have ever attended," said Evelyn to Isobelle as they strolled over the lawn, fingers entwined.

"I suppose we shouldn't tempt fate, but so far it has been brilliant," agreed Isobelle.

"Your family are so kind. I really do like Fiona so much. She is one of the most down-to-earth and friendly of people that I have ever met."

"Knowing Fi as I do, I can say that she also likes you very much. And I love you, so that must make you likeable and loveable!"

As the major throng of the guests had congregated around the entrance to the marquee in anticipation of being allowed in, Isobelle and Evelyn hung back. It was far too hot a day to be without breathing space and the hope of catching an errant breeze. It was not long before they saw Gordon and Rebecca extract themselves from the mass and head over to join them.

"And I thought that it was hot enough in the Middle East," griped Gordon, running an already sodden handkerchief over his wet forehead. He peered up at the sun as if accusing it for it's excessive output.

"I suppose that the kilt is not your usual regalia for the Middle East though," answered Isobelle. "Not unless you are setting a new standard. I seem to recall that you lived in shorts, socks and desert boots most of the time."

"I have managed to get him into cotton shirts now, although not without protest," chimed in Rebecca.

"Good for you, Rebecca! Are you confident about your speech now, Gordon?" asked Isobelle. She felt a little guilty about asking him when she knew perfectly well that he abhorred any public speaking, but it was her sweet shot of revenge as she could see that he was angling himself round for the best sidelong view down Evelyn's cleavage. It had the desired effect, for his face suddenly assumed a worried look and his hand shot to his sporran to check for the umpteenth time that his notes for the speech were indeed still there.

"When mother asked me to do it, it seemed such a good idea, but I am having big reservations about it now." As if to underline his reservations, he swept a long glance over the large clusters of assembled guests.

"Don't worry, Gordon, it will all be over much quicker that you think. Just try not to rush it though or all your jokes will be missed."

Isobelle was not sure if he had any jokes, but she had expressed the right sentiments. Fiona had actually been upset that her mother had gone ahead and asked Gordon to make the speech, as she had wanted Isobelle to fulfil that role. Isobelle herself had felt somewhat hurt, not so much by the fact that it was Gordon, but rather more the fact that of all people, she was the closest to her sister. Her mother had obviously known that and it would have been such a logical step. However, most mothers tend to have a special affinity with their sons, a mild Clytemnestra complex the psychologists would say, and so Gordon had been persuaded despite not being at all enthusiastic.

"How long are you staying on in the UK after the wedding?" asked Evelyn, pointedly including Rebecca in the question as she had noticed how Gordon appeared oblivious to her presence.

"Only a day," piped up Gordon. "I've got to get back ASAP. Business calls. No rest for the wicked!" He grinned as if the statement was original, amusingly his.

"And how about you, Rebecca?" asked Evelyn without hesitation.

"I will go back with Gordon. I was hoping to see some friends while over here, but it was not to be. Unfortunately Gordon has to get back as they are expecting a large number of German tourists in next week." Her heart was definitely not in her words, and Evelyn did feel for her, but she was young and, it seemed from Gordon's lack of attention, she was on the way out. Hopefully she would rebound and learn from this episode. As long as her self esteem remained, to some degree, intact.

Fortunately Isobelle and Evelyn were spared from too much more awkwardness by the fact that the guests were now making their way into the marquee. A large seating plan had been positioned on either side of the marquee entrance, so with the advanced knowledge and efficient help of ushers, the guests quickly found their places on numbered tables. Evelyn and Isobelle were sitting opposite Piers and Fiona. Mrs. Swanson was to Fiona's left, followed by Gordon and Rebecca. To Piers' right were his mother, father and Nigel. Evelyn felt much happier knowing she was not next to Gordon, although she experienced little waves of guilt that she was unable to take to him when the rest of Isobelle's family had taken to her. Almost immediately on seating, a veritable army of waiters and waitresses streamed from the entrance to the kitchen area with a first course of a selection of sliced gala, water and honeydew melons.

"Oh! Incidentally darling, I hope you don't mind, but I put you down for vegetarian with me. There were not many among the guests and I felt that I needed support, so who better than you to volunteer. Besides," Isobelle added, "since you met me I think you have almost become vegetarian. Do you mind? I did mean to ask you, but it kept slipping my mind."

"Beginning to take liberties with me now, Miss Swanson. My, oh! My. This will just be added on to the debt that you already owe me from this morning!"

"Keep this up and I will only be able to imagine you in a corset and thigh length boots, swishing an article of correction back and forth as I kneel vulnerable before you!"

"Now there is a furtive imagination! Nevertheless, I shall store your obvious fantasy in mind for a rainy day. And don't go peeking in my shopping bags again!"

The meal progressed at a fairly sedate pace during which Evelyn and Isobelle discovered Nigel to be as witty as he was intelligent. Everyone on the table was in good spirits with the exception of Gordon, who was looking more and more anxious as the time for his speech approached. Isobelle, being the person she was, began to feel sorry for him and it was while she was offering him encouragement that her mother dropped her small bombshell.

"Oh! Gordon. The bridesmaid's gifts! I have left them over in Fiona's room," she lamented, obviously perplexed that she could have forgotten anything.

"Don't worry, mother, you can give them to the girls later," assured Isobelle.

"No, I want to give them out after Gordon's speech, when he thanks them," she continued. "I'll just have to go and get them."

"You cannot go now, mother!" replied Isobelle, incredulous. "The speeches are going to begin at any moment. You cannot possibly miss them."

"I'll have to," she announced, determinedly. Isobelle was fuming inside. How could she offer to miss the speeches for a few gifts that could easily wait until afterwards. Unfortunately, she had a stubborn streak and it was virtually impossible to change her mind once made up.

"What's wrong, love?" asked Evelyn who had been chatting with Nigel, but who could sense Isobelle was annoyed about something. Once she had told Evelyn the cause, Evelyn immediately stood up.

"Off to the loo?" queried Isobelle.

"No. It's important for you and your mother to be here during the speeches - you're family. If she wants these gifts so much, she can tell me where they are and I'll go and fetch them." She gave Isobelle's hand a squeeze.

"Oh! Evelyn. You are a gem. I would go, but I know it would upset Fiona and it seems so trivial an issue at such an important moment. I hope you don't mind."

"Don't worry. I understand. Hopefully I can get back before the speeches end." She edged round to Mrs. Swanson to collect the key to Fiona's room in the main house before quietly slinking out of the marquee. Isobelle watched her go, silently raging at her mother, a thousand whys and wherefores forming in her mind, the principle being why couldn't she just have waited? Because of her obduracy, someone was fated to miss out on this important occasion, namely Evelyn. And because she was cross, she knew now that the enjoyment would be spoilt for her.

CHAPTER THIRTY-EIGHT

Outside the marquee it was as if stepping through a seal of some sort, for the hum of voices died almost immediately. No one was about with the exception of a few of the staff lingering around what must have been the marquee's kitchen entrance. To make her walking easier over the lawns, she slid off her shoes. The grass was cool under her feet. No doubt it had been regularly sprinkled in this heat to retain its lush green and healthy colour. As she walked, her face angled heliotropically to the sun, she sifted through the events of the day, cataloguing the highs and lows. The chapel wedding had to be a high with its mystical air, a charmed cool glade in the heat of the day. Meeting Gordon had to be a low, more from disappointment than from anything else. Despite Isobelle's warning on his womanising, she had hoped that he would have inherited enough of the good Swanson qualities to excuse his rakish ways, but within minutes of meeting him, she found it impossible to like him. She could find none of Isobelle or Fiona's magnanimity or graciousness, only self-charity and vainglorious, disrespectful of anyone who did not see him or his ideas as cardinal. Quite often families had their black sheep, but Gordon was one step on, a wolf in black sheep's clothing. How he came from the same stock as Isobelle and Fiona would always puzzle her, particularly as she had so hoped to love all Isobelle's family. At least she was comforted to know that it was not just her who felt this way. Isobelle obviously found something troubling in him, for she had herself admitted that they had never been close. Still, she was adamant that she would keep her views to herself as much as possible, because, at the end of the day, he was Isobelle's brother and she would not wish to do or say anything to upset Isobelle if humanly possible.

So tied up in her thoughts was she, that when the world began to creep back in to her consciousness, it seemed excessively loud. She could hear on a sheltered lawn nearby the swishing sound of a water spray jetting it's timed cycle over the appreciative grasses, she heard the prosaic, yet tranquil drone of a distant lawn mower, as easy on the ear as a hummingbird hovering over a bloom. Amidst these noises so reminiscent of summer days interjected one, fast and alien, so fast that she was unable to react before her legs were swept violently from under her. The shock instantly numbed her brain, she could not understand why she was on her hands and knees staring at the grass beneath her until the pain lashed through her calves. What could possibly have hit her in this plethora of open space? Grasping at straws, her mind thought perhaps one of the children had ploughed into her accidentally. But when a hand cruelly grabbed a fistful of her hair and used it to twist back her head, the horror of the situation began to flood through her limbs so that they were barely able to support her.

"Thought you had seen the last of me, did you? You and your bitch think you were rid of me? You stupid woman, you must know you are a part of me as I am of you. You can't do without me, can you?"

Trying to curl herself into a foetal position, Evelyn was too terrified to speak. Her brain could only register that a psychological line had now been crossed, that Richard Bleach was now no longer annoying, but very dangerous. It frightened her so much that she had lost the power of speech, even to agree with him, to placate him until help arrived.

"What's that? I couldn't hear you, Evie dear. You owe me an answer.... can't do without your Richard, can you?" To prompt an answer from her, he jerked her hair viscously, the pain causing her to scream out.

"Shut up, Evie! We don't want prying toffee-nosed bastards down here trying to ruin our little get-together now, do we?"

Without warning, he lifted an arm and slapped her across her cheek with the back of his hand. Her head wrenched in response, tearing at the hair wrapped in his other hand. She gritted her teeth to stifle the scream that was ringing in her head. Through tear-stained eyes, she was able to see that from where they were, no one at the marquee would be able to spot them as they were hidden in a depression, a simple ha-ha that concealed them from view. She couldn't help thinking the irony of it. *I'm going to die in a ha-ha, murdered in an English garden joke.* She could almost see Miss Marple now, chastising some heartless constable for his quip, 'last laugh from the ha-ha'.

Sharply, she was rocked from her imaginings as Richard once again pulled at her hair, using it to twist her body into a kneeling position where she had no option but to look up into his aggressive features. His lips were curled up as he spoke and his eyes were deep, black pits with no emotion whatsoever. It was this that terrified her most, for now she knew that he was beyond reason and that he was here with the sole purpose to kill her. She felt herself begin to cry. *But I don't want to die,* she pleaded in her head. *For the first time in my life I have found true happiness and I don't want to die.* The tears were now streaming down her face as she sobbed silently, her body wracked with the grief.

"Thinking about your bitch, Evie? Well you might as well forget her. It's just going to be you and me now. See, we're going to go on a journey together, you and I. And if I cannot have you here, then I'll take you where I can. Follow my drift, do you?" She felt his spittle flecking her face as he accentuated each word.

"Please let me go, please….I won't tell anyone. Please." She had found a small voice deep amongst her fear. A barely heard voice, full of entreaty.

"Of course you wouldn't tell anyone. Think I was born yesterday? I have waited many years for you. I knew that one day you would come to me, that you would want me. That bitch was just a distraction. She confused you when it was me you were saving your love for. Well, she is not going to have you anymore. Now you are mine and will always be. You'll be happier now with me."

As he was ranting, he had loosened his grip on Evelyn's hair as he struggled with something in his pocket. Instinct compelled her to react. She leaned towards his hand as if in supplication, suddenly jerking forward and scrambling to her feet, the pain searing through every hair root in her head. Having been so subjugated, her sudden bid to escape caught Richard by total surprise. He had hidden a handgun in his pocket while pretending to be one of the waiting staff and it was this he had been struggling to extract. Having to decide quickly between the gun or pursuit, he chose the gun. Fortunately for Evelyn, his erratic efforts were snagging it in his pocket, so that by the time he had ripped it free, she had managed to run a fair distance from him. She guessed that he had been grappling with a gun and she knew that she would have to clear a lot more open ground before she would be safe, so she ran for all she was worth. The whole time she was waiting for the report, tensing her shoulder blades in anticipation of the shove that would fling her forward like a discarded rag doll.

When the shot did come, the speed of it all took her totally by surprise. No sooner had the sound carried to her then she experienced the most painful wrench on her upper arm that sent her spinning onto the grass. For seconds, it was as if the world had stopped, for she could hear nothing and she was convinced that her heart had stopped beating. Then, just as suddenly, her senses returned some twenty-fold, along with an agonising pain careering up and down the length of her arm. With her face pressed close to the ground, she was almost intoxicated by the earthy, verdant smell of the crushed grass and soil beneath her. There was a strange sensation on her hand. Moving her eyes slightly, she was at first puzzled, then panicked. Blood, bright glossy red and frightening, was running down her arm and over her spread fingers, snaking rivulets greedily soaked up by the summer-dry loam.

Move! She screamed at herself. *Move, Evelyn, or he'll take another shot and kill you. I don't want to die. I don't want to leave Isobelle.* As if in response, she heard another shot violate the still afternoon and a split second later she registered the dull thwack of a bullet striking the dry earth to her left, throwing up a small plume of soil dust into the air. Gritting her teeth against the pain in her arm, Evelyn hauled herself up onto all fours and began to crawl towards the house.

Don't look back, she coaxed herself. *Keep on going. Get to the house. Someone will be there to help. Keep on going!*

Richard had been amazed when he took the first shot. Firstly, not having ever fired a gun, he had not anticipated the recoil, which had nearly broken his wrist with its force. When he had bought the gun through some distinctly unsavoury connections, he had thought that he would only need it at close range. With Evie's escape, that had changed. He was going to kill her, along with himself. That was also why he was amazed, for once he had retrieved the gun from the ground having jolted itself from his hand, he could see that Evie was lying prone on the lawn. He thought he could also see blood against the royal blue of her dress. Had he miraculously hit her from that distance? He smiled to himself. Why not? He had always been good at most sports at college. He felt an exhilaration within him. Soon he would be with her forever as it rightfully should have been all along. Oh! Yes, she had resisted him, but she had been naïve. She had not really known what she wanted. Why take up with that lesbian tart? She had been confused, but no longer. He was with her now and everything would be orderly and neat. All knots tied off.

As he started to amble towards her, he noticed with dismay that he must have just wounded her, for she had managed to start crawling away from him. On impulse, he levelled the gun, this time using two hands to hold it and standing as he had seen in various detective films. However, when he pulled the trigger, he could see by the dirt kicked up that he had missed by some six feet. *Must be due to the ache in my hand*, he thought. Moving the gun fractionally over to his right, he carefully squeezed off another shot, half expecting to see Evelyn drop lifeless to the ground. He was stunned when this time he saw the plume of dust rise about four feet short of her. Up a little, that's all it needed. However, after the last shot, Evelyn had angled her path slightly and the bullet hit the earth beyond where she had been crawling.

Idiot, he cursed himself. *I only had six bullets and I've already used…..* his mind counted them off….*four! That is two left!* One was meant for himself, so the next one on Evelyn had to count. I must get nearer, much nearer, he thought as he started to lope after her crawling shape.

In the marquee, Piers' best man, Nigel, had not long risen to give his address and Isobelle was trying to calm herself down enough to appreciate it, when the first shot went off. Most people looked round at the entrance, but assumed that it was a car backfiring or a particularly virulent champagne cork, but as soon as Isobelle heard it, she knew it for exactly what it was.

"Oh, God, no! Not Richard!" she screamed, everyone around her jumping visibly with surprise. Tearing off her shoes and girding up her dress, she took off through the marquee exit before anyone had time to react. Once out of the marquee, she stopped to quickly get her bearings. It had to be towards the house, but she could see that the ha-ha masked what was happening from her view. Using muscles honed with years of swimming, she ran as fast as those muscles would take her. As she neared the crest of the ha-ha, she heard another three shots ring out, one after the other.

"Evelyn, hang in there, don't let him have shot her, please, please, please," she begged of whichever deity would listen and take mercy. Tears were streaming down her face as she ran over the crest and saw that Evelyn was still alive, but crawling agonisingly slowly, some twenty yards or so from

Richard, who was loping in an almost arrogantly casual way behind her. Calling on reserves that she had never utilised before, Isobelle propelled herself down the ha-ha, using the momentum to give that extra speed. So absorbed was Richard in his quarry, he had not heard her approach yet.

Evelyn was screaming. Her arm was screaming in pain, her mind was screaming for survival, and she was screaming a garbled help for anyone. Her consciousness was slipping, fading in and out, and she knew that she was hardly making any progress. However, it was when her wounded arm gave way on her that her spirit finally flagged and she curled up in a foetal ball, preparing for her death. She looked up, seeing Richard almost upon her, gun arm swinging casually at his side.

"That's right, Evie. Don't fight the inevitable. We'll be happy together where we're going."

"But I don't want to die. I don't want to go with you!" she screamed at him with what little strength she had left.

"Denying your true love even to the end. It is touching. Unfortunately though, there is not really time for us to chew the fat. I'll see you soon though, in the beyond."

As he lifted the gun, she felt black spots and garish stars move across her vision, her limbs going spongy and limp as she fainted, no longer caring as the gun went off.

So conceited was Richard in his purpose, it did not occur to him that he could be approached as deftly as he had crept up behind Evelyn earlier, so as he prepared to fire, he was totally relaxed as Isobelle cannoned into the small of his back. The impact generated by her speed was enough to catapult Richard beyond Evelyn's prone figure, but not before he had pulled the trigger. As she fell heavily beside Evelyn, she noticed with a heart crushing horror that there was a crimson bud, opening like a blossoming flower over the waist of Evelyn's dress. From within her a primeval cry welled up and rent the afternoon, sending cold fingers up the napes of anyone who happened to hear it.

"NNNNNNooooooooooooooooo! Oh, God, help me. Evelyn, please, please be alive. Please don't leave me." The tears gushed from her eyes as the grief tried to compress her internal organs. She was finding it difficult to breathe. Ignoring everything around her, she pulled herself to Evelyn's side, gently brushing her hair away from her eyes with wildly trembling hands, crooning softly in her ear, over and over, "Darling, stay with me, don't you dare go and leave me, please." Her tears were dripping down onto Evelyn's cheeks, little runnels sweeping them down to her still lips. "Evelyn, I love you. Stay here with me. I am not sure I can carry on without you."

Although Isobelle had a head start out of the marquee, it had not taken Fiona a second to realise what was happening and to urge Piers, Nigel and Gordon to follow. As they left, she called over one of the waiters and asked him to call the police and ambulance service as quickly as possible. The police were obviously required. She prayed that the ambulance would not, but with what she now guessed to be gunshots, she thought they best be on hand.

Meanwhile, the men flew after Isobelle, never quite able to gain, but close enough so they hoped they could be of support when the time came. Each blinking away the running sweat that threatened to cloud their eyes, they saw Isobelle barrel into Richard and heard the shot, noticing Evelyn's supine body jerk as the bullet hit home.

"I'll take Evelyn!" wheezed Nigel to the other two as he veered slightly towards her. Piers and Gordon carried on in the hope that they could get to Richard before he sufficiently recovered. Unfortunately, he was on his knees and had the gun aimed their direction faster than they had predicted, forcing them to come to an immediate halt.

"Spread out," mumbled Piers to Gordon in an attempt to make a harder target.

"Stop! That's close enough," threatened Richard. "I don't particularly want to kill either of you, but I will if you attempt to come closer."

"Easy does it. Let's make sure that no one else gets hurt. Why don't you call it a day? All you have to do is drop the gun and step away from it." Piers was trying to keep his voice level, but it was proving difficult as his chest heaved with the effort of running.

"Just shut the hell up will you. You can't fool me with all that psychological bullshit. I'm not going anywhere without Evelyn."

By this time, Nigel had carried out a quick, but thorough inspection on Evelyn's condition. After taking her pulse, checking her eyes, and listening to her chest, he looked up with anger on his face. "She won't be going anywhere with you, you bastard! You've killed her!"

Richard looked searchingly at Nigel's face, before uttering a manic laugh. "That's where you're wrong, shit-face, because now I'll be joining with her forever." With that, he put the barrel of the gun in his mouth and blew off the back of his head.

CHAPTER THIRTY-NINE

Isobelle stood almost touching the tall glass lounge window. She could just about see her reflection, although the room behind her was dimly lit by a couple of table lamps. Outside it was raining heavily in preparation of the forthcoming storm that rumbled in the near distance. Every now and then, a gust of wind would throw the rain like a handful of pebbles against the glass, the rivulets straining against their horizontal path by the force of the wind. In this faint light, the reflection of Isobelle's red hair looked liquid, like wine pouring both down her back and the window. The first glimpse of lightening forked through the pitch-blackness, but Isobelle barely noticed, being so wrapped up as she was in her thoughts.

Three weeks had alternatively raced or crawled by since the wedding. Piers and Fiona had been urged to go on their honeymoon as planned. It was deemed to be a good thing for Piers in particular, as he had been in shock following Richard's symbolic suicide. Fiona had been very reluctant to leave, knowing what pain Isobelle was going through, but in the end Isobelle had ordered her away, saying how guilty she would feel if the whole wedding and honeymoon had been ruined by one callous madman.

"For me, it was both the best day and the worst day of my life, Fi. The wedding was obviously the best part. Don't make the whole thing any worse for you and Piers. Take the good aspects and enjoy them. A totally different country couldn't be better. Please go, Fi. I'll be fine now."

Fiona's presence of mind at the wedding had prevented what could have been a catastrophe, for once Piers, Gordon and Nigel had left the marquee, she had tried to ensure that everyone carried on as normal. No one had been permitted to leave that side of the marquee, a replacement exit being opened on the south side. Despite being curious, most guests either grasped that something was wrong and played along, or didn't really care as long as the food and disco were good.

"Don't ever berate yourself over the wedding," Fiona had retorted firmly. "This was never any of your doing or Evelyn's doing. It was all the work of that evil stalker and Piers and I will not have you guilty over it. You would never have considered blaming Evelyn for his attack on you. Likewise I blame no one but him. Don't let him win over us, Issy. Don't carry any guilt." Fiona had reinforced her wish by gripping Isobelle's shoulders. Isobelle had cried again. She had cried so much recently that she was amazed there were any more tears within her. Even now, as she stood at the rain-streaked window, she could feel the makings of tears.

And so they had departed for that mystery location, somewhere hot and sunny with plenty of beaches. Nigel, the only one not overly affected by the suicide, had driven them to the airport. Gordon had been admitted to hospital with shock, both on account of the horror of Richard's death right before him, but also due to the near hysteria he had witnessed in Isobelle. If anything good could be said to have come out of the situation for him, it was that he had seen how perilous life was and as a consequence, had been visibly more attentive and responsive to Rebecca. He had delayed his return by a week in order that they could go and visit some of her family and friends, an act that had not gone unnoticed by Mrs. Swanson, who crossed her fingers and quietly prayed. For some reason, it made Isobelle remember the quote that she always found mesmerising at the breakfast table as a girl. It was off the distinctive tins of Lyle's Golden Syrup and read *'Out of the strong came forth sweetness.'* Would that be the case with Gordon?

Strangely enough, it had been Mother who had been most effected by the whole episode. She had obviously reflected on just how her stubborn need to have the bridesmaid's gifts had almost resulted in an ending to the wedding that could only have been conceived in a television thriller. The outcome had been horrific enough, but the hair-raising scenarios of what might have been had frequently played upon her mind. She had telephoned Isobelle virtually every day to apologise for her intransigence, as if hoping that it might turn back the clock and that everything could end happily as per her agenda. Although Isobelle told her that all was forgiven, she had to admit that within her was a small, but insistent, voice that continued to blame her mother for behaving so thoughtlessly at such an important time over such a trivial issue. As with Gordon, she sincerely hoped that her mother would not beat herself remorselessly over this, but instead would learn sensibility, to be flexible towards and considerate of other people's feelings.

She was suddenly shocked back into the present by an arcing flash of lightening that had jaggedly split the darkness into two, like a violently ripped photograph. She glanced at her watch as the chasing thunder cracked through the night, awesome in its resounding power. It was 8pm and time for medicine. Isobelle made her way down to the kitchen and extracted some vegetable soup that she had made on the weekend from the freezer. Heating it up, she added a few slices of bread to a plate, some antibiotic tablets and a long glass of water. Once the soup had heated sufficiently, she poured it carefully into a bowl and placed it on a tray. To accompany this, she cut a stem off one of the pink roses she had brought in earlier that afternoon and placed it in a small crystal vase. Adding water, the vase went on the tray along with a serviette. Picking up the tray, she moved carefully through to the bedroom, gently easing the door ajar and slipping into the darkened room within. She stood still for a moment as her eyes adjusted, then moved to the bedside table where she placed the tray.

"Isobelle? Is that you, darling?" Evelyn's voice had the thickness of newly awoken.

"Yes, sweet pea. I have brought you some soup. Can I turn on the bedside lamp?"

"Just a minute....okay. Do your worst." Evelyn lay on her back, her one arm thrown over her eyes to protect them from the immediate glare of the lamp. Slowly she eased it down as her sleepy blue eyes became accustomed to the illumination. Isobelle leaned over and gave her a kiss.

"Did you have a good nap? I looked in a couple of times and you were completely out of it. Even in this noisy old storm"

"Mmm! I slept like a log. What have you been up to, love?"

Isobelle carefully held the delicate Evelyn as she helped her slide up into a seated position. "That's it, lean forward a little while I fluff up your pillows. Well, I have been thinking back over the last few weeks and how thankful I am that I did not lose you."

"You have been an angel, Isobelle. I suppose because my injuries are more physical, people tended to make more of a fuss over me, but I can see that you have been through as much hurt as I, if not more." She reached up with her good hand and stroked Isobelle's cheek.

Since the wedding, Isobelle's plaster had been removed and a clean bill of health given to her arm. Luckily for Evelyn, both her wounds had been flesh wounds and although immensely tender, they were bound up and would certainly heal with time. Isobelle lowered the tray onto Evelyn's lap and then raised the rose to her nose. The fragrance was heavy and pink in the confines of the bedroom.

"Since that day I never take anything for granted any more. The smell of that rose, for instance. Doesn't that alone make you want to live forever?" Isobelle took up the soup and held the bowl close to Evelyn's chest to make it easier for her while she ate. "When I believed that I had lost you and Nigel then told Richard you were dead to fool him, it was as if my heart had stopped. I couldn't breath and, to be honest, did not really want to again. I would have quite happily gone with you there and then. I lost touch with reality around me at that point, but what I do remember is the things that I wished we'd had the opportunity to do together.......visit Edinburgh in the festival season, go for a romantic meal for two, wrap each other warm for a winter walk, grow plants and flowers together..... there were so many in a few seconds. Like flashbacks. Now we have been given another chance, I am going to make sure that we do all those things we want to do together."

"And we will, love. I promise. I am healing, somewhat slowly, but once I am better, we are going to live life to the fullest and visit those places we've always desired to go to. We are lucky in that we have the money to do so. Talking of which, how is it going with your flat? Did the agent call today?"

Isobelle broke off the bread into manageable pieces for Evelyn. "No, I called them as I did not want the phone to disturb you. The good news is that the agent received several offers, but the last was thirty thousand pounds more than my asking price. He recommended that I keep it open, but the person who made the bid is a young woman such as myself and I want her to have it. I think I have got more than enough for it. So, effectively it is sold."

"That's marvellous, darling. You certainly did not have to wait long."

"That's for sure. I am going to have to whiz over there in the Land Cruiser tomorrow to sign some papers with the solicitor and then it can all go ahead."

Evelyn had finished her soup and bread and dutifully downed her tablets. "It's a shame I am on these and cannot join you, but go and get a glass of wine for yourself and a grape juice for me. We should celebrate. Have you eaten?"

"I had some soup myself about an hour ago. Let me go and get the drinks." She left the rose on the bedside table and took the tray back to the kitchen. She poured out a grape juice for Evelyn and uncorked a German white wine from the fridge. She popped some crisps and pretzels into small bowls and went back to the bedroom.

"I've locked up for the night and doused all the lights, so you now have my undivided attention for the rest of the evening," she beamed.

"Well, you can slip out of that dress and hang it up for starters," Evelyn grinned, "before you get rid of the rest of your clothes and hop into this bed beside me."

Isobelle stripped off very slowly and seductively, teasing Evelyn as she did so. When at last naked, she slipped into the bed, already warmed by Evelyn's body. She raised her glass to Evelyn's. "Cheers! Here's to a successful sale, but more importantly a loving and adventurous life together."

"I'll second that," replied Evelyn as their glasses clinked together in a toast. After a sip of her juice, she feigned struggling with a memory. "Now, if I recall correctly, on the evening of the wedding you were in debt some serious love-making. I think it is time to deliver."

Isobelle's eyes widened. Lovemaking had been a little out of the question of late, what with Evelyn's very tender wounds. "Are you sure, Evelyn?" she whispered, her lips damp with wine and fluttering near Evelyn's ear, the breath around her words clearly conveying her want.

"I'm sure, sweetheart. You may have to avoid my right arm and waist, but all the other parts should work beautifully. Make love to me, Isobelle."

And Isobelle lost herself deep within those Morning Glory Blue eyes, plunging into their limpid effulgence and luxuriating in all the love that Evelyn had for her.

About the Author

Selyna was born in 1956 in RAF Abingdon, Oxfordshire. The family then moved to Nigeria and Bahrain, before settling in the United Arab Emirates. Most of Selyna's childhood was spent either there or at boarding school in Wales.

Selyna later became a management accountant with a major North American bank. It was during this time that she met her partner and moved with her into the northern suburbs of London, where they live happily with their two children.

She has written a specialist aircraft book, as well as a few poems published in anthologies. *Deep Within The Morning Glory Blue* is her first foray into the realms of the novel.

Her ambition is to become a middle-aged full time writer.

Printed in the United States
35733LVS00010B/1-6